ANDREW MCDONALD & BEN WOOD

Twig Friends

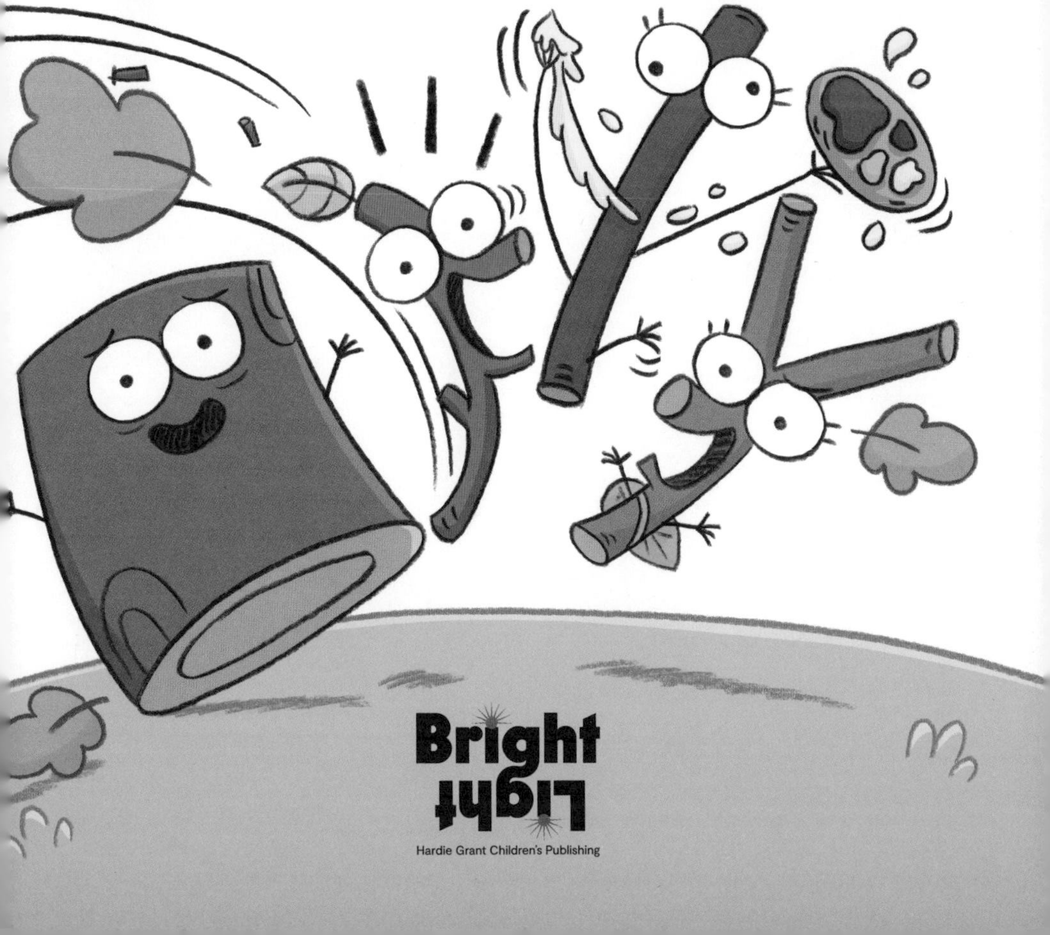

Bright Light
Hardie Grant Children's Publishing

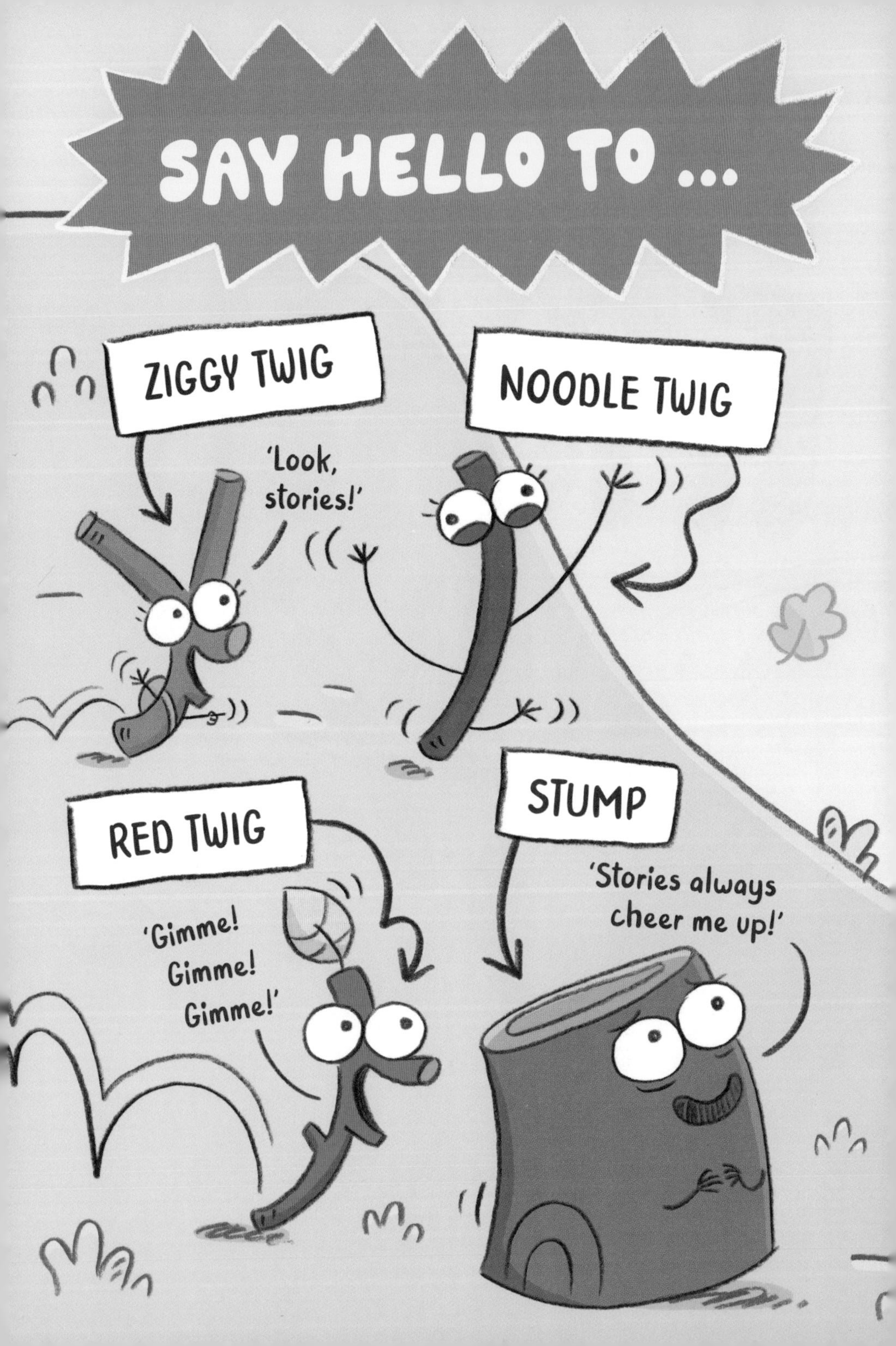
SAY HELLO TO ...
ZIGGY TWIG
'Look, stories!'
NOODLE TWIG
RED TWIG
'Gimme! Gimme! Gimme!'
STUMP
'Stories always cheer me up!'

CONTENTS

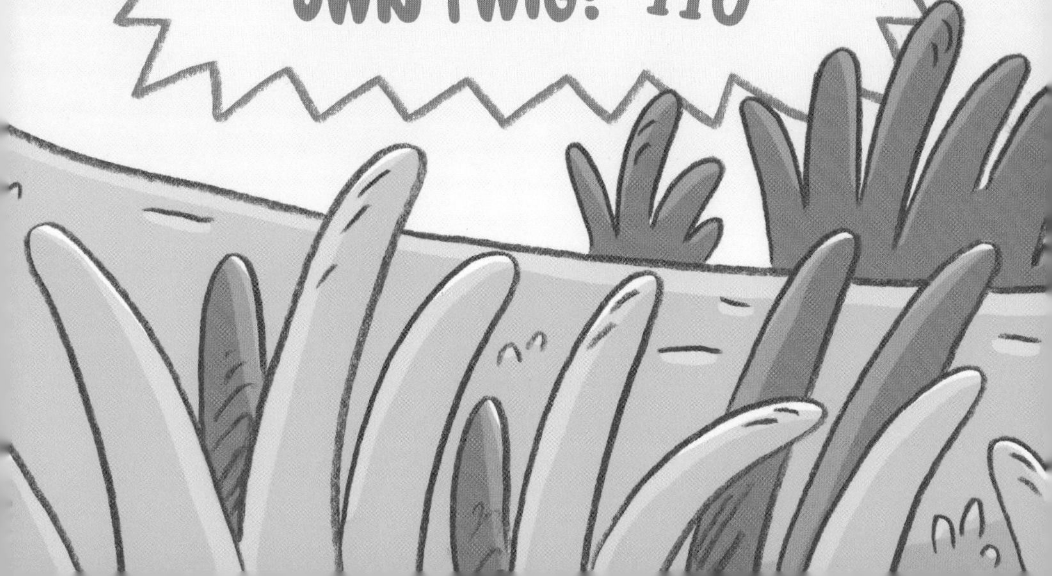

1. SURPRISE!

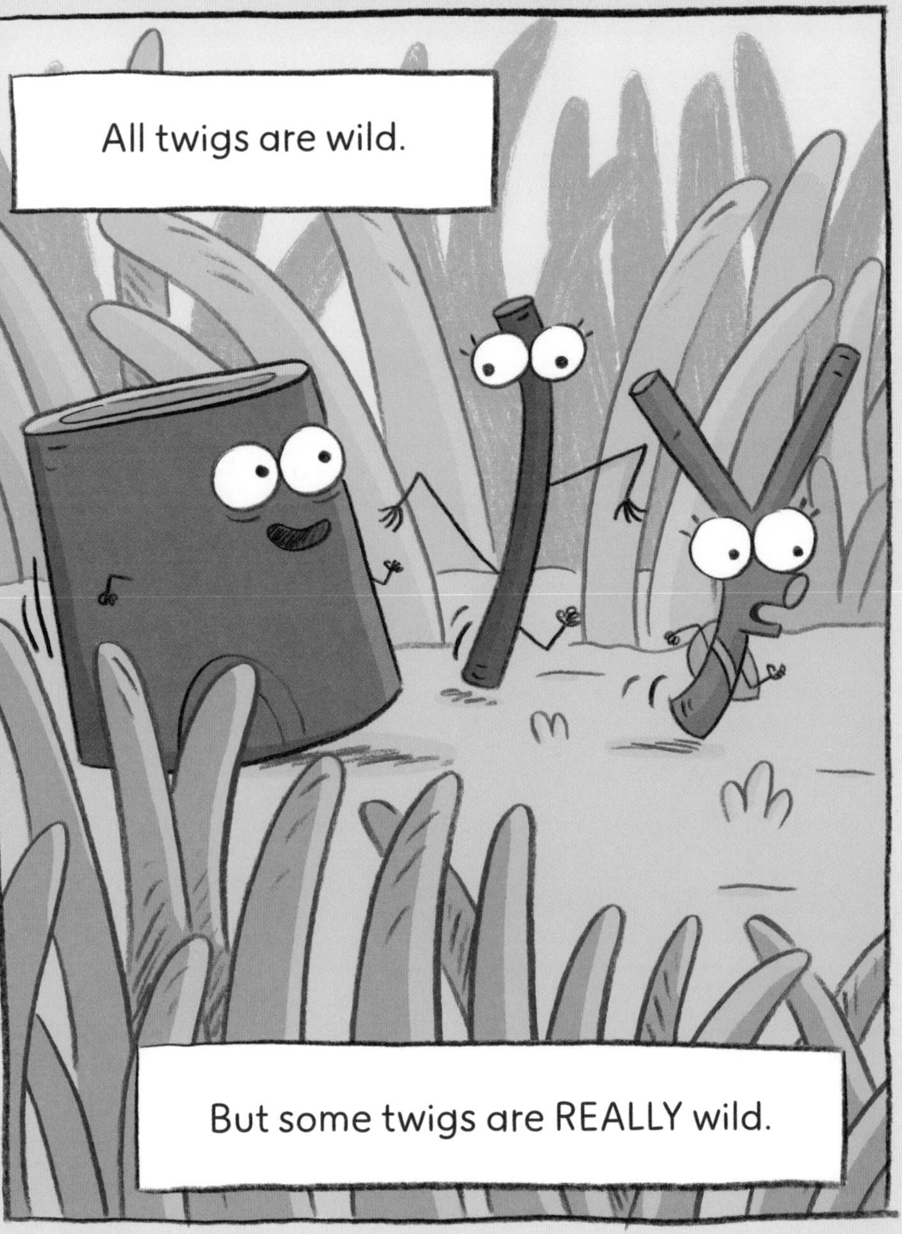
All twigs are wild.
But some twigs are REALLY wild.

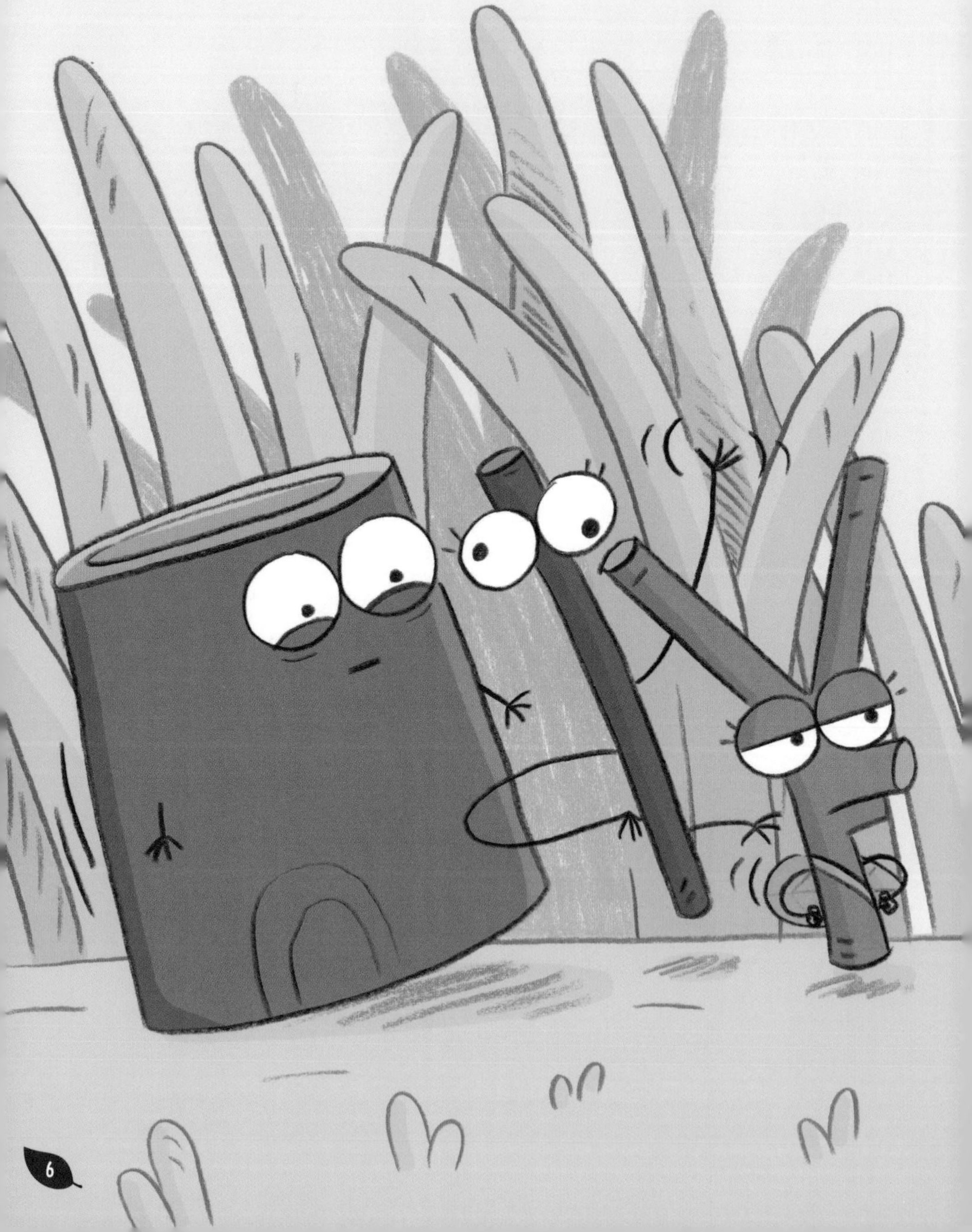

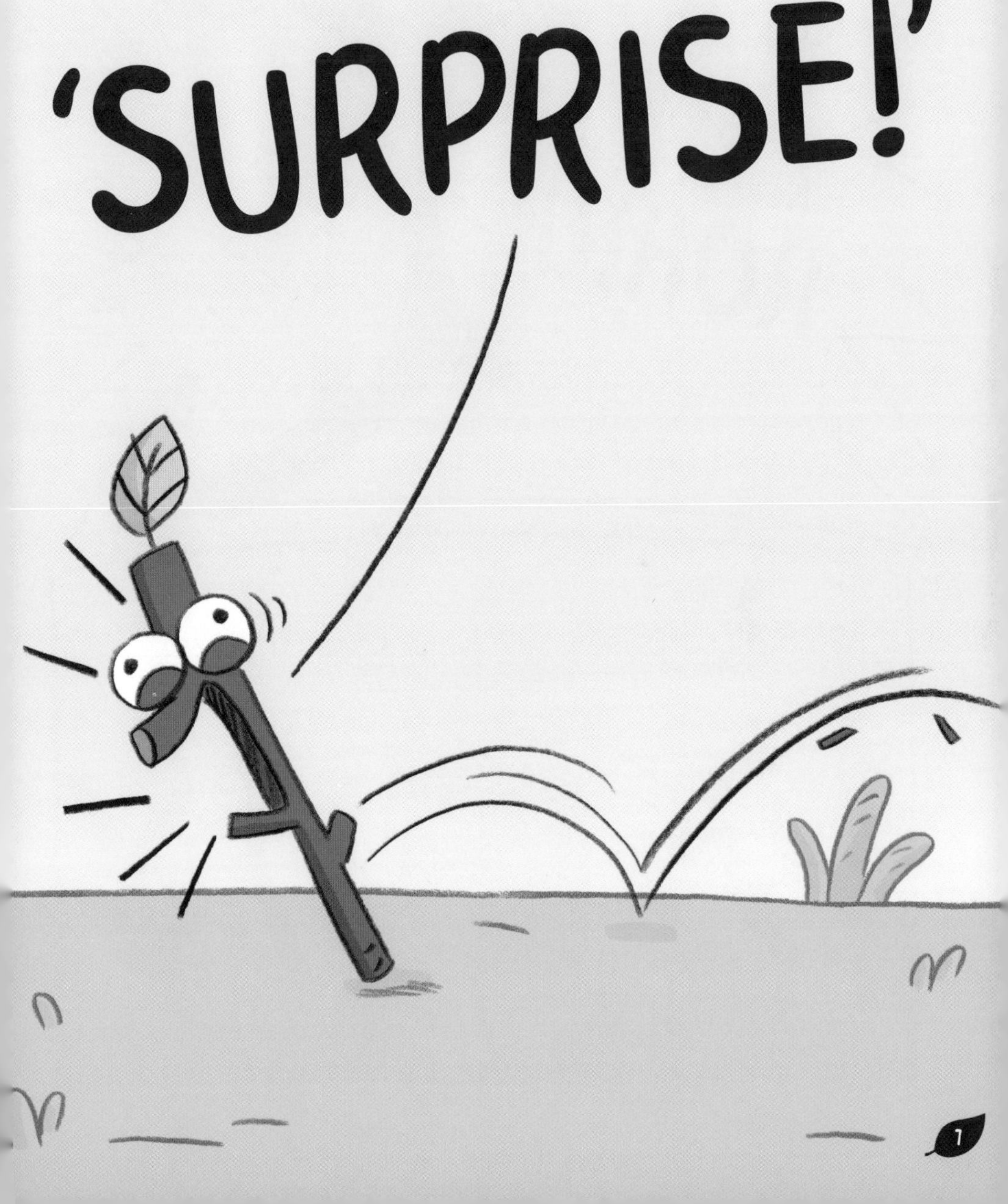
'SURPRISE!'

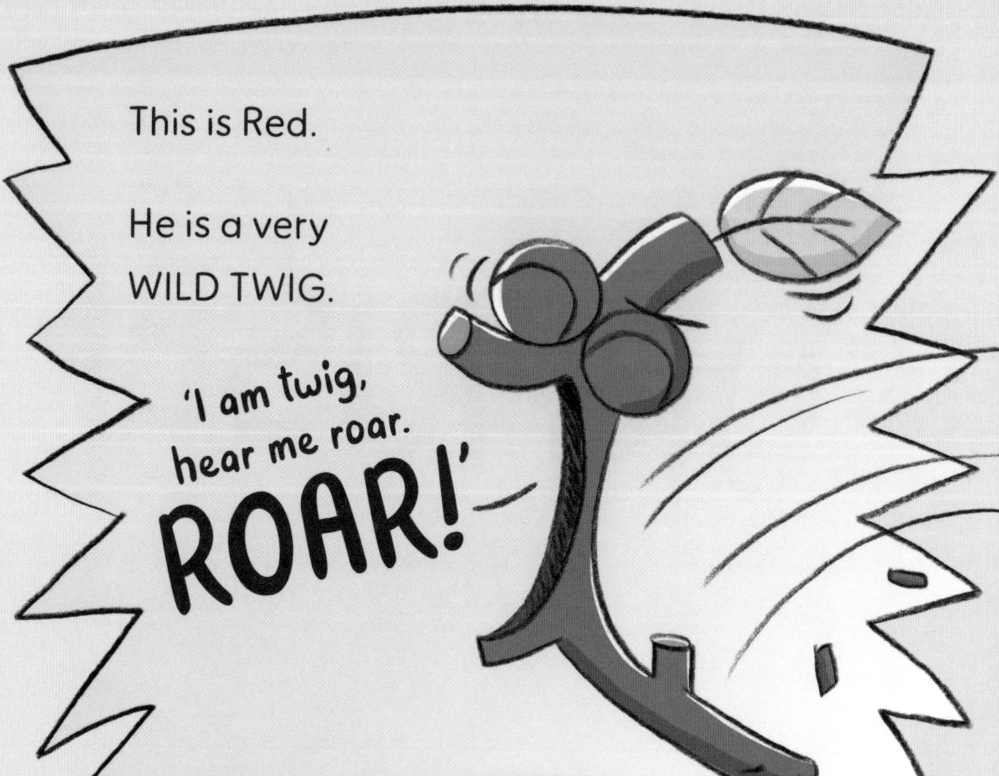
This is Red.
He is a very WILD TWIG.
'I am twig, hear me roar. ROAR!'

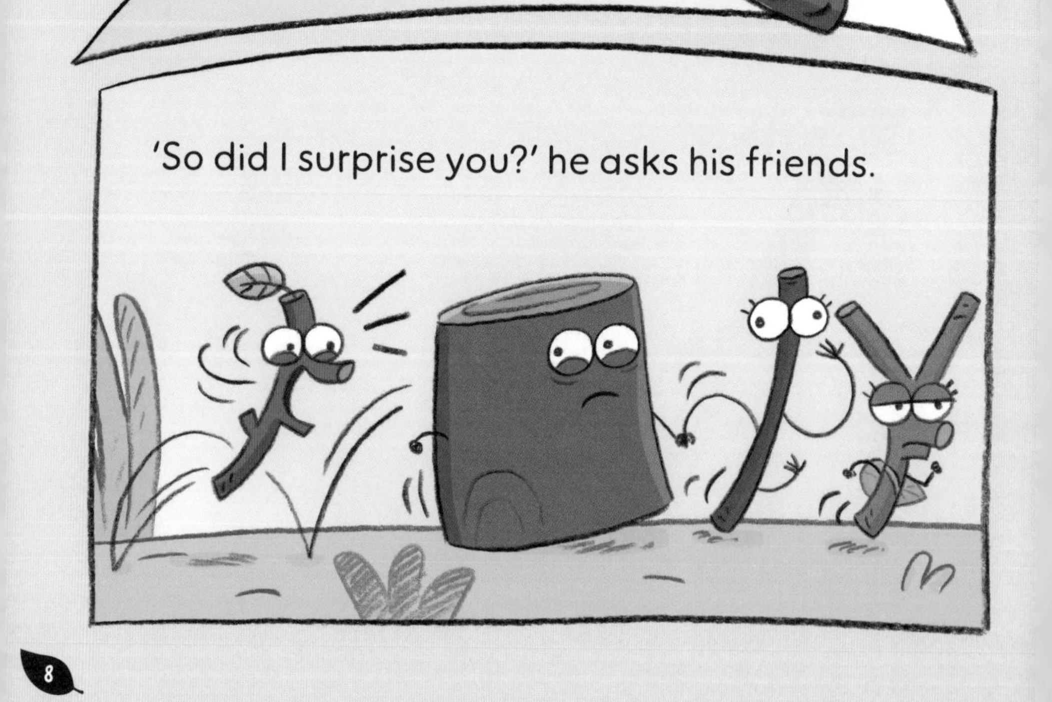
'So did I surprise you?' he asks his friends.

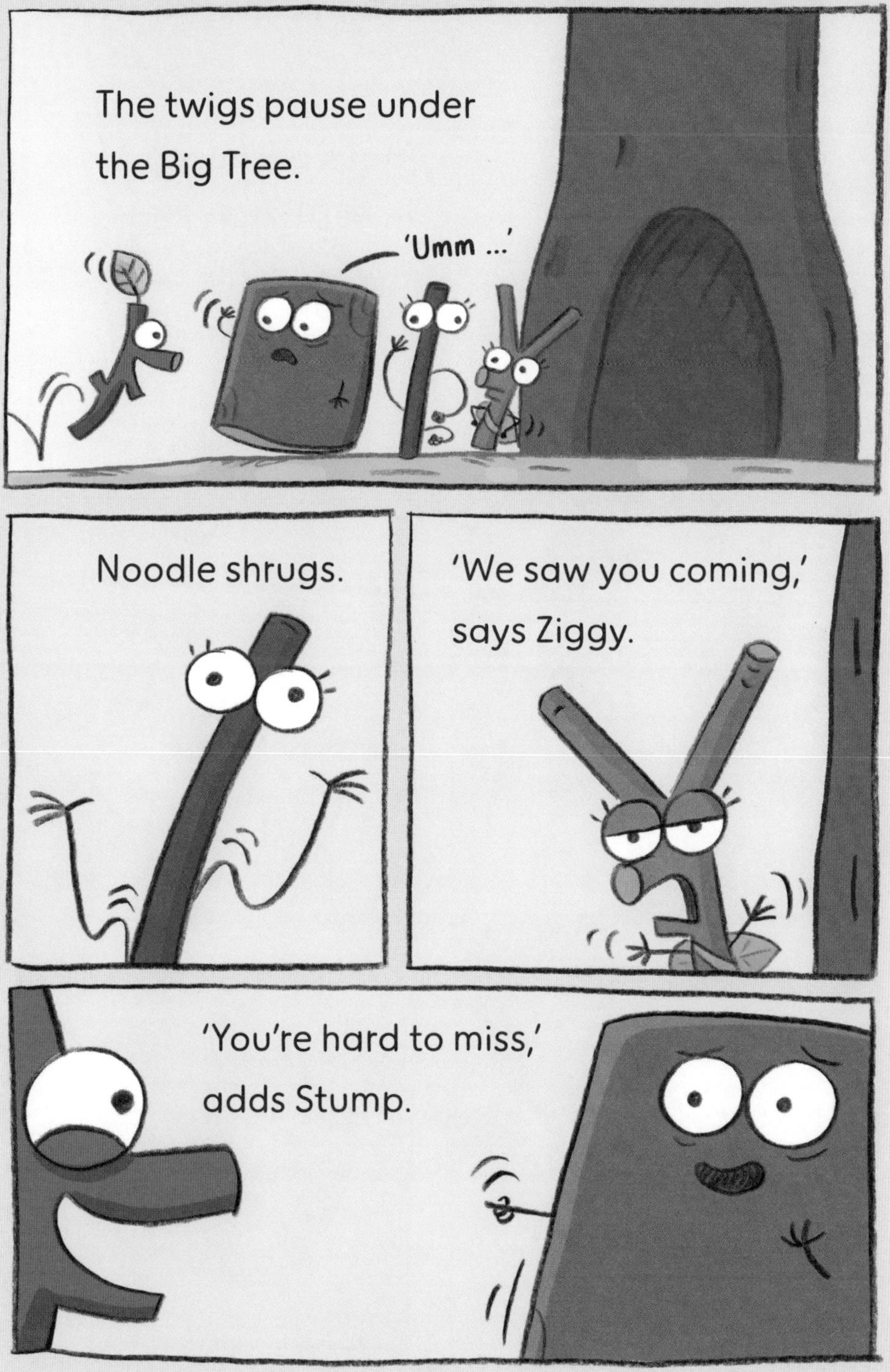
The twigs pause under the Big Tree.
'Umm ...'
Noodle shrugs.
'We saw you coming,' says Ziggy.
'You're hard to miss,' adds Stump.

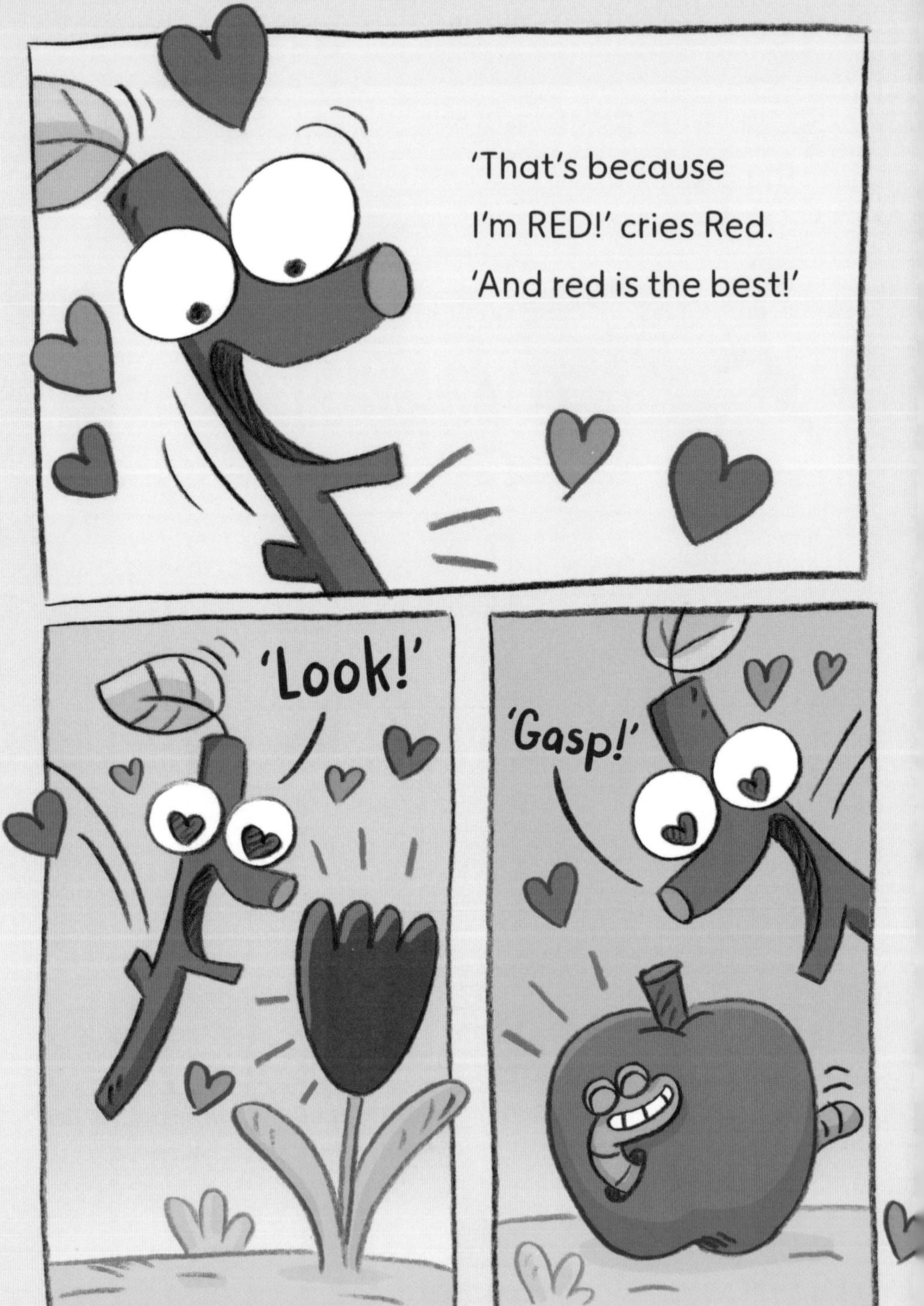
'That's because
I'm RED!' cries Red.
'And red is the best!'
'Look!'
'Gasp!'

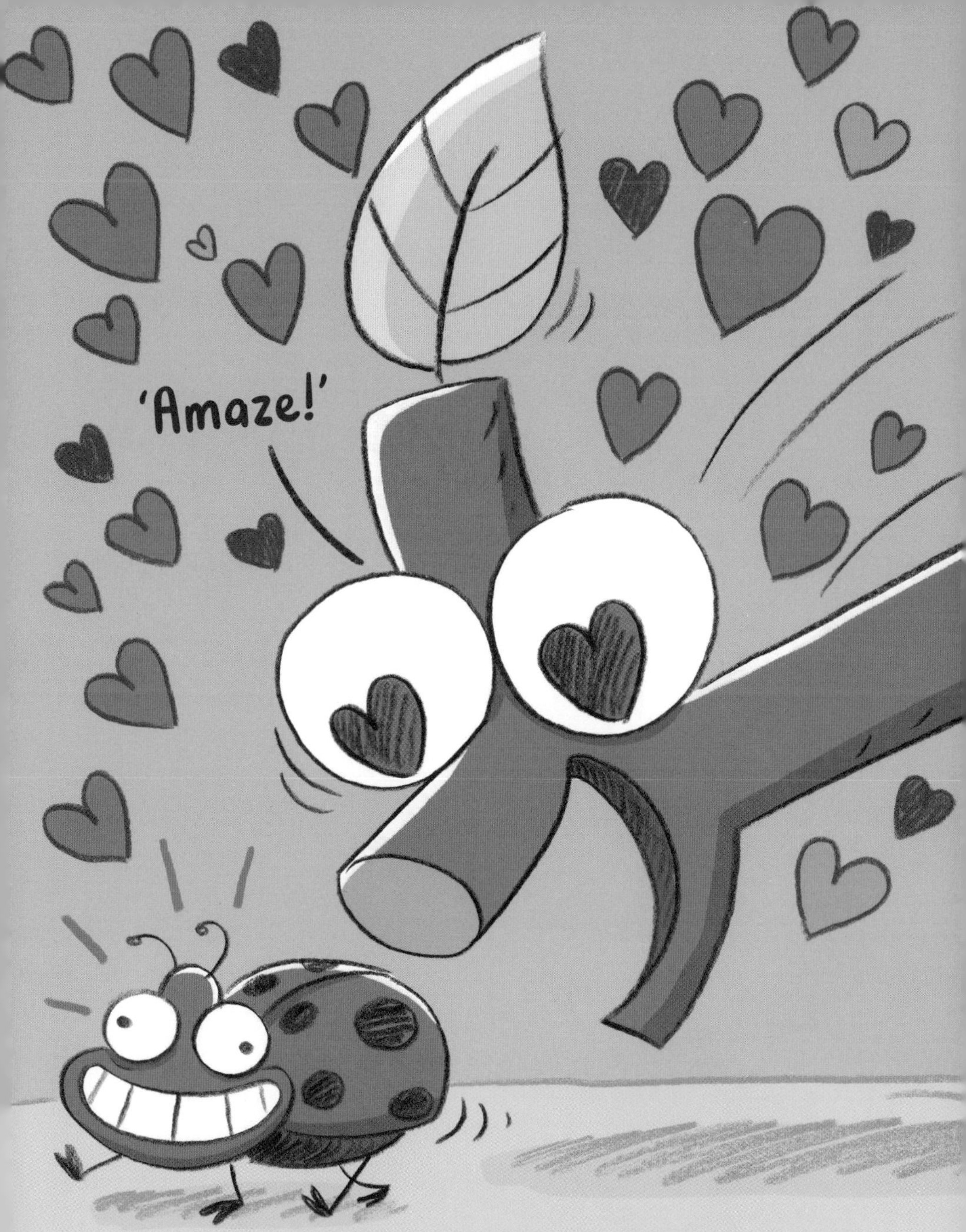
'Amaze!'

Yeah. He REALLY loves red.

Now the other twigs are over by some fall leaves.

And they look serious.

'I will give them better SURPRISES!' says Red. 'Then they will jump and laugh and be less serious!'

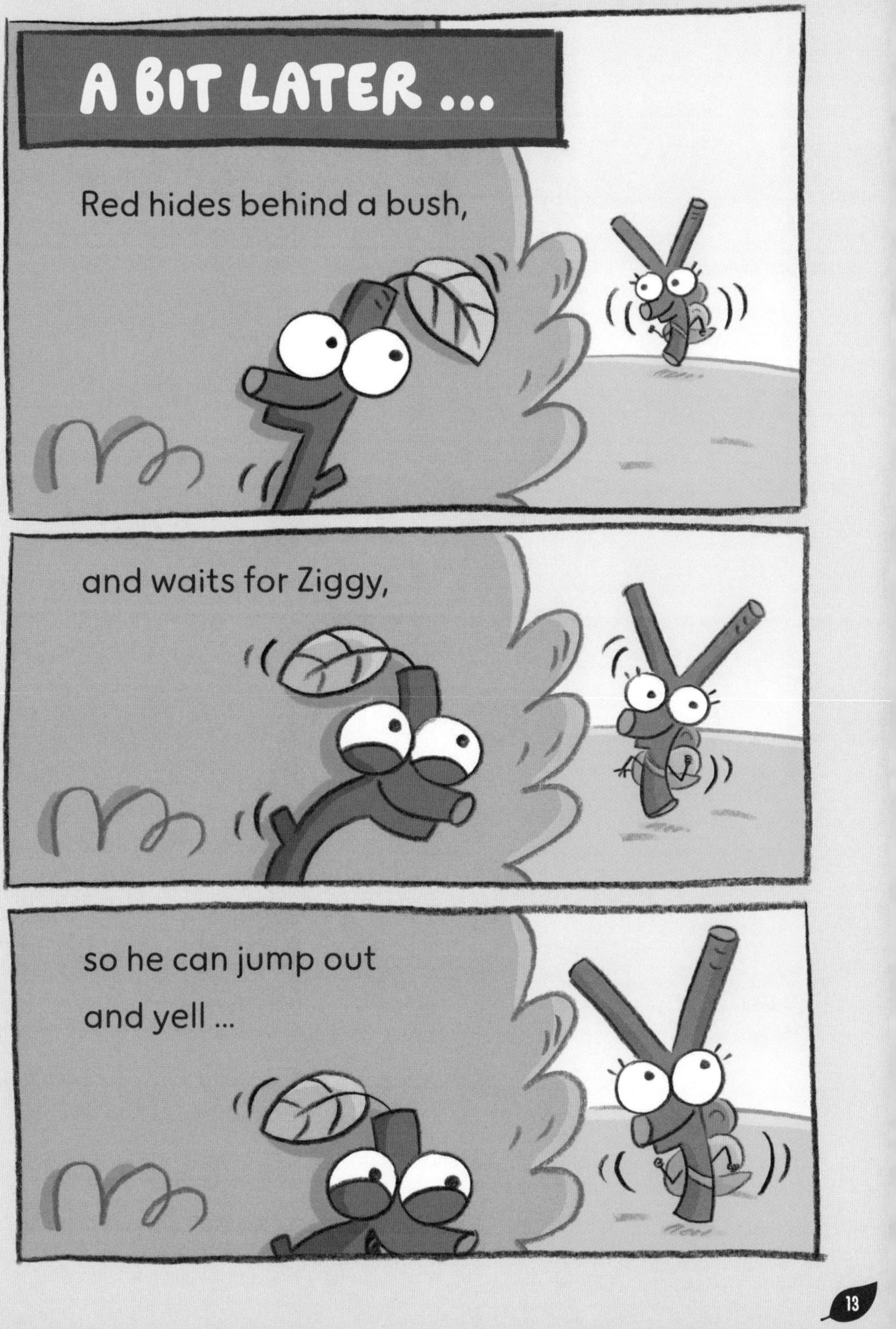
A BIT LATER ...
Red hides behind a bush,
and waits for Ziggy,
so he can jump out
and yell ...

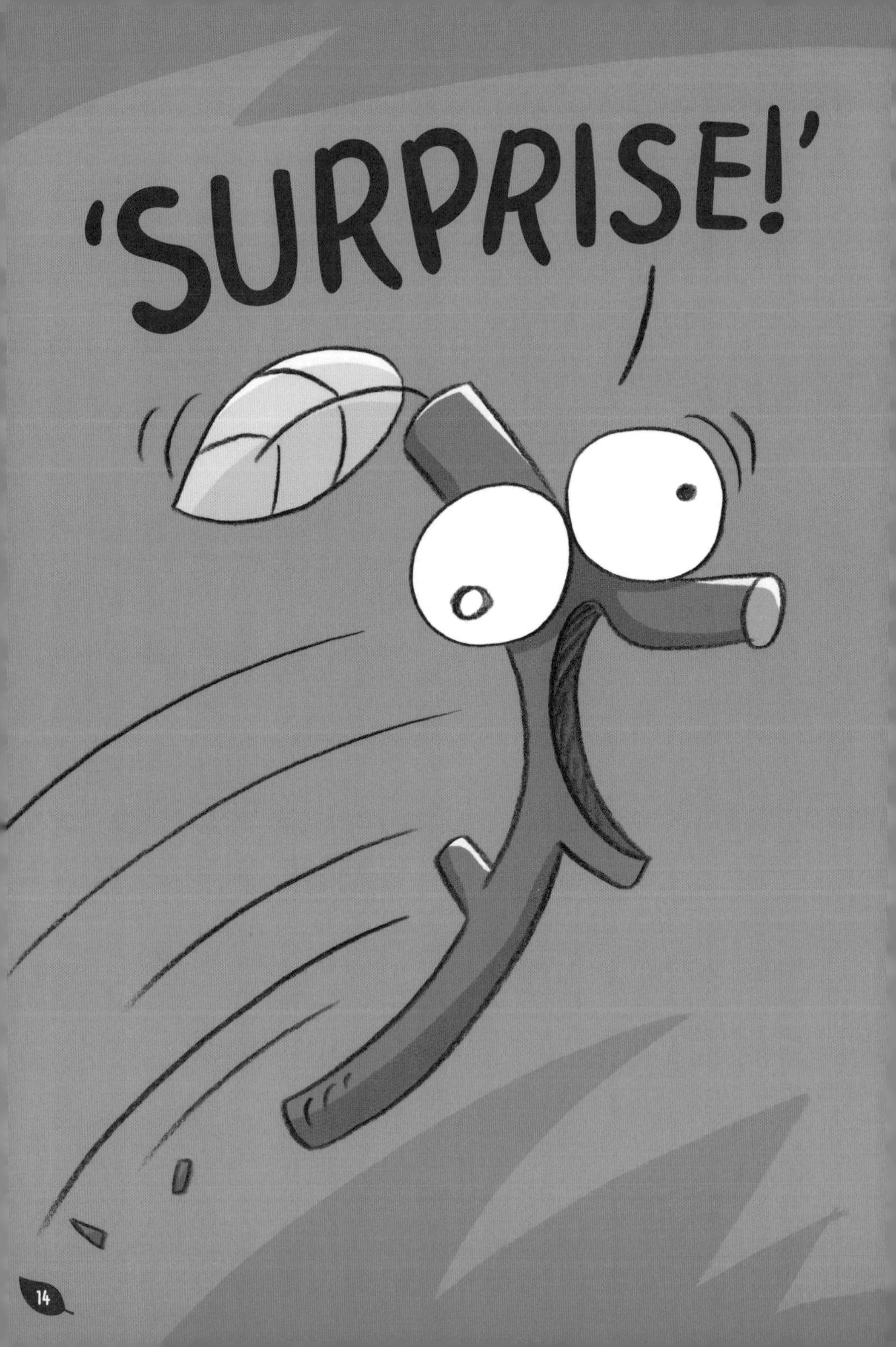
'SURPRISE!'

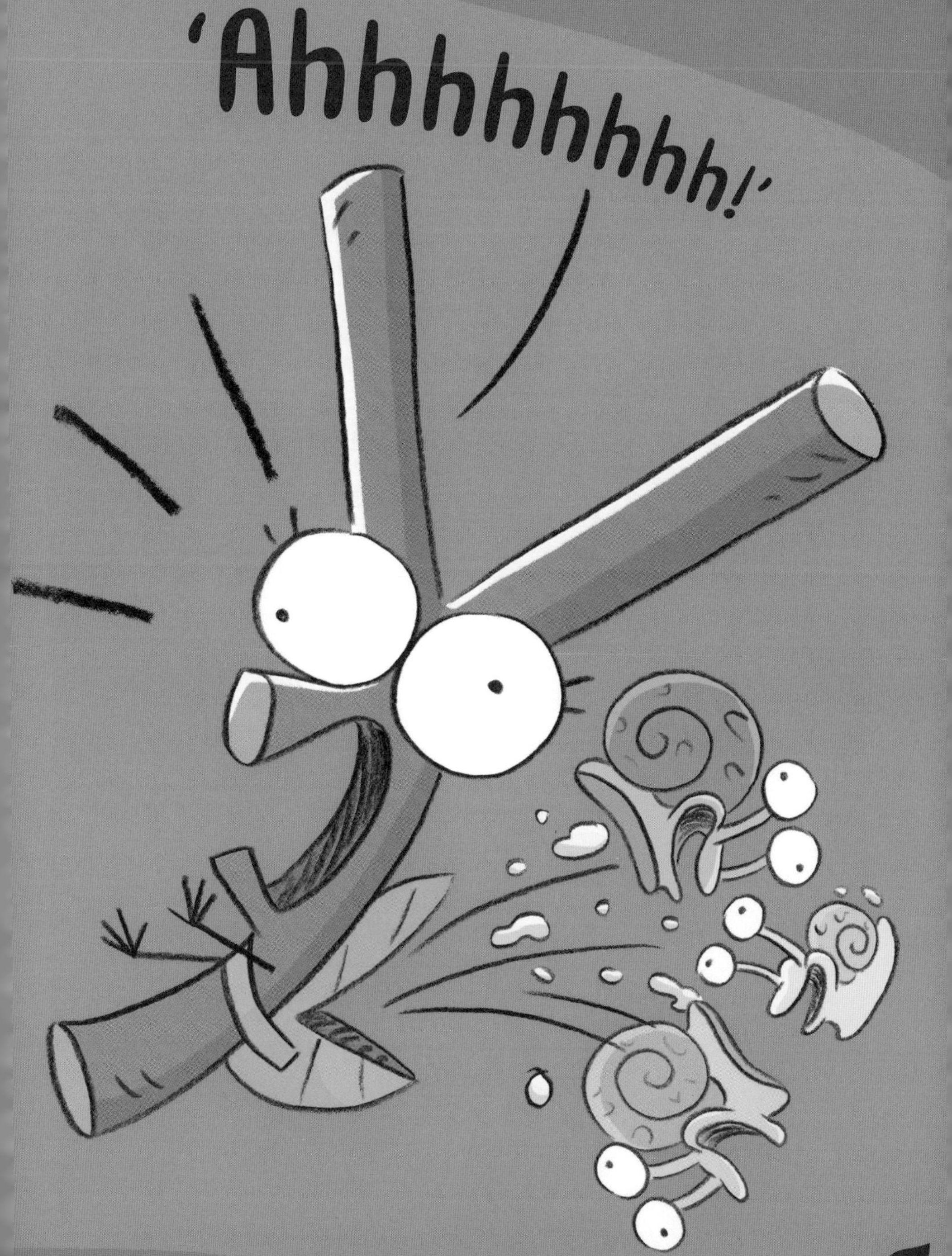
'Ahhhhhhhh!'

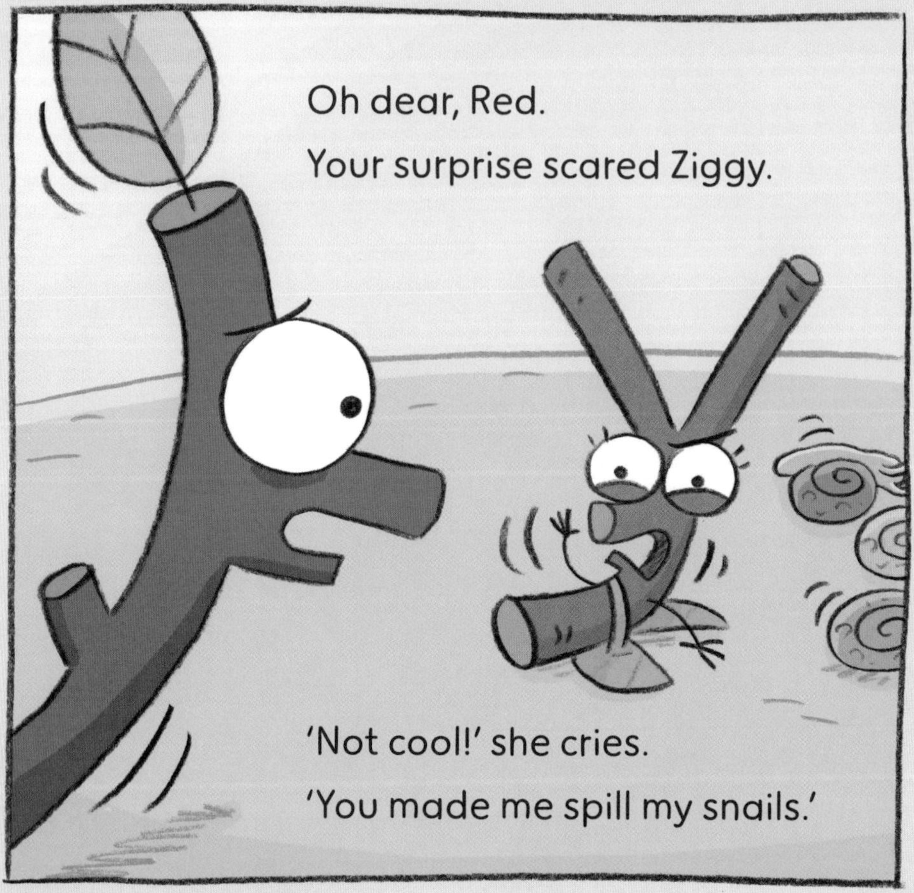
Oh dear, Red.
Your surprise scared Ziggy.
'Not cool!' she cries.
'You made me spill my snails.'

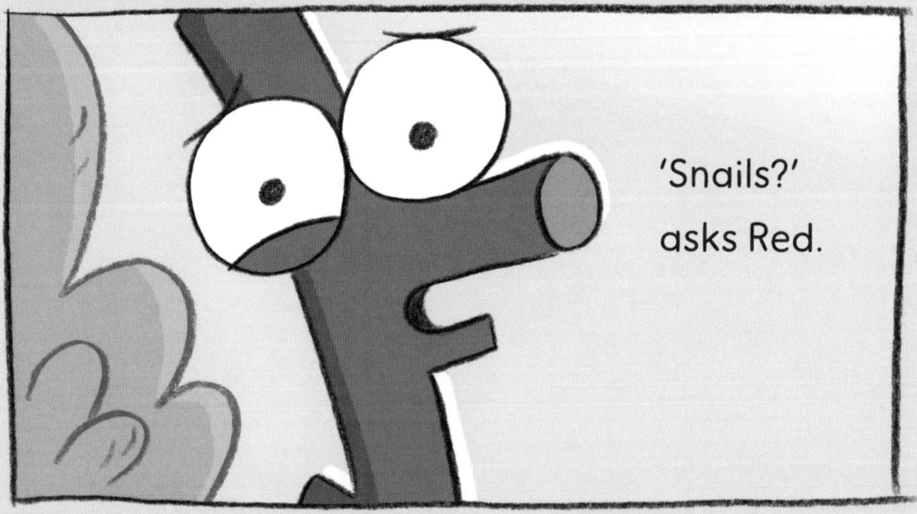
'Snails?'
asks Red.

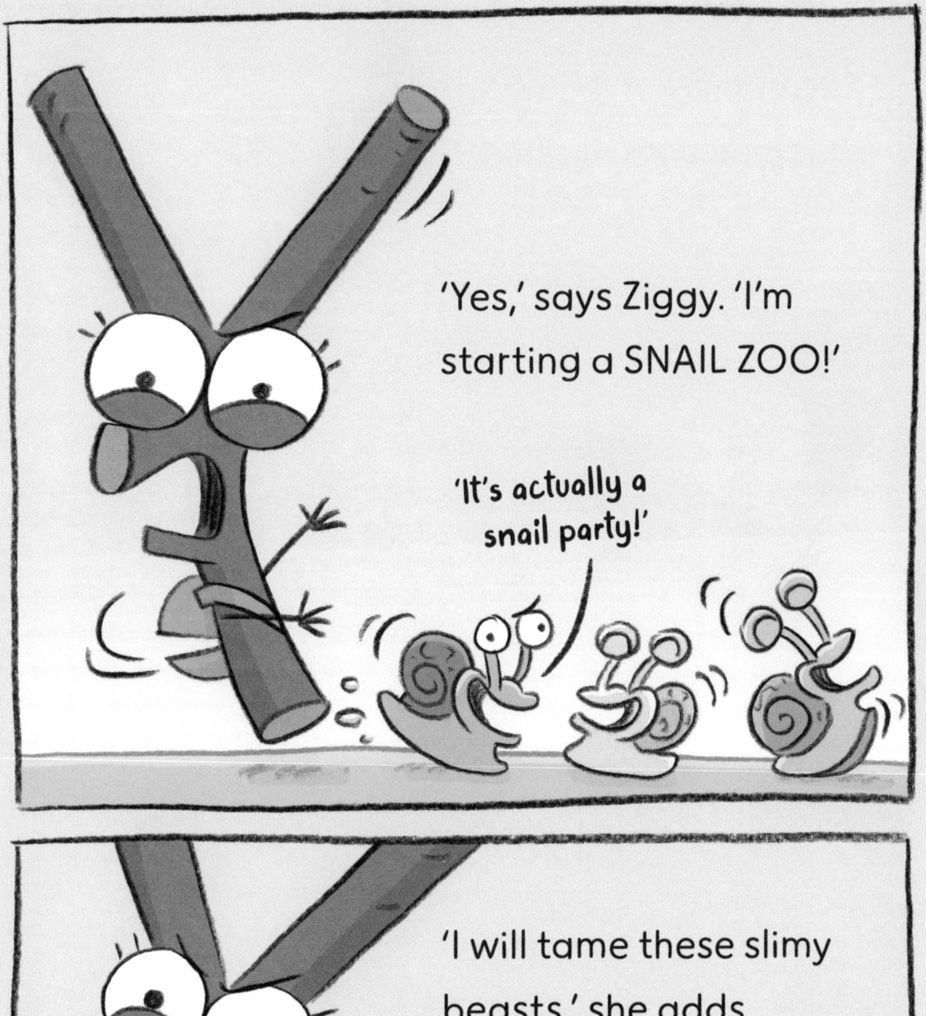
'Yes,' says Ziggy. 'I'm starting a SNAIL ZOO!'
'It's actually a snail party!'

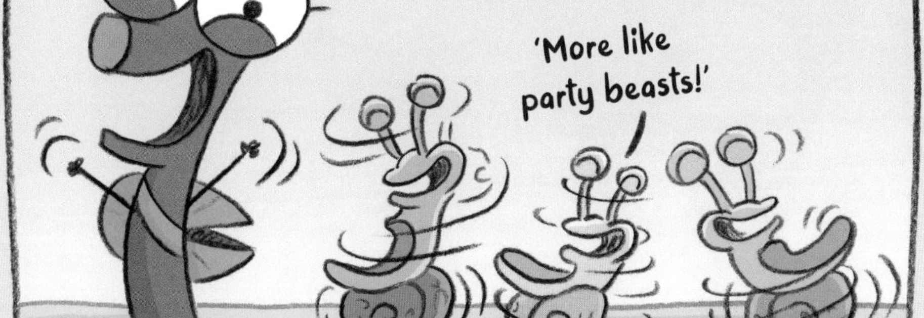
'I will tame these slimy beasts,' she adds.
'More like party beasts!'

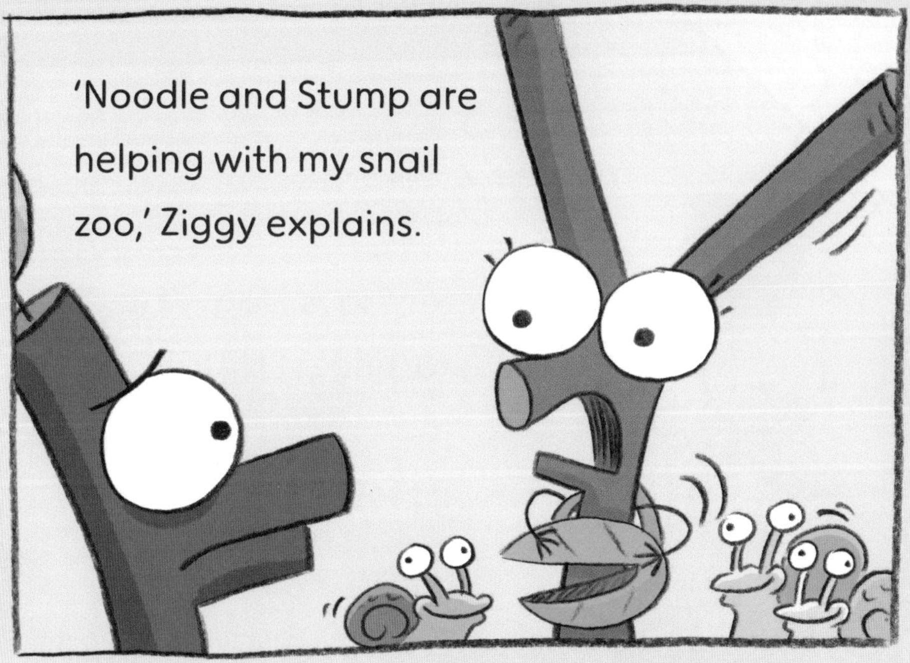
'Noodle and Stump are helping with my snail zoo,' Ziggy explains.

No wonder they were so serious before.

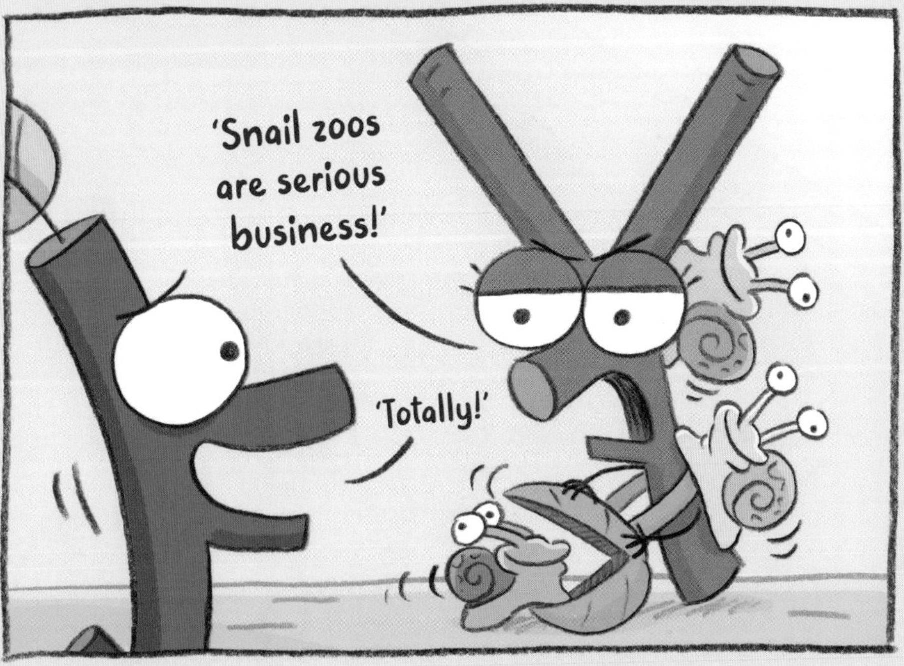
'Snail zoos are serious business!'
'Totally!'

Ziggy hops off.

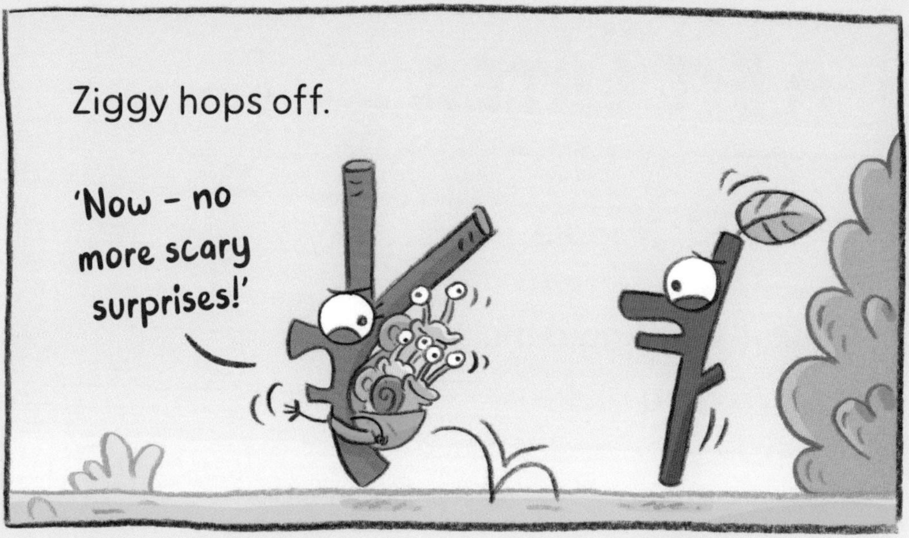
'Now – no more scary surprises!'

Maybe it's time to do something else, Red?

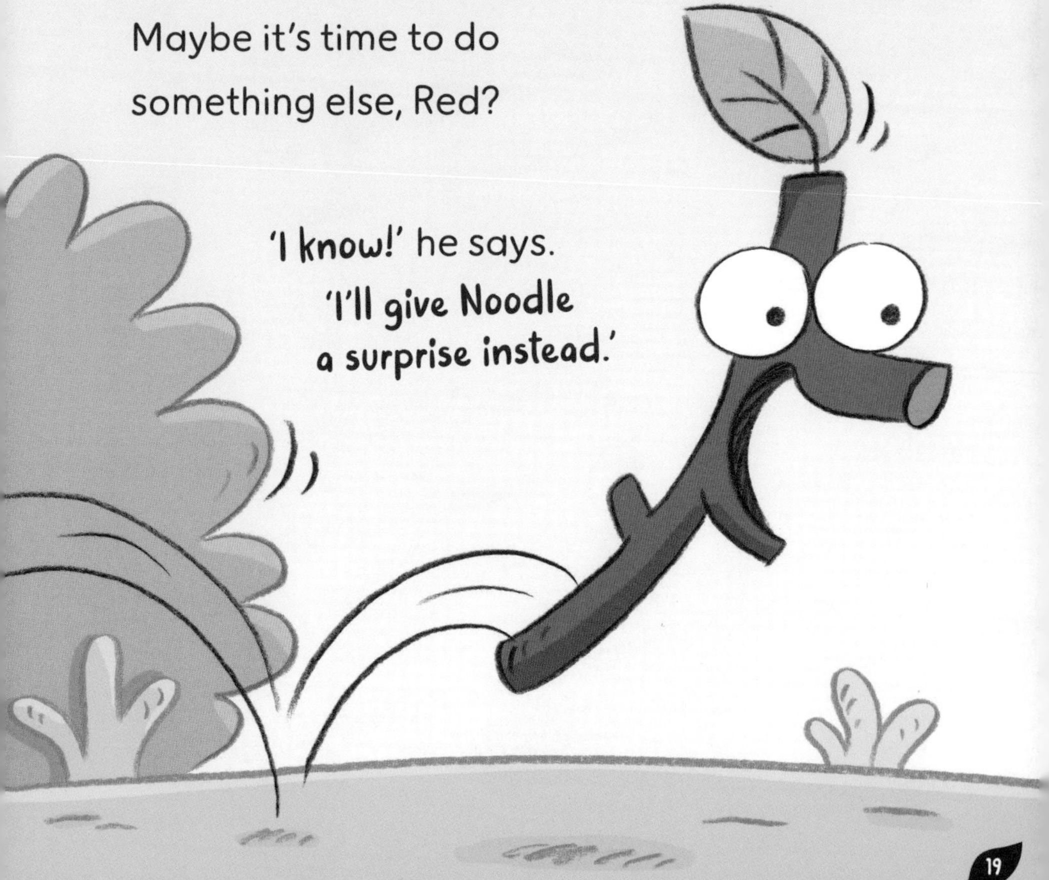
'I know!' he says.
'I'll give Noodle a surprise instead.'

A BIT LATER ...

Red finds Noodle.

She is painting a muddy sign onto a rock.

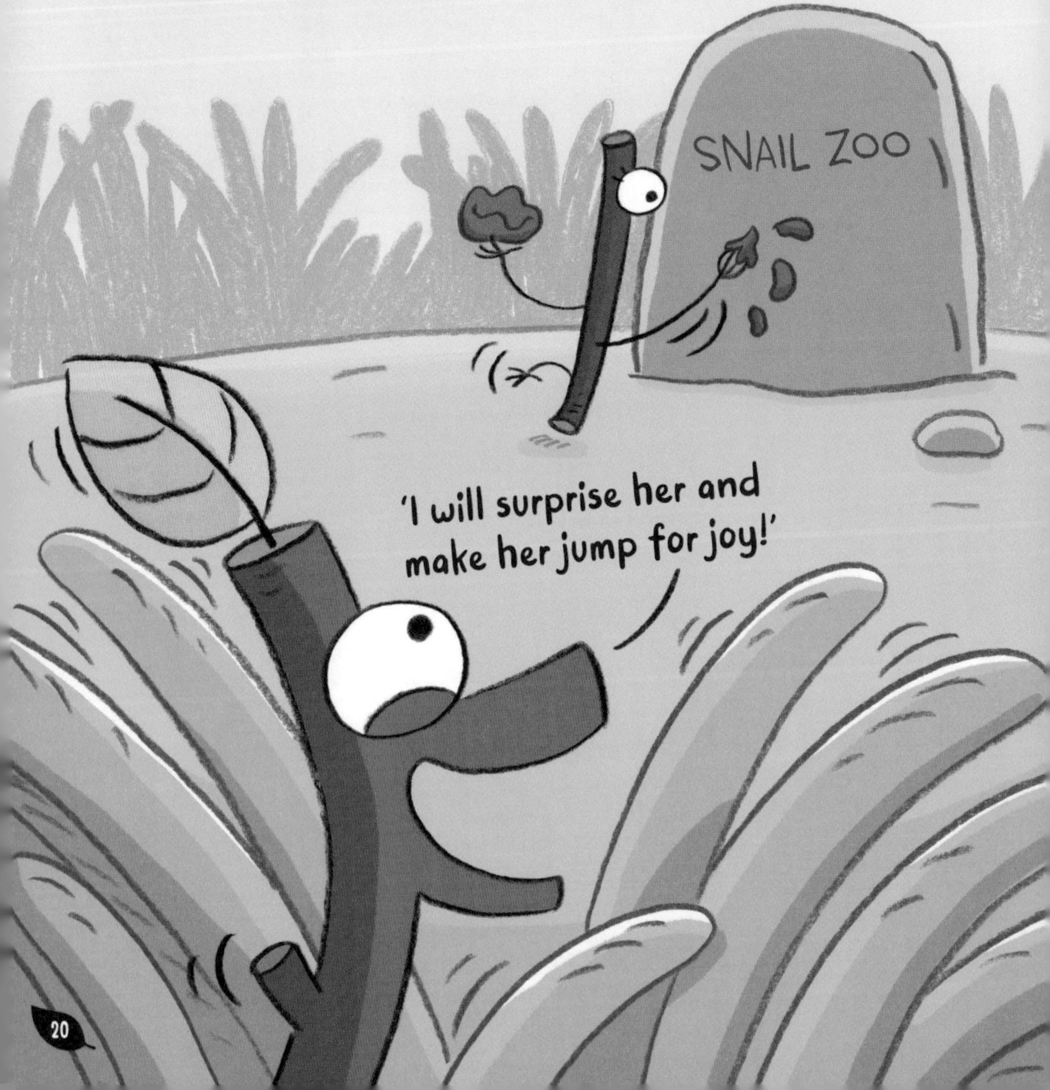
SNAIL ZOO
'I will surprise her and make her jump for joy!'

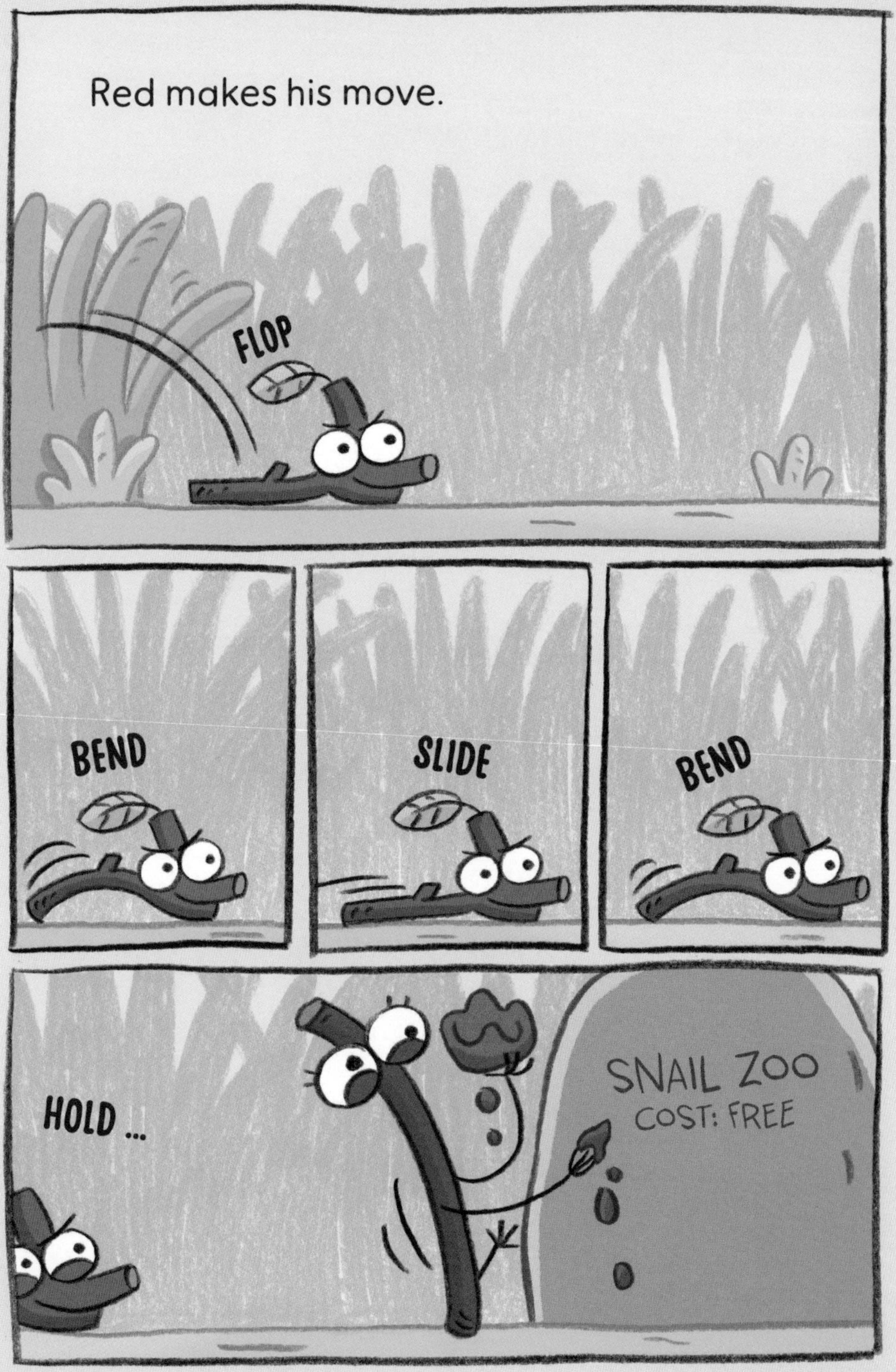
Red makes his move.
FLOP
BEND
SLIDE
BEND
HOLD ...
SNAIL ZOO
COST: FREE

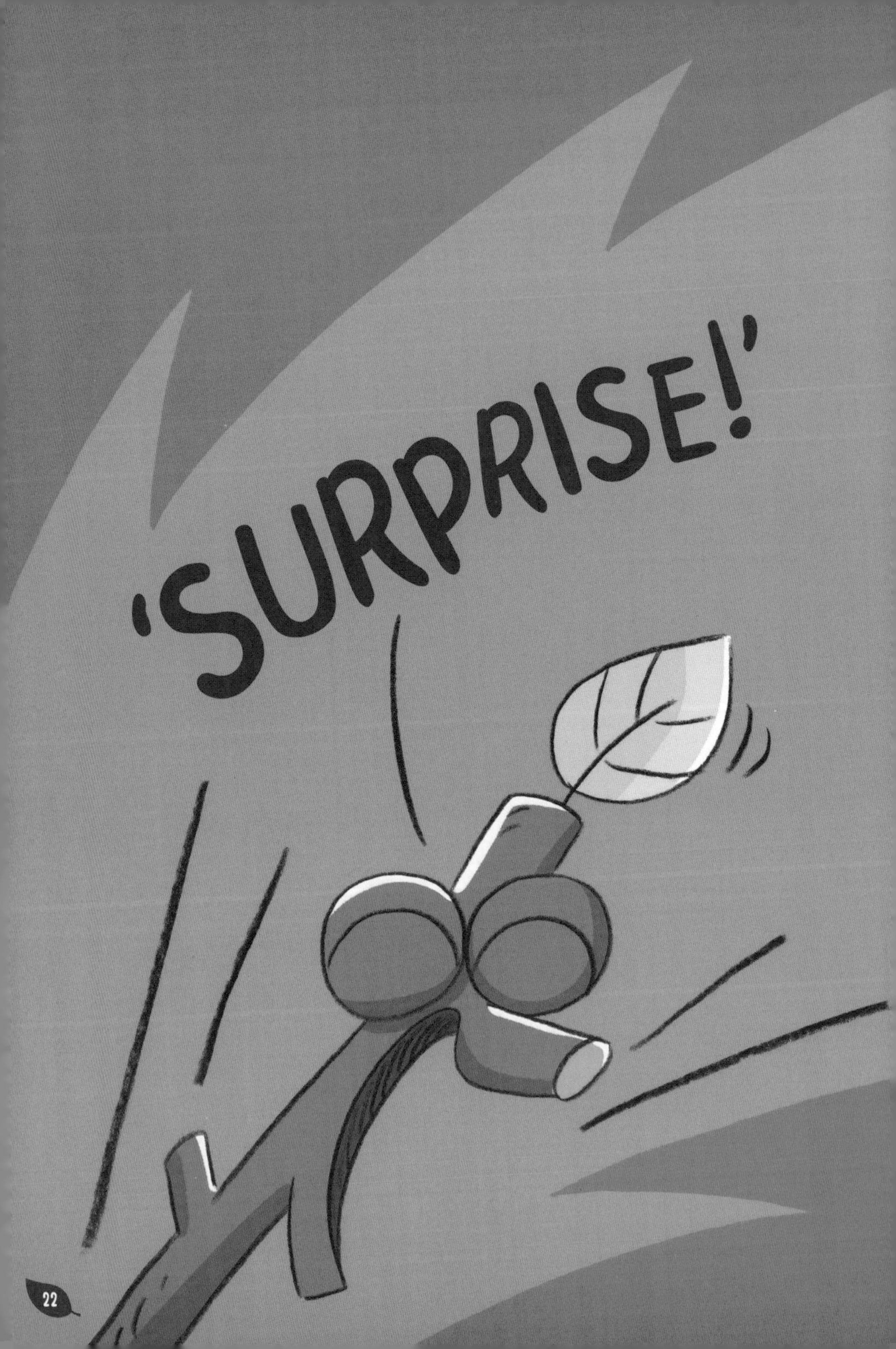
'SURPRISE!'

Noodle is so shocked, she jumps high in the air.

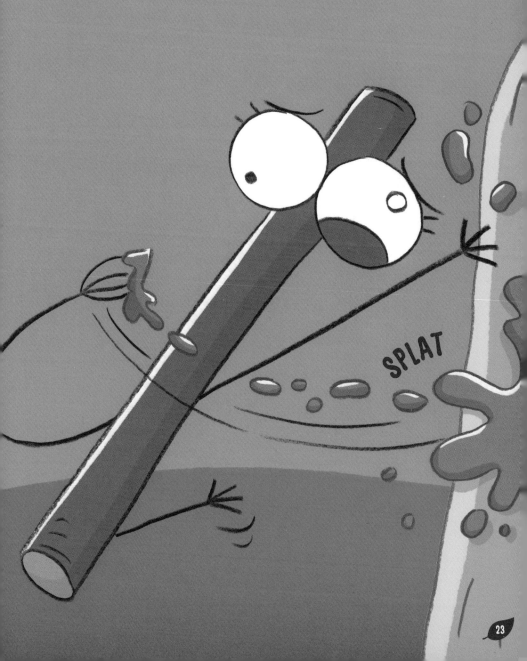

SPLAT

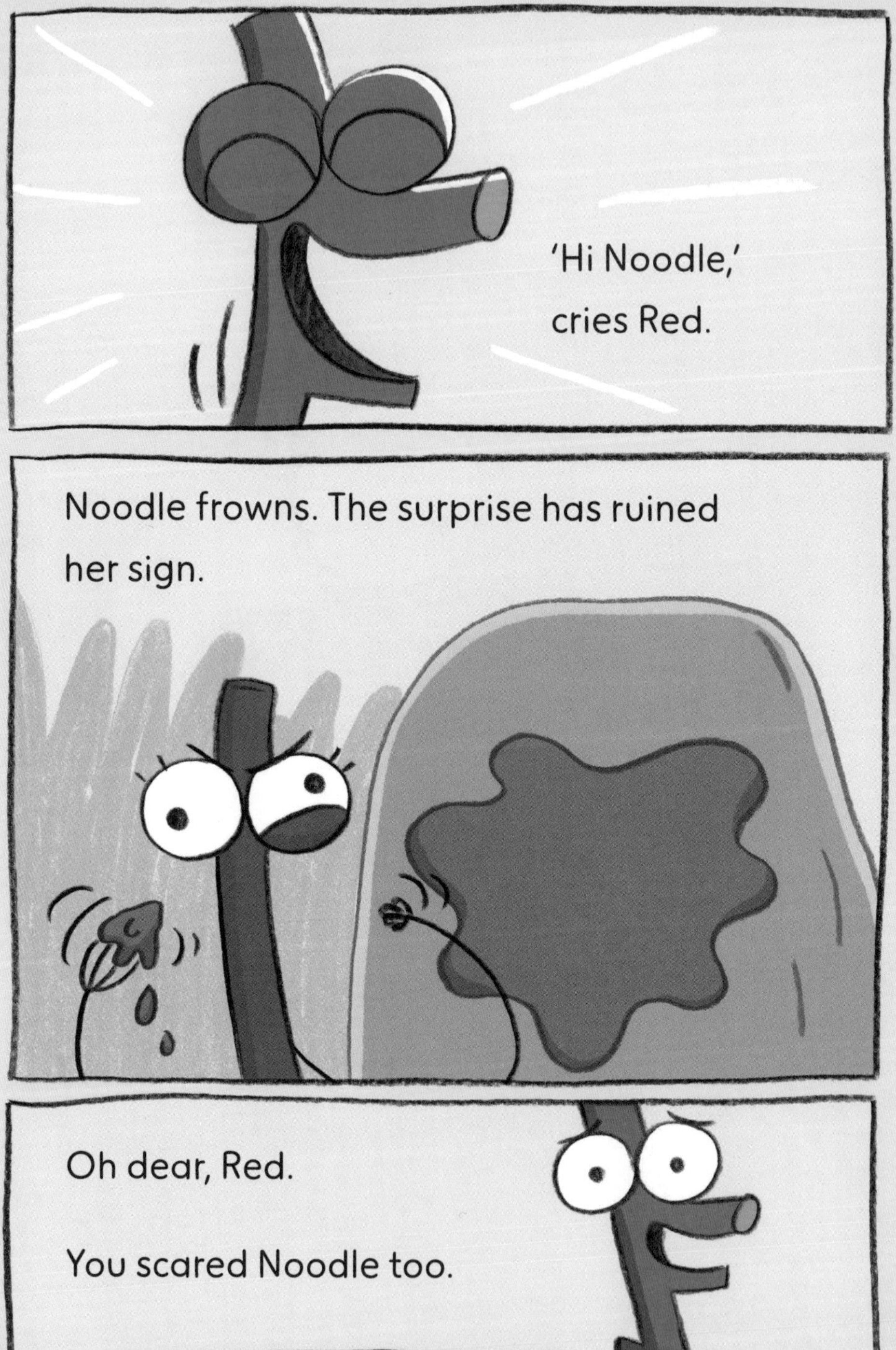
'Hi Noodle,'
cries Red.
Noodle frowns. The surprise has ruined her sign.
Oh dear, Red.
You scared Noodle too.

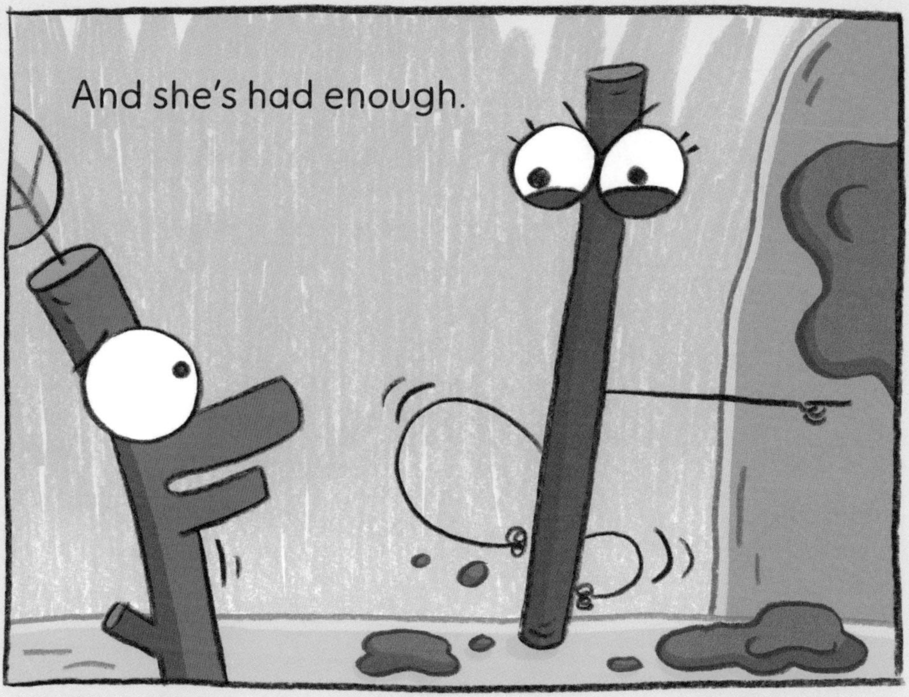
And she's had enough.

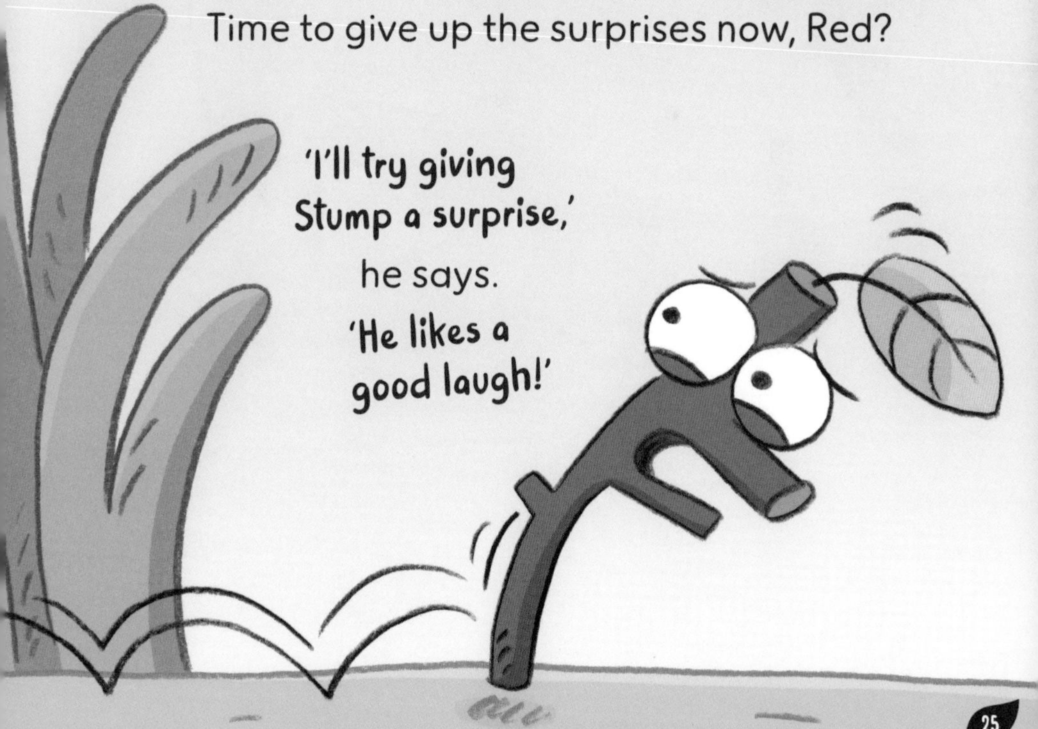
Time to give up the surprises now, Red?
'I'll try giving
Stump a surprise,'
he says.
'He likes a
good laugh!'

MORE LATER AGAIN ...

Red spots Stump carrying some stones.

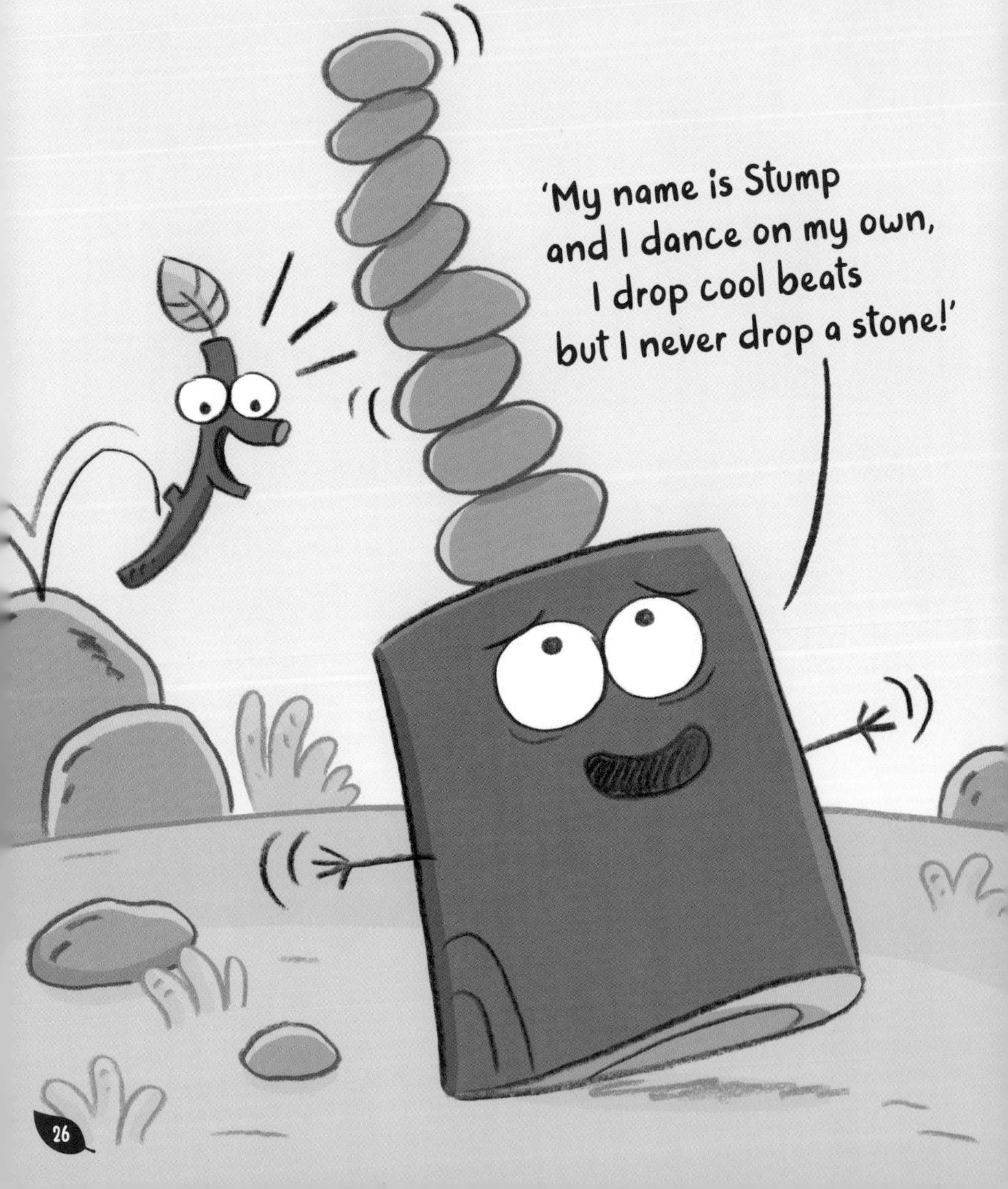
'My name is Stump
and I dance on my own,
I drop cool beats
but I never drop a stone!'

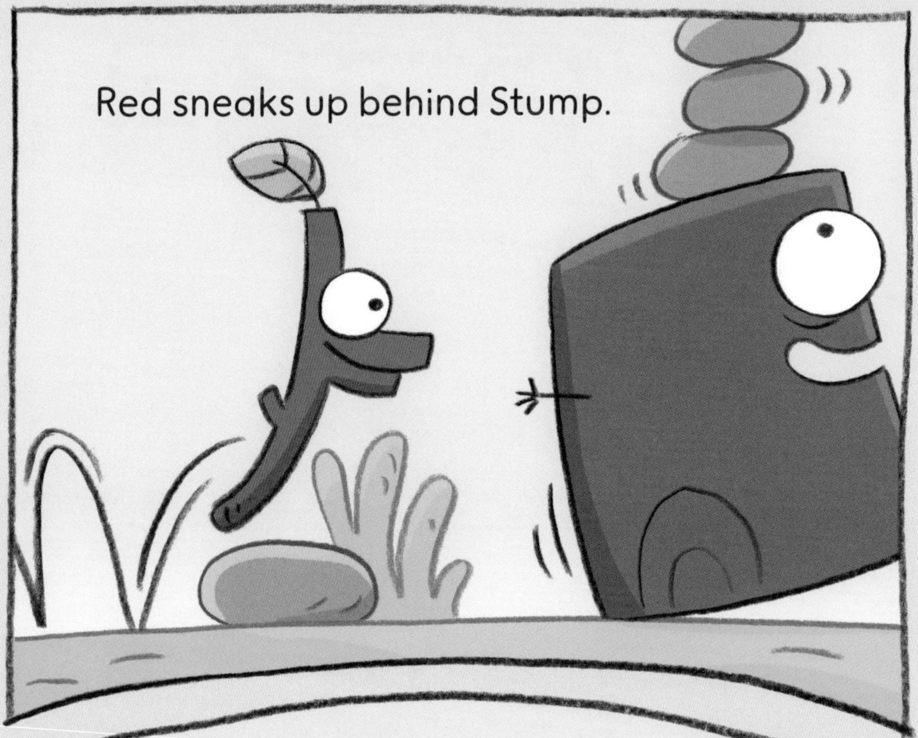
Red sneaks up behind Stump.

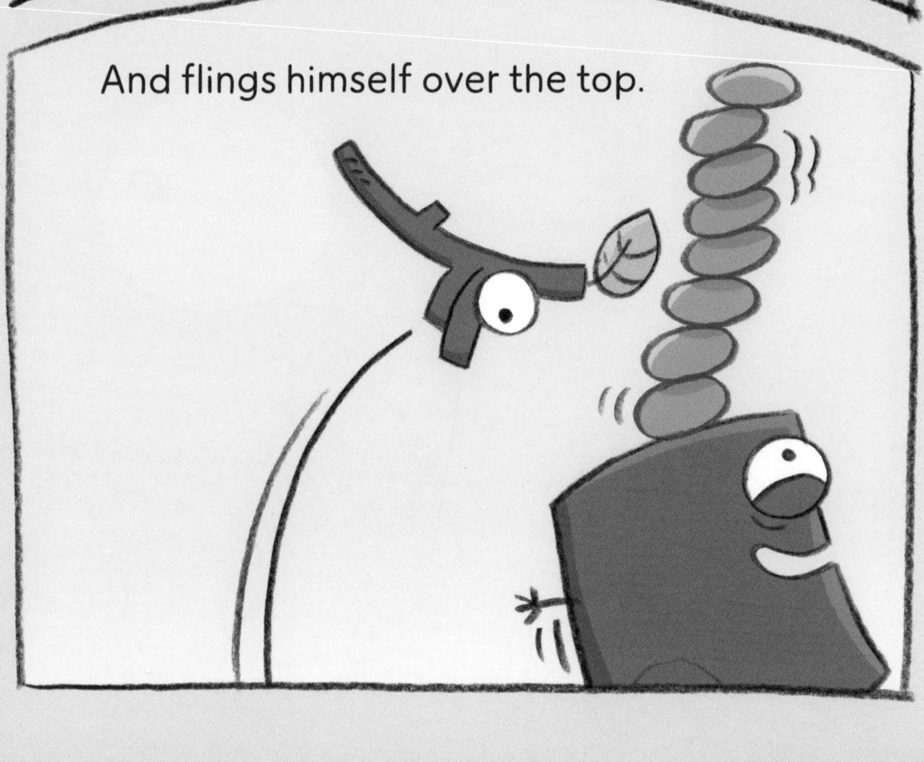
And flings himself over the top.

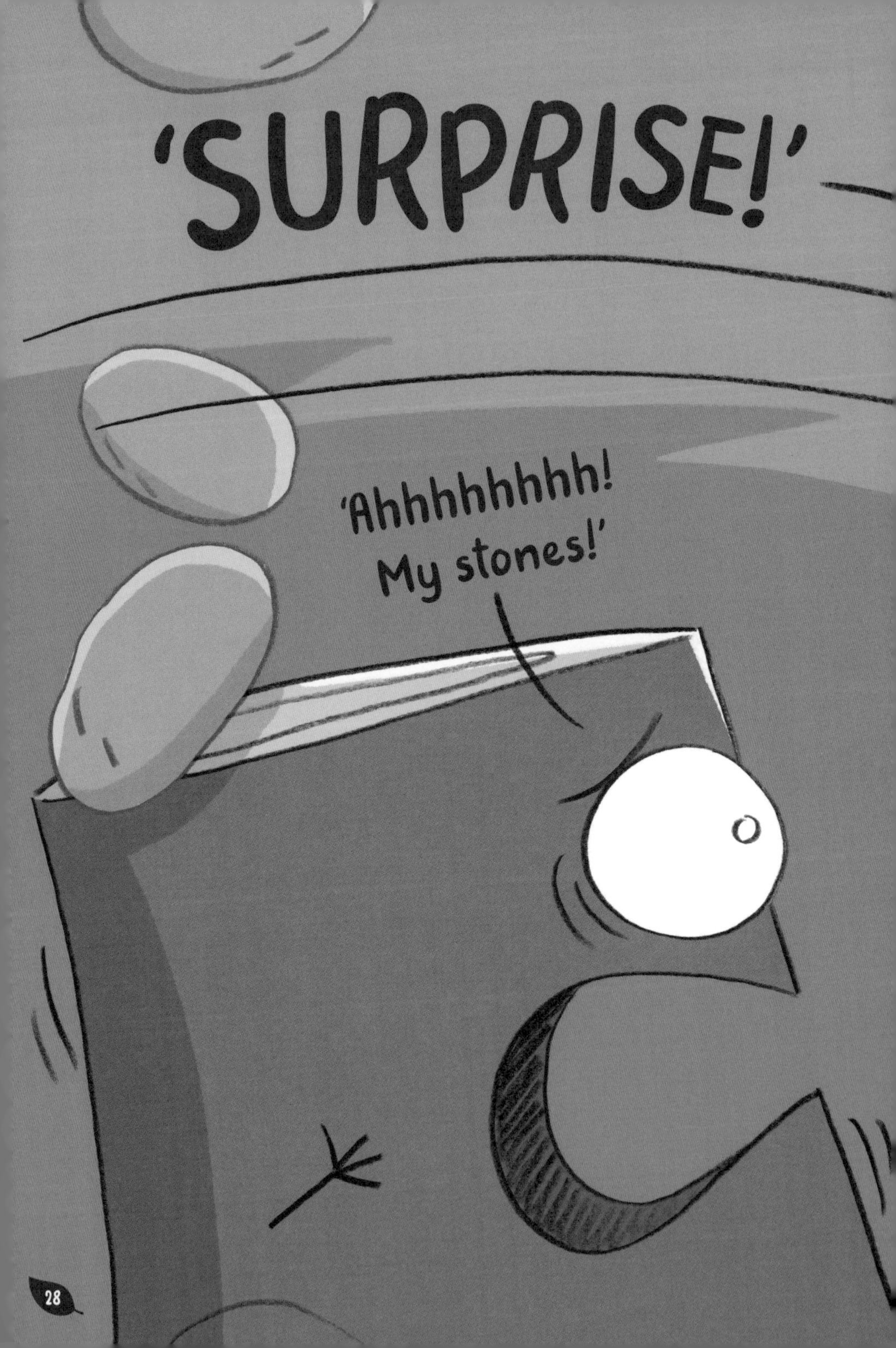
'SURPRISE!'
'Ahhhhhhhh!
My stones!'

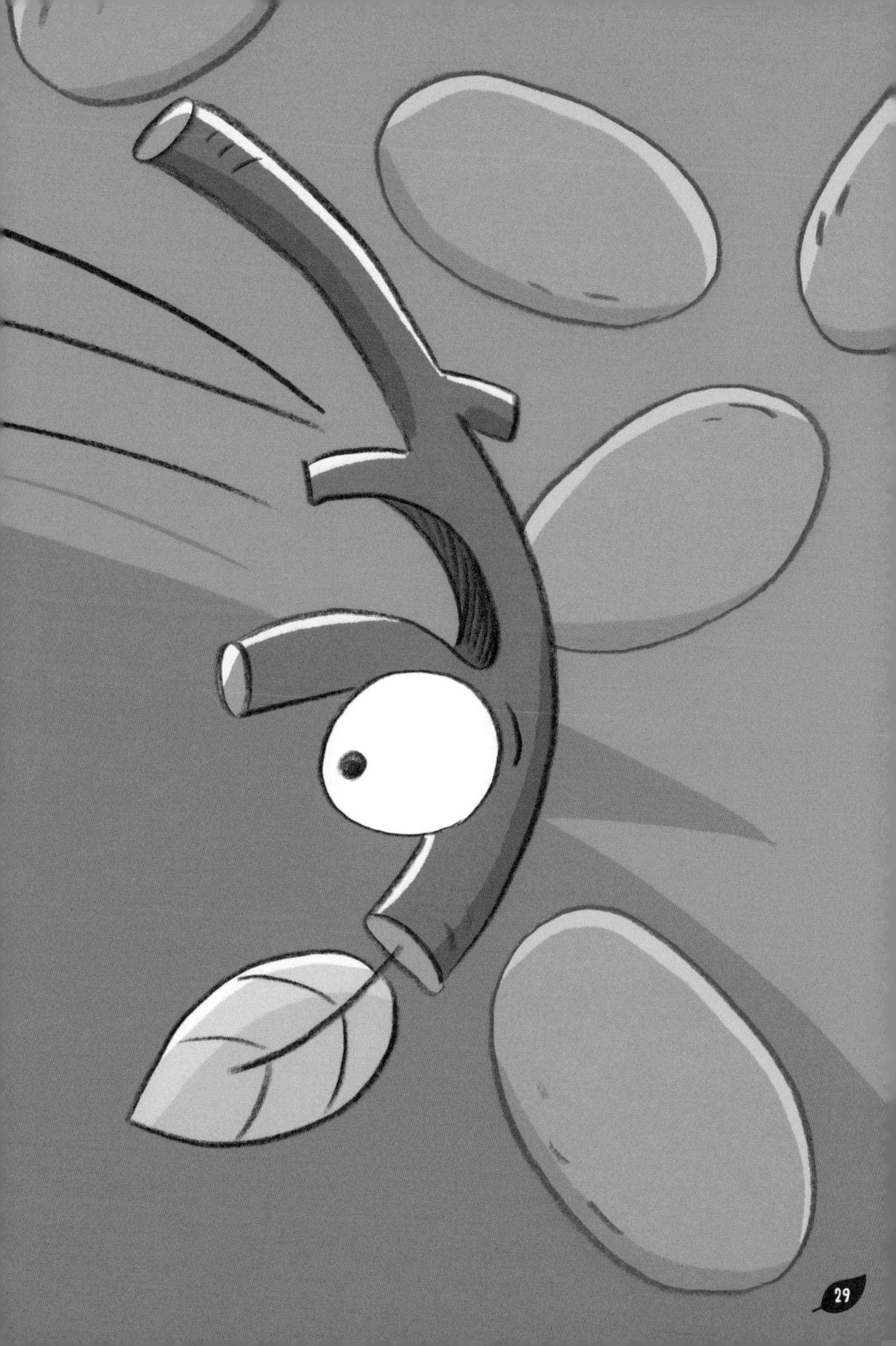

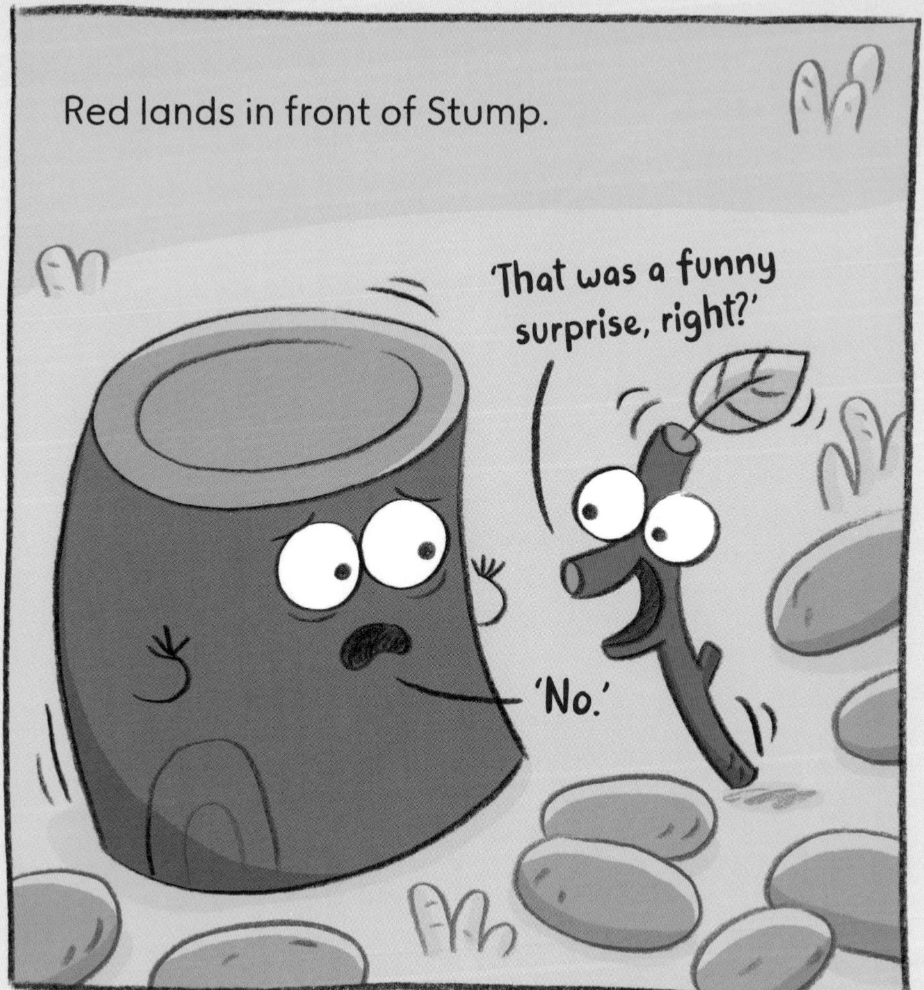
Red lands in front of Stump.
'That was a funny surprise, right?'
'No.'

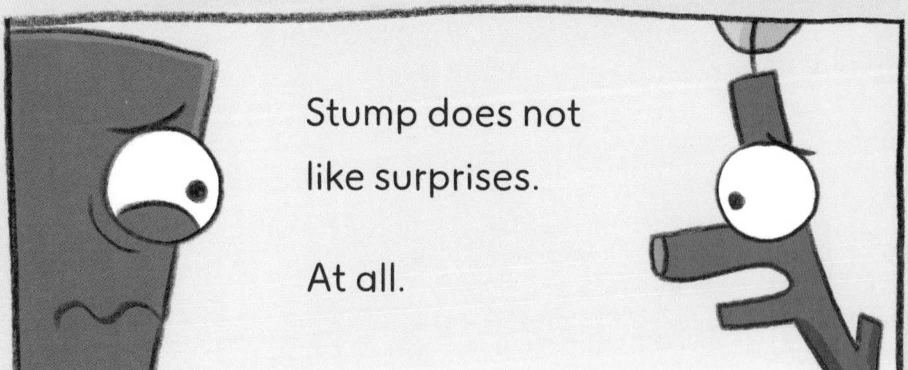
Stump does not like surprises.
At all.

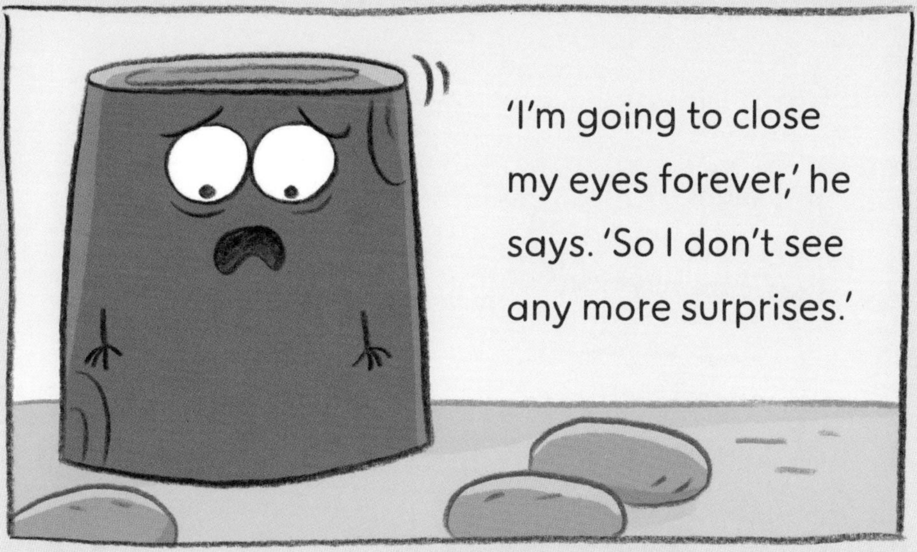
'I'm going to close my eyes forever,' he says. 'So I don't see any more surprises.'

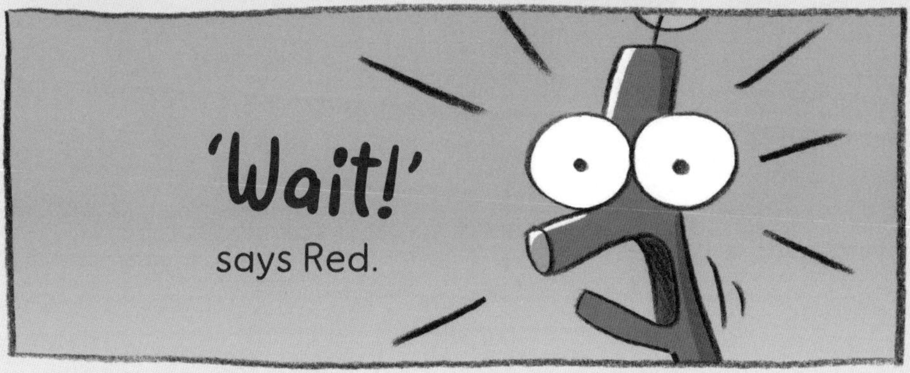
'Wait!'
says Red.

But it's too late.

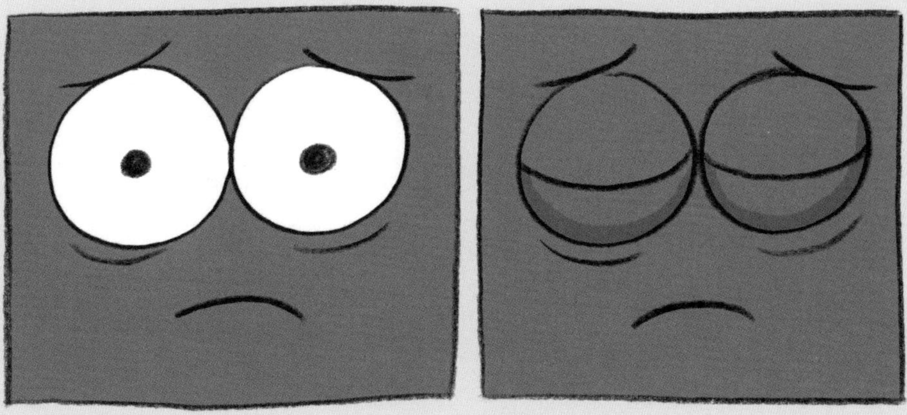

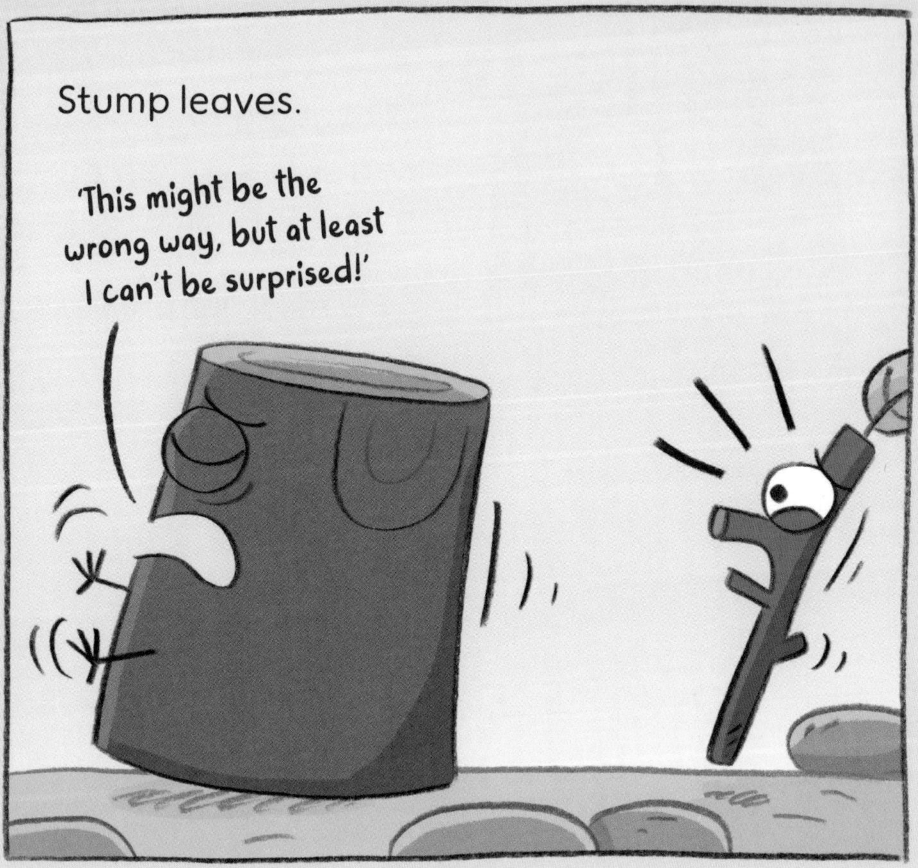
Stump leaves.
'This might be the wrong way, but at least I can't be surprised!'

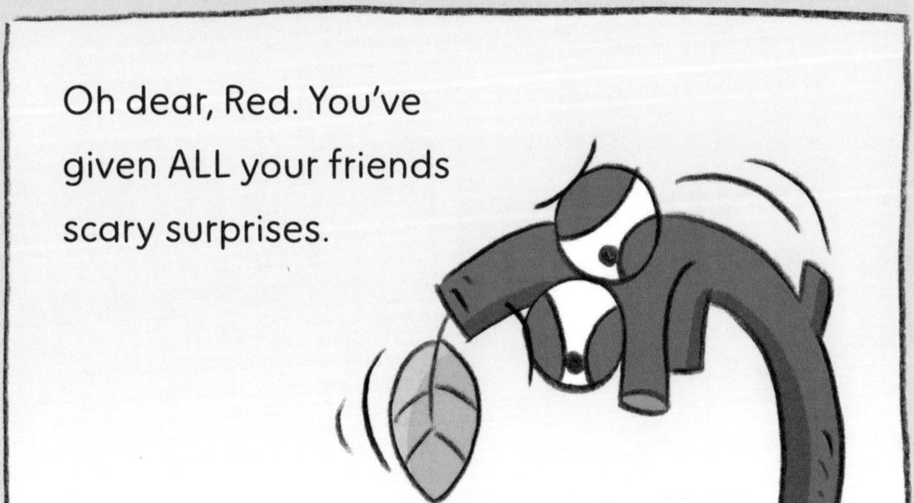
Oh dear, Red. You've given ALL your friends scary surprises.

Red flops down.

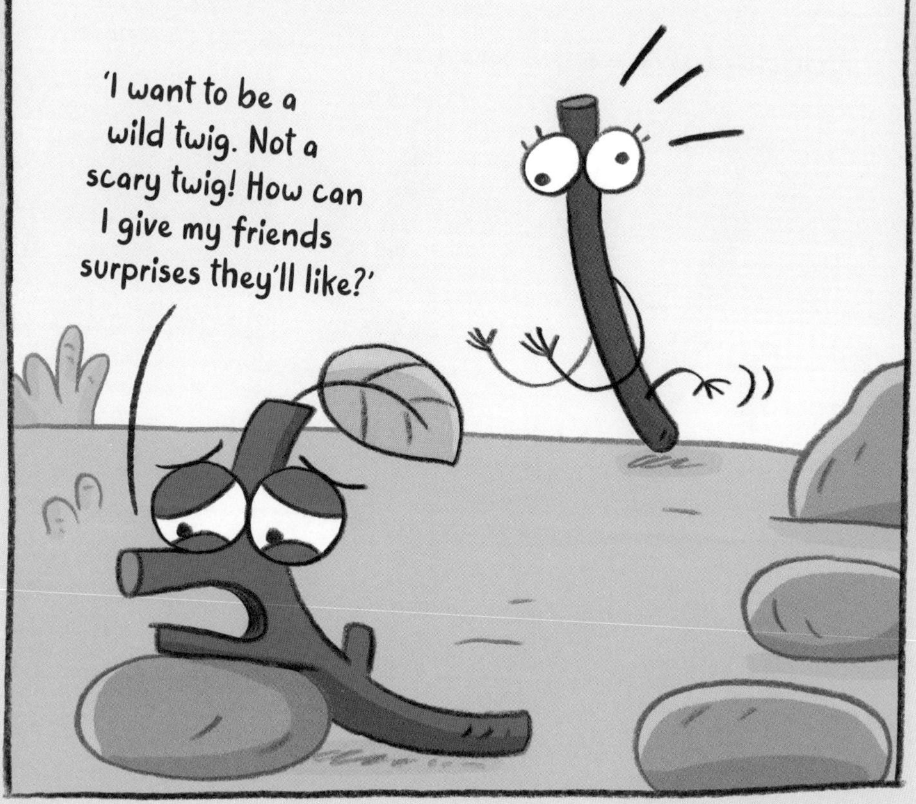
'I want to be a wild twig. Not a scary twig! How can I give my friends surprises they'll like?'

Noodle is nearby,
and gets an idea.

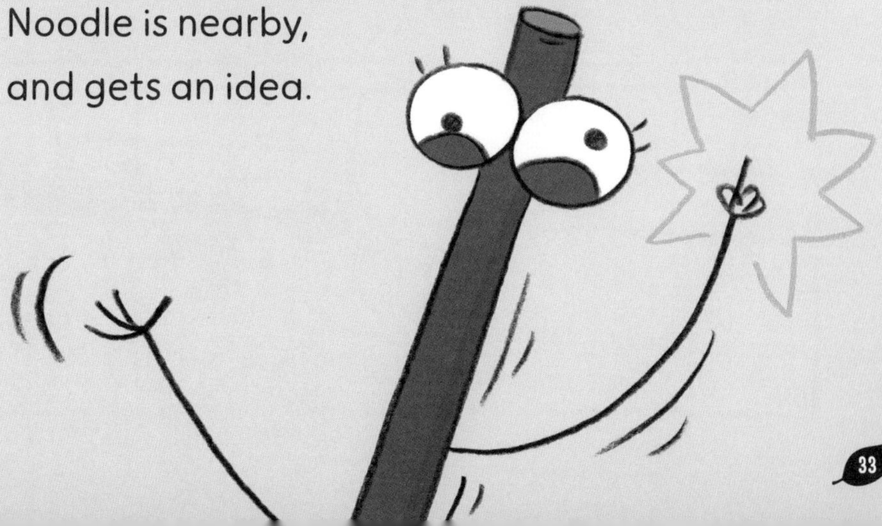

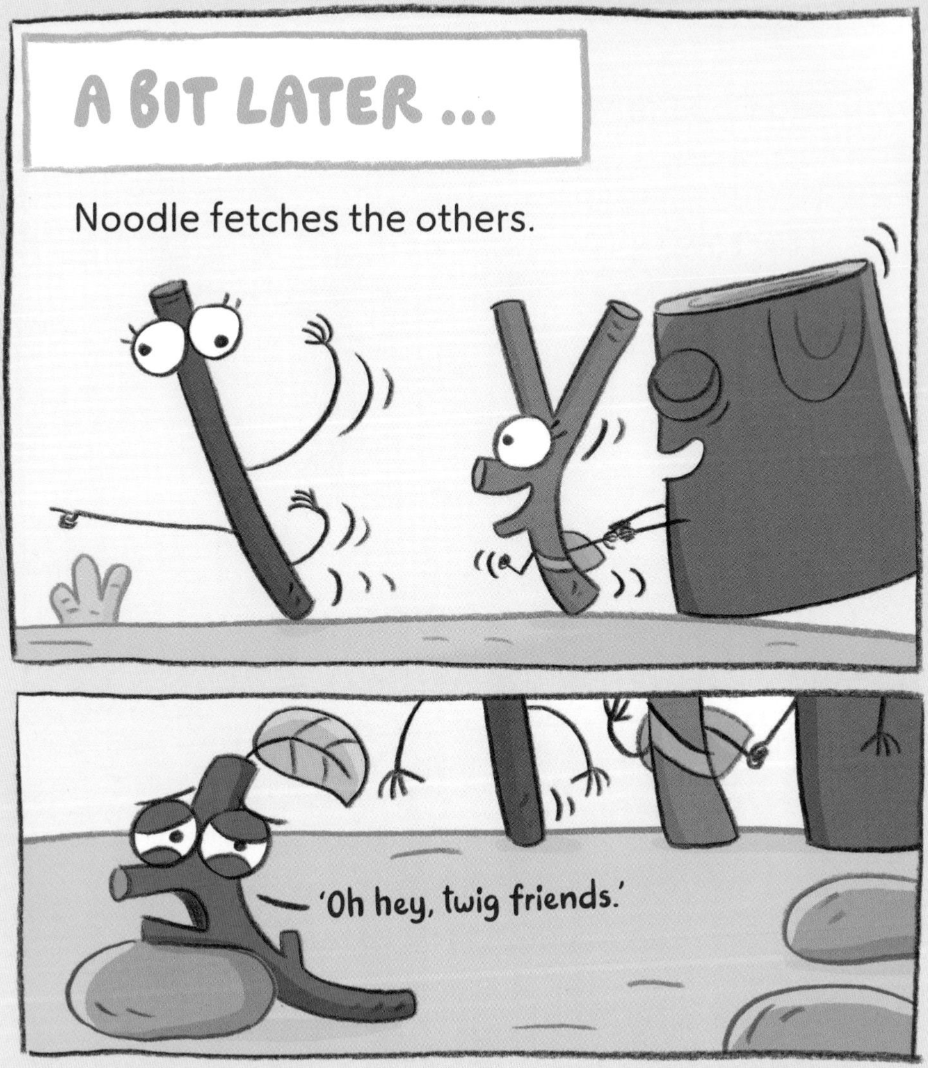
A BIT LATER ...
Noodle fetches the others.
'Oh hey, twig friends.'
And they all grab Red.
'Huh?'

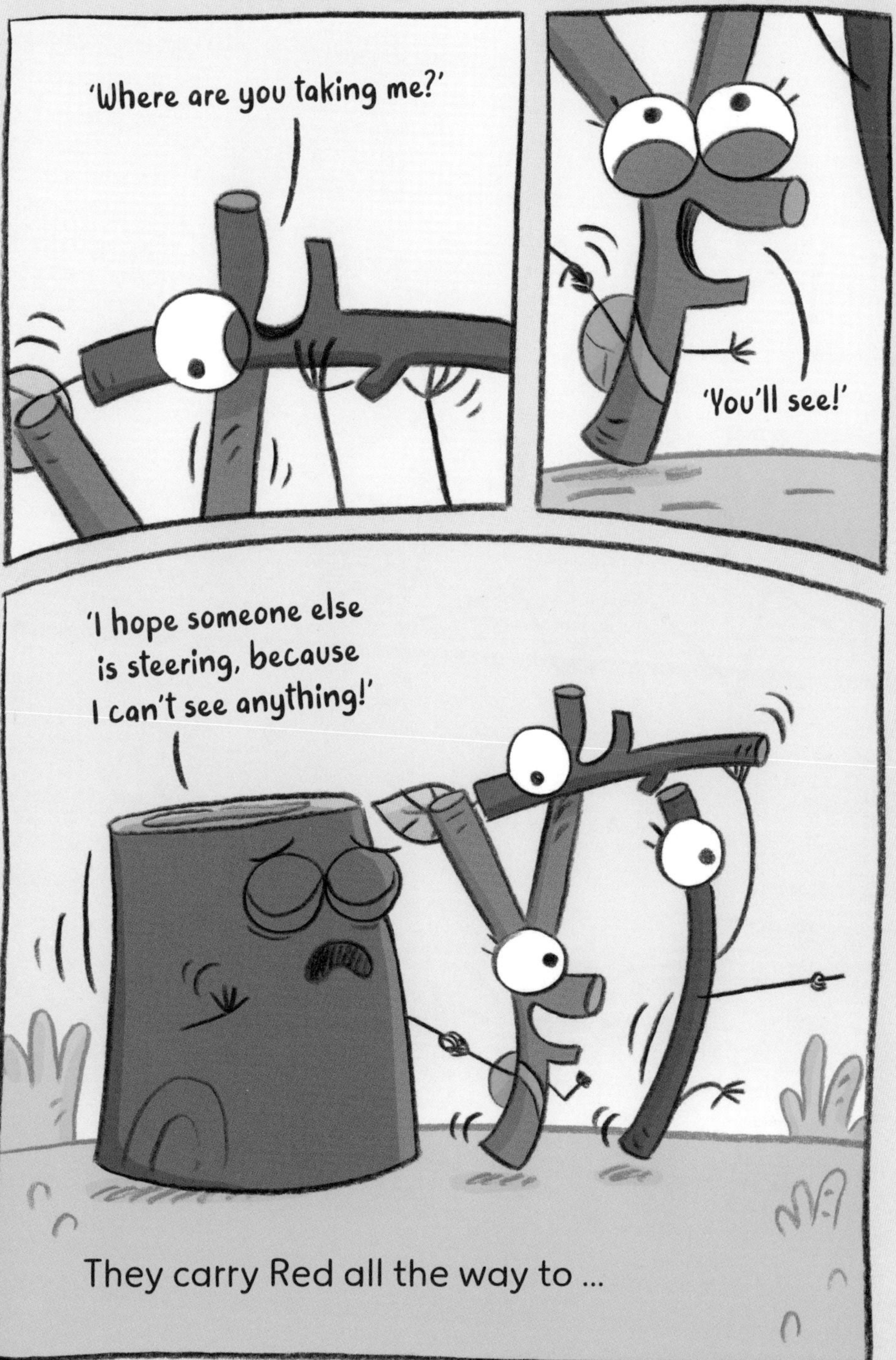
'Where are you taking me?'
'You'll see!'
'I hope someone else is steering, because I can't see anything!'
They carry Red all the way to ...

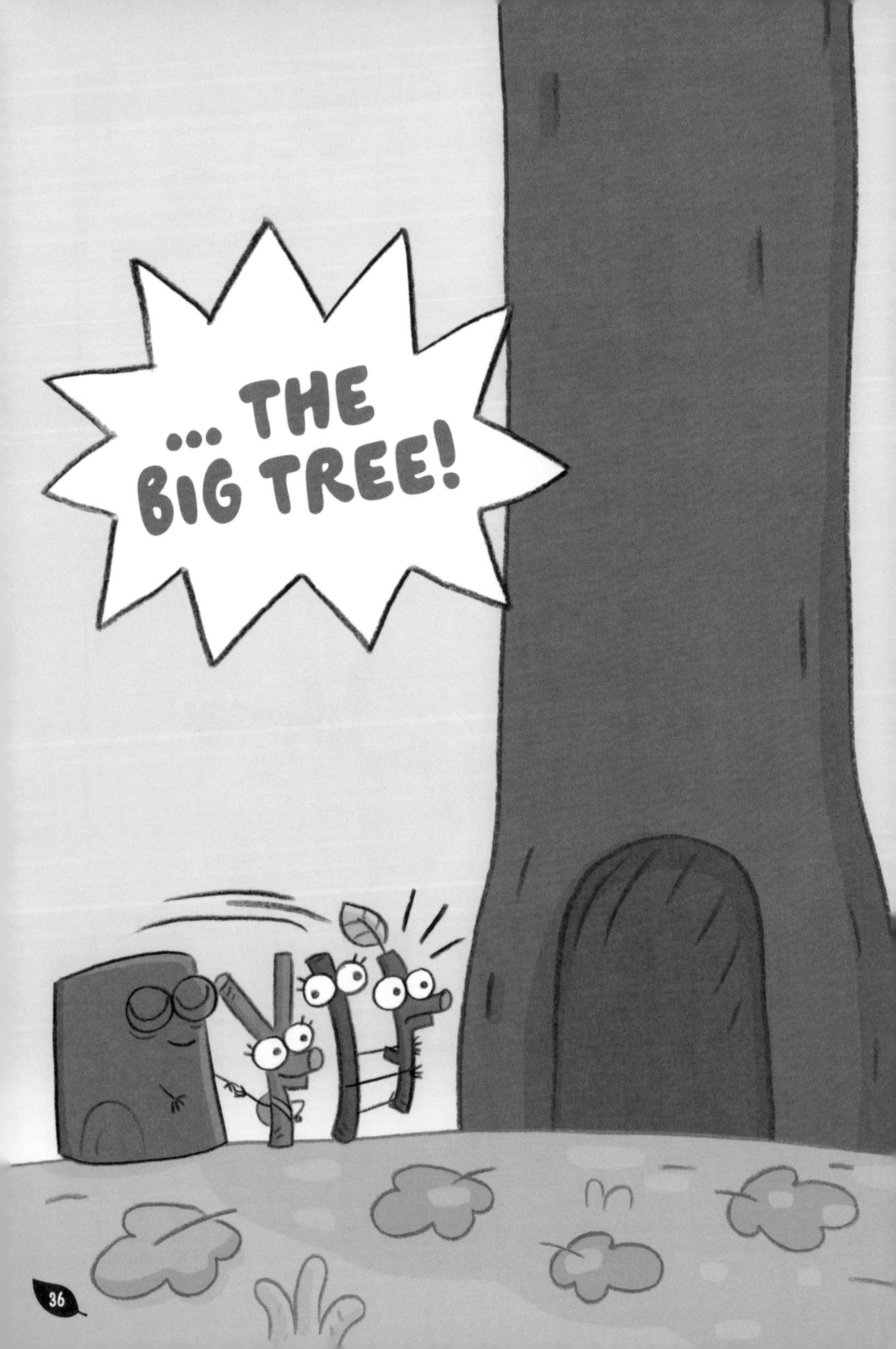
... THE BIG TREE!

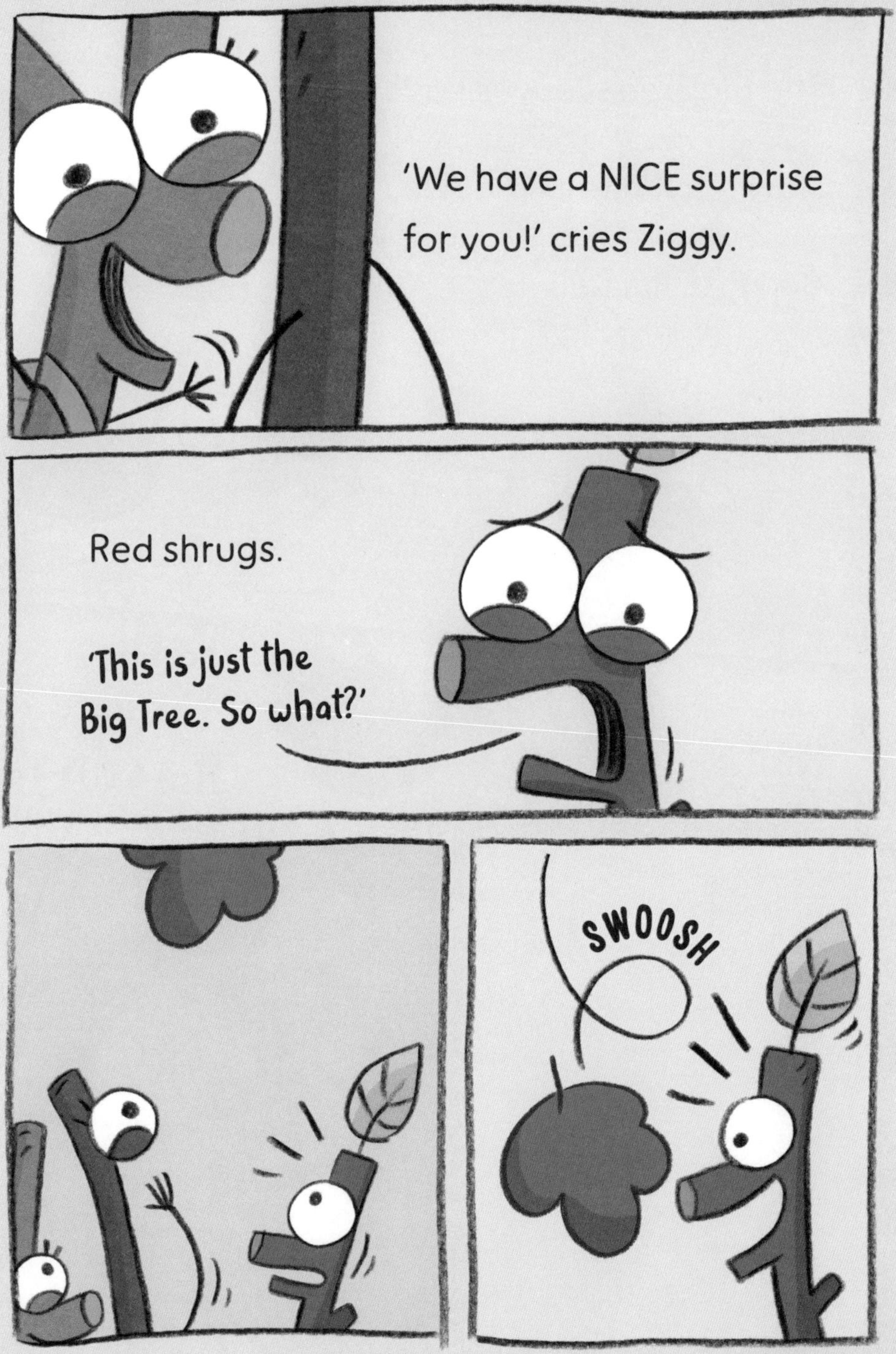
'We have a NICE surprise for you!' cries Ziggy.
Red shrugs.
'This is just the Big Tree. So what?'
SWOOSH

The Big Tree's leaves have turned RED.

Now they're falling down.

Because it's fall!

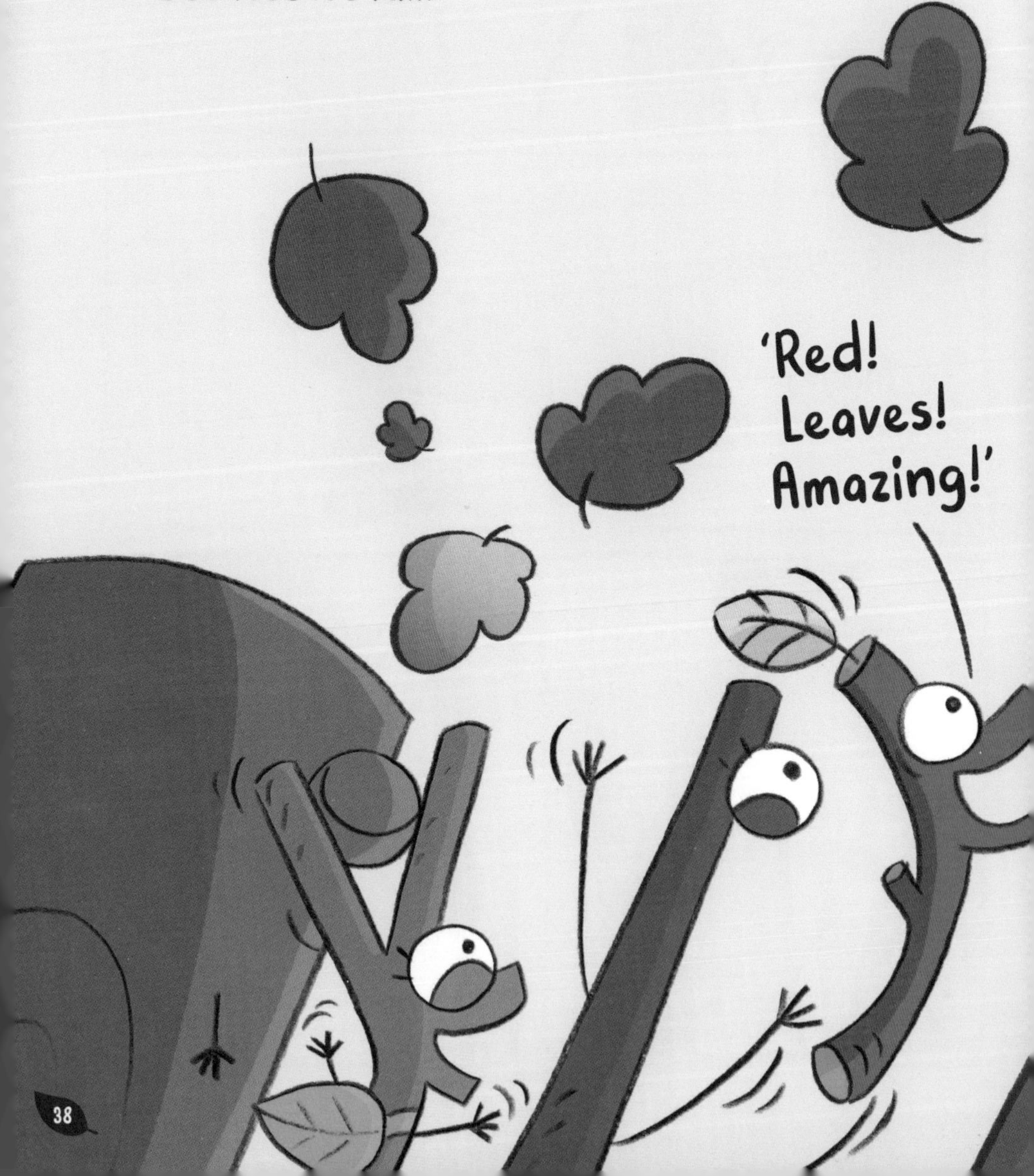
'Red!
Leaves!
Amazing!'

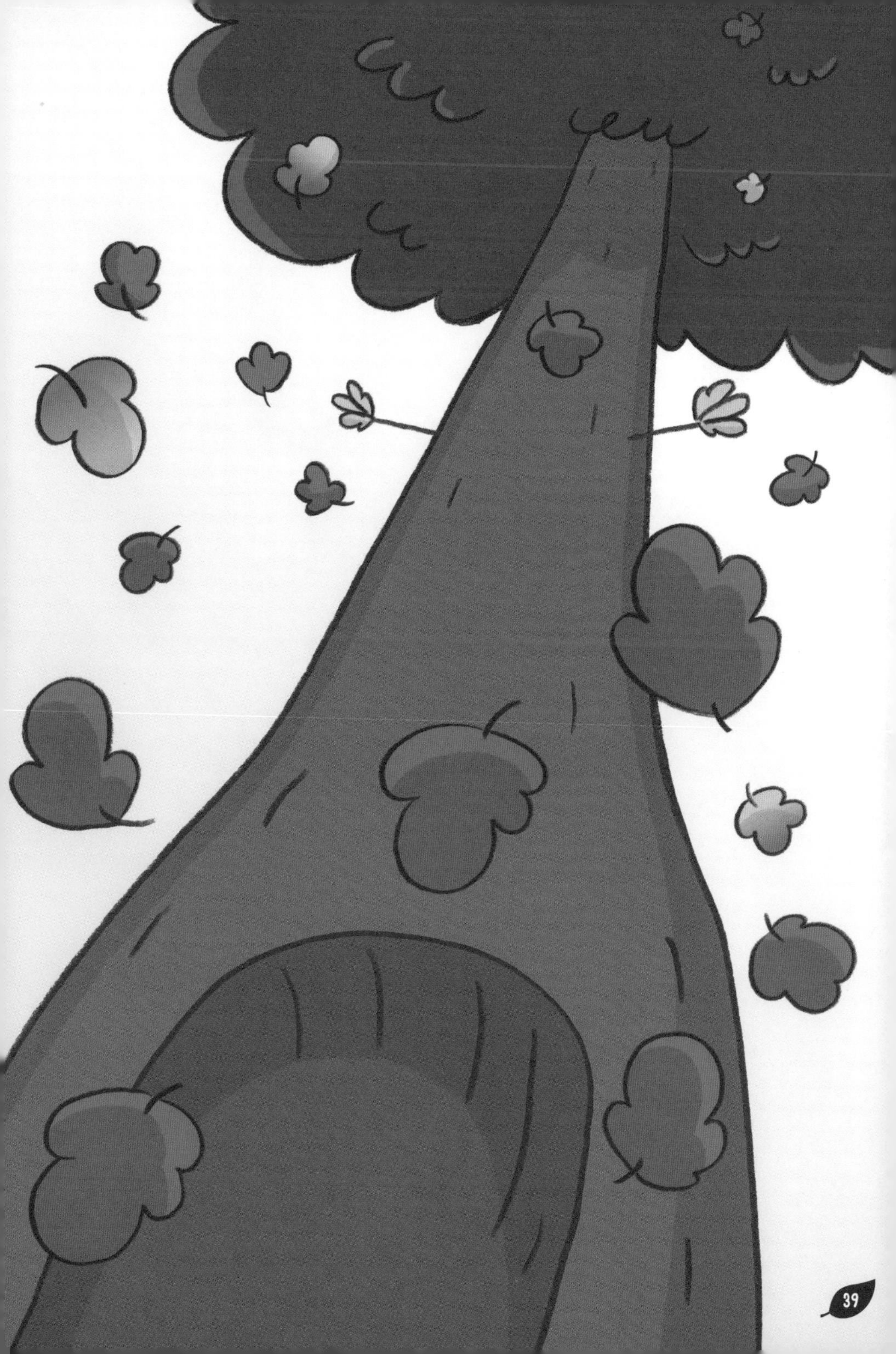

Suddenly, Red understands.

The best surprises are NICE SURPRISES!

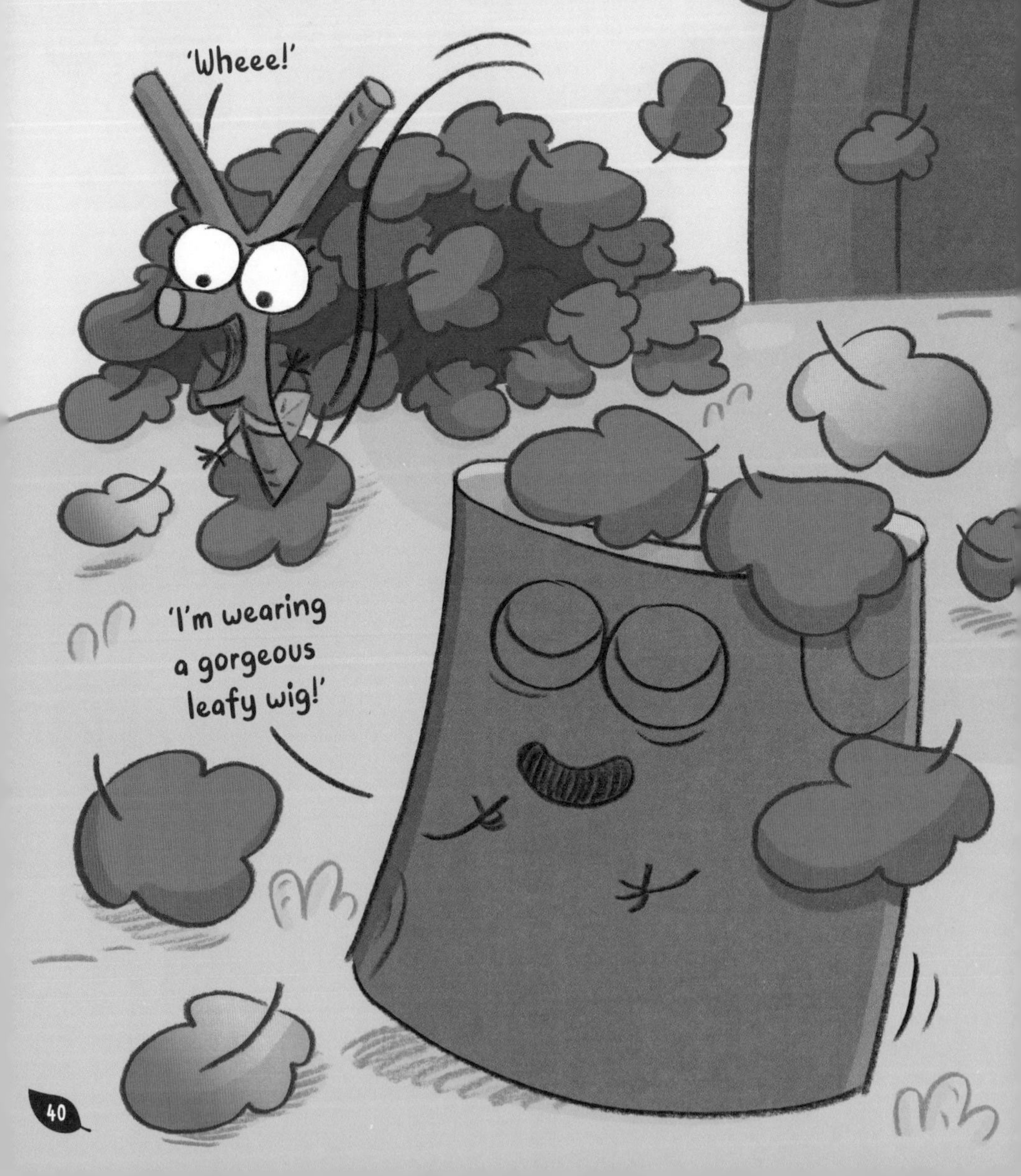
'Wheee!'
'I'm wearing a gorgeous leafy wig!'

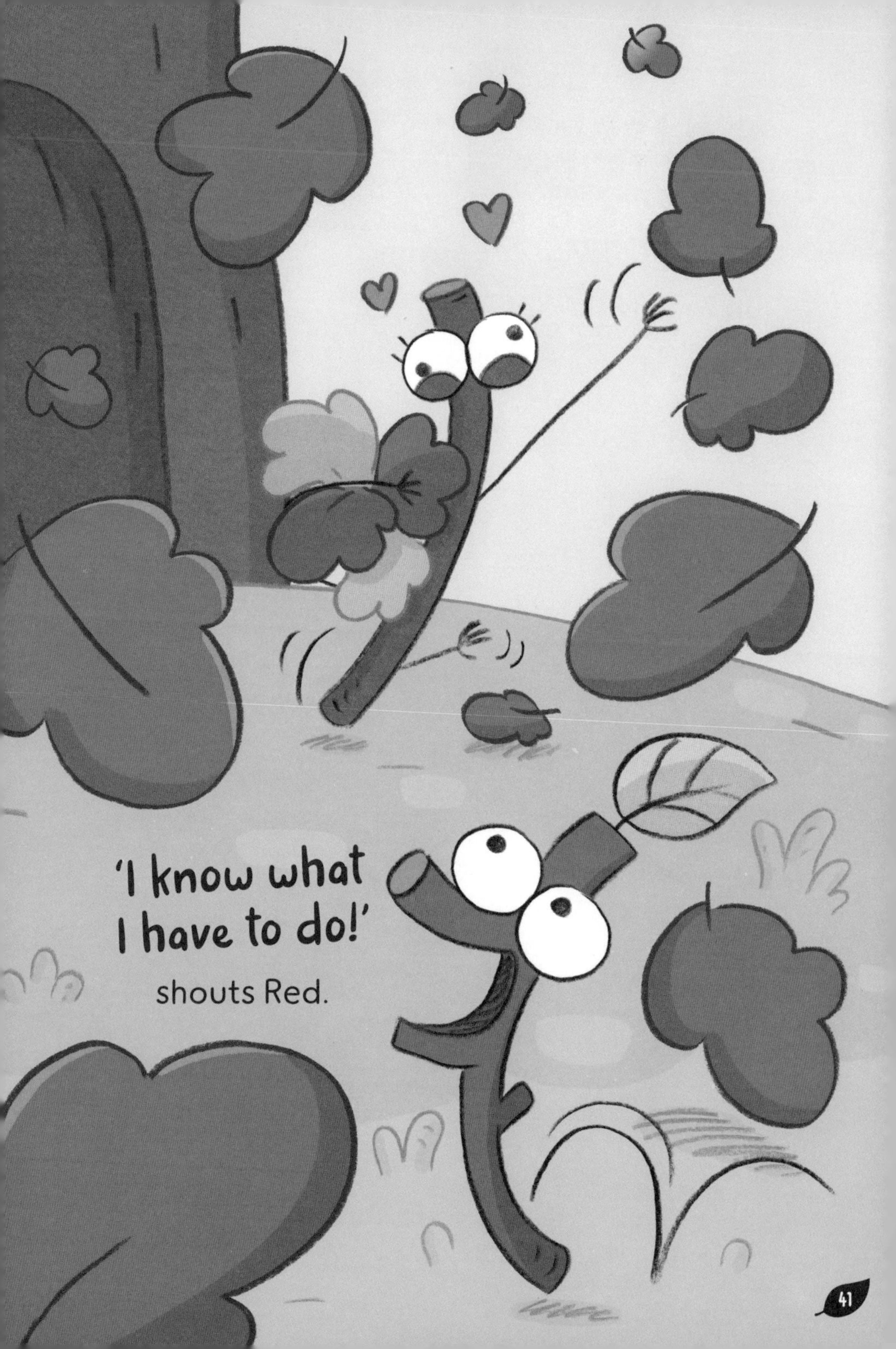

'I know what I have to do!'

shouts Red.

SOON ...

The other twigs are setting up the SNAIL ZOO.

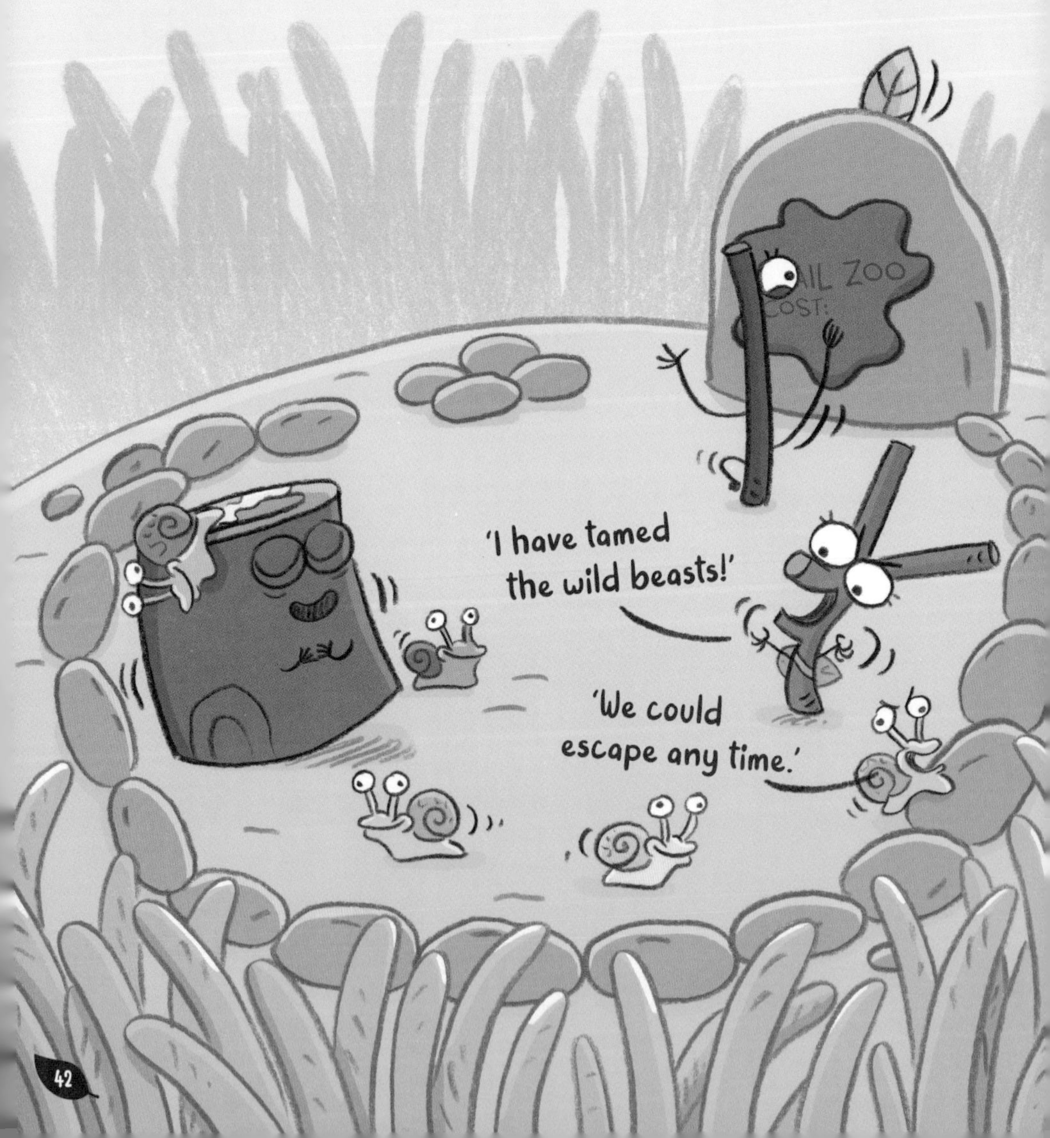
'I have tamed the wild beasts!'
'We could escape any time.'

While Red watches from behind a rock.

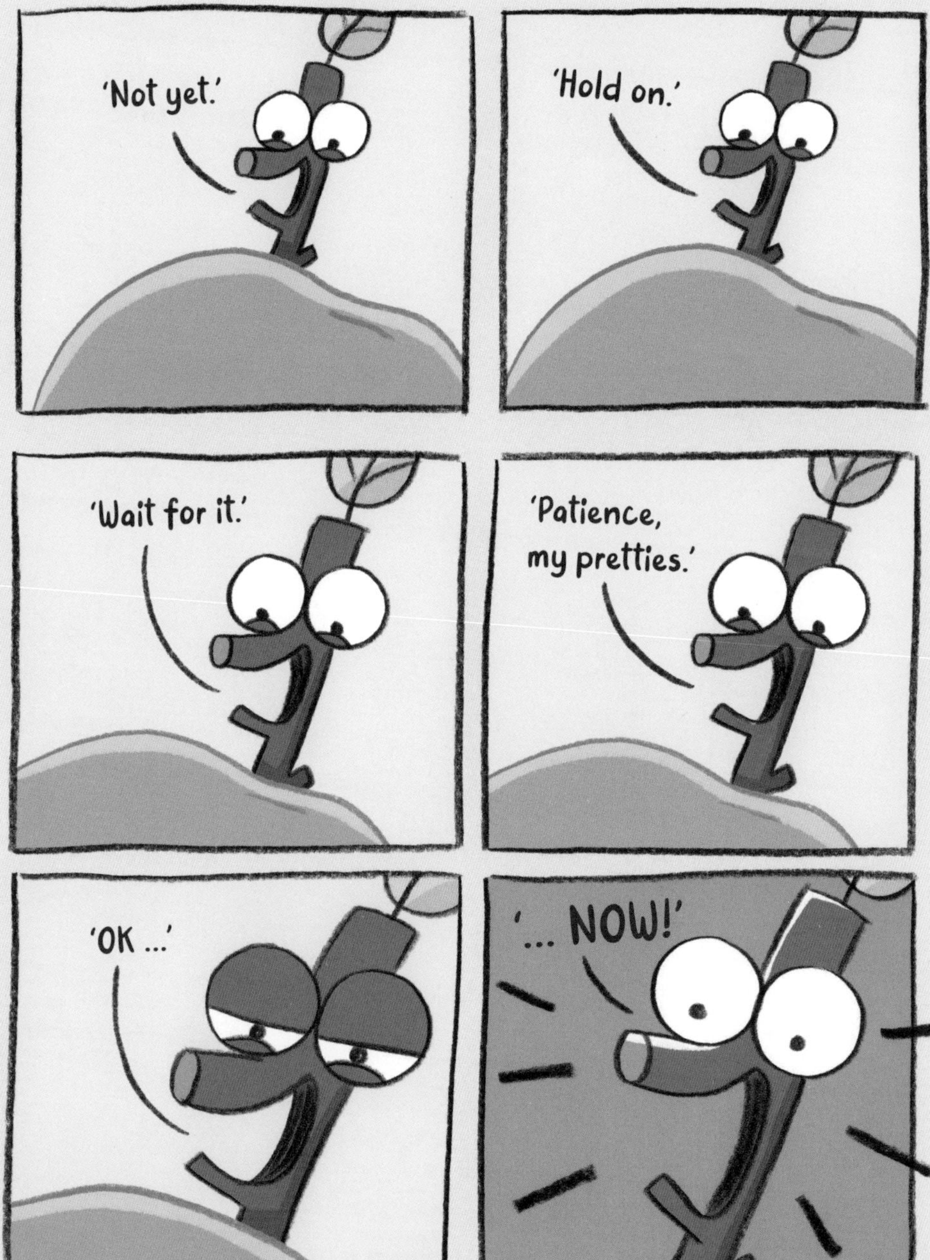
'Not yet.'
'Hold on.'
'Wait for it.'
'Patience,
my pretties.'
'OK ...'
'... NOW!'

He leaps out.

With a hundred snails.

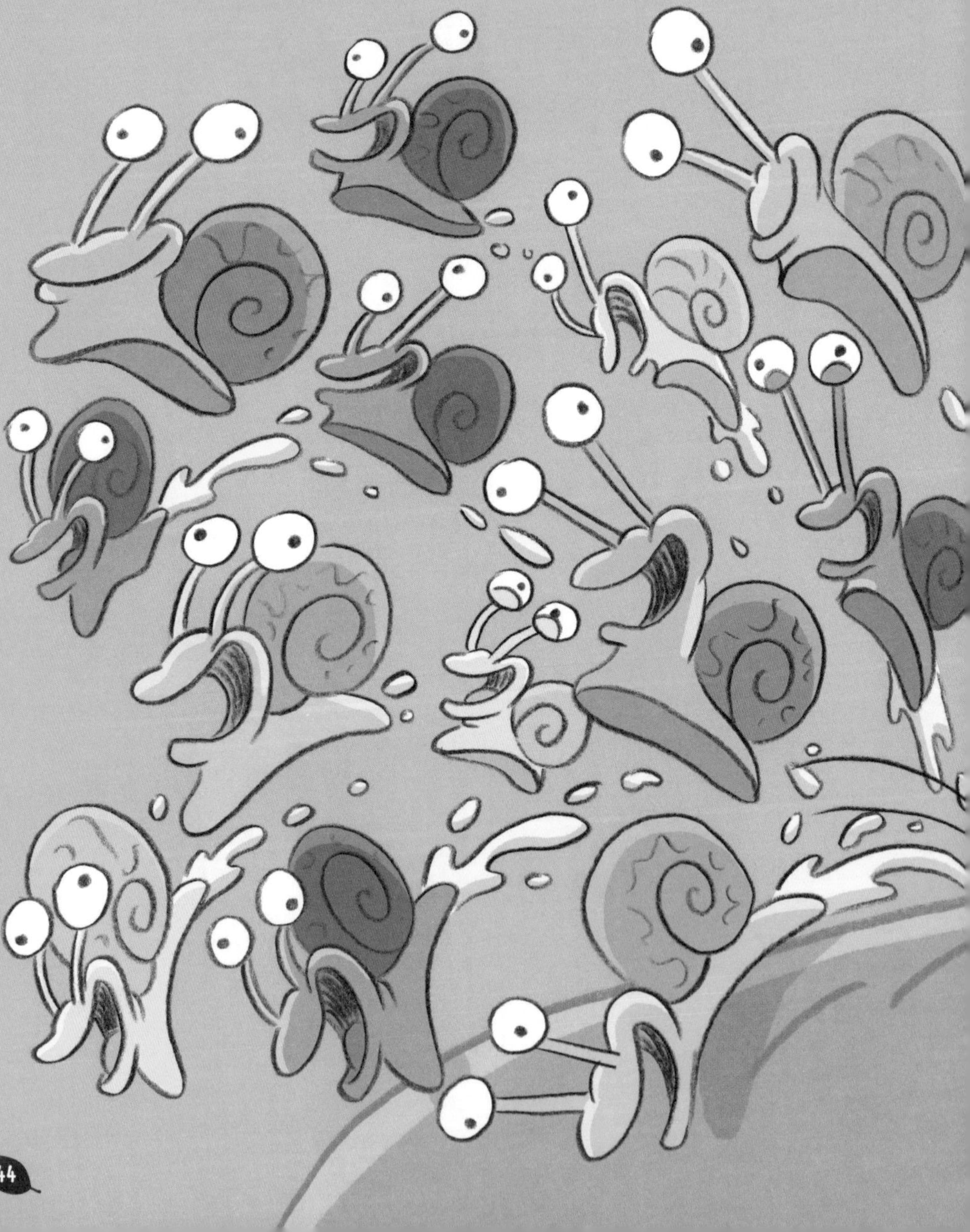

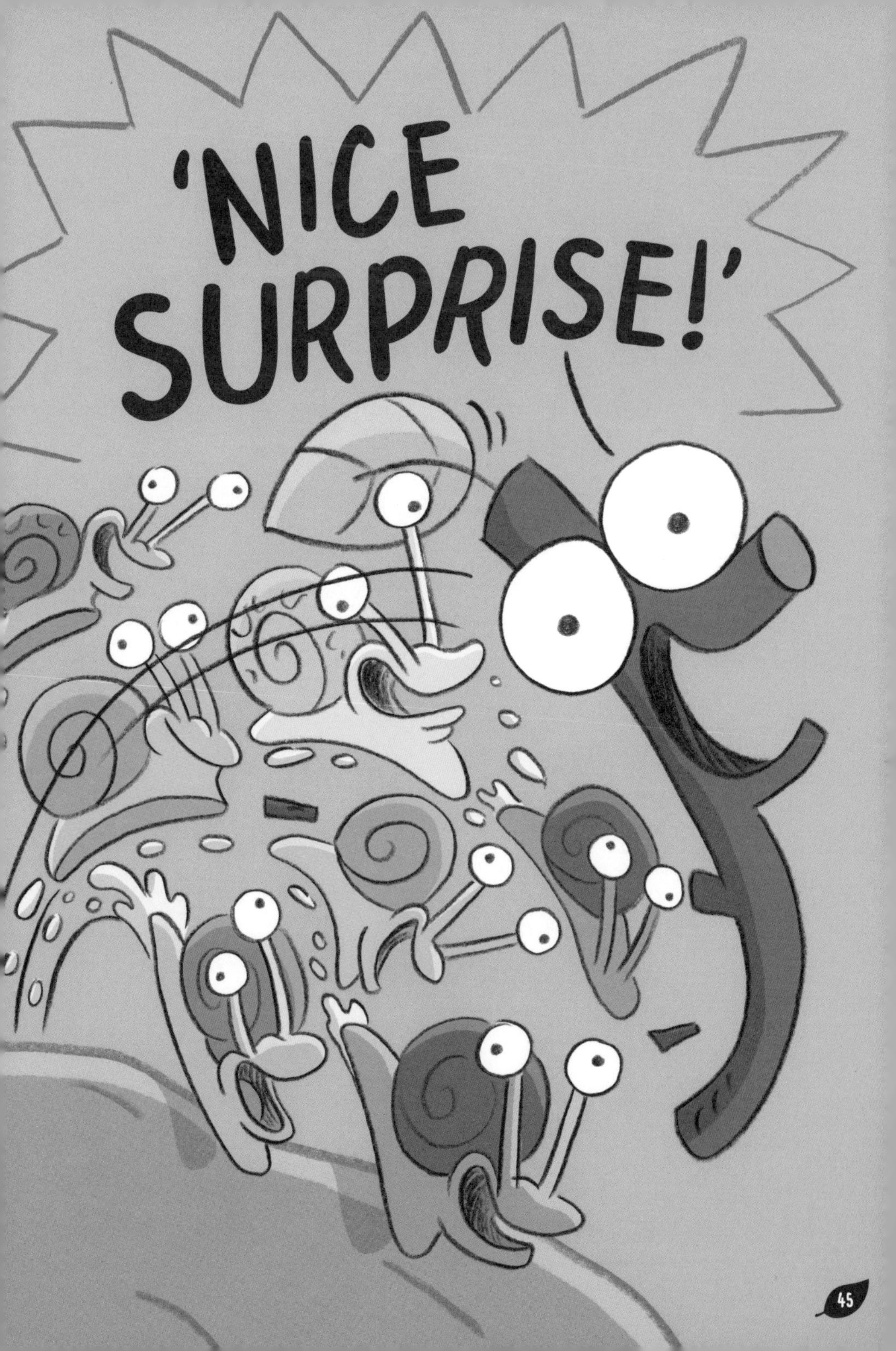
'NICE SURPRISE!'

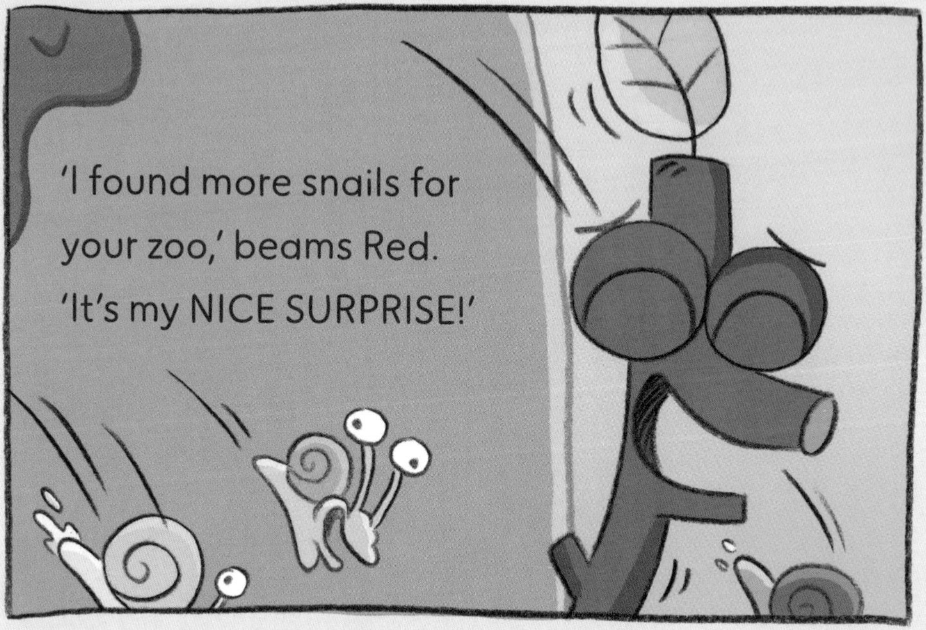
'I found more snails for
your zoo,' beams Red.
'It's my NICE SURPRISE!'

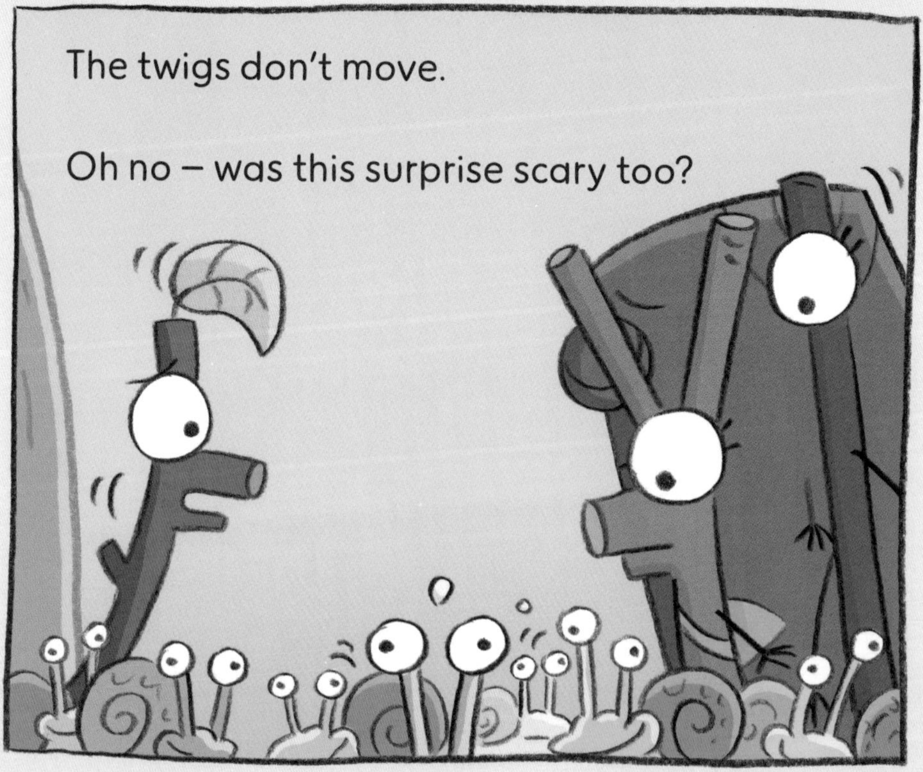
The twigs don't move.
Oh no – was this surprise scary too?

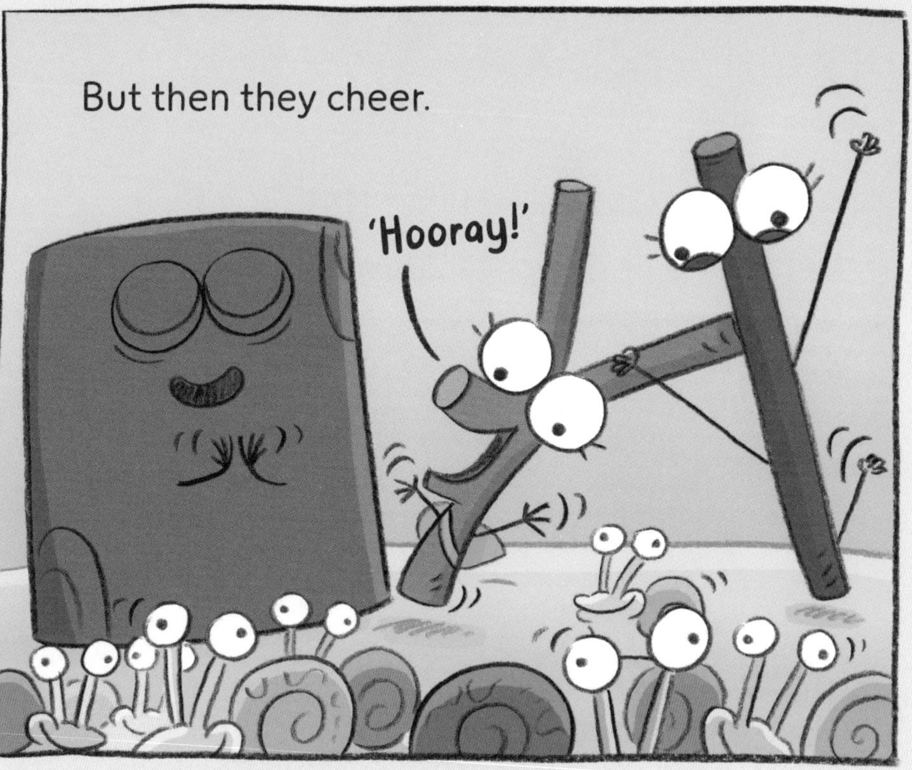
But then they cheer.
'Hooray!'

'I need to see this,' says Stump.

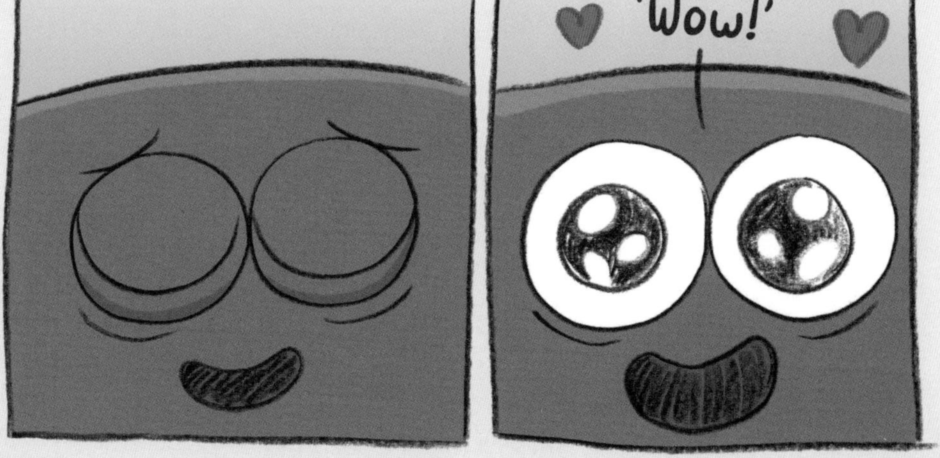
'Wow!'

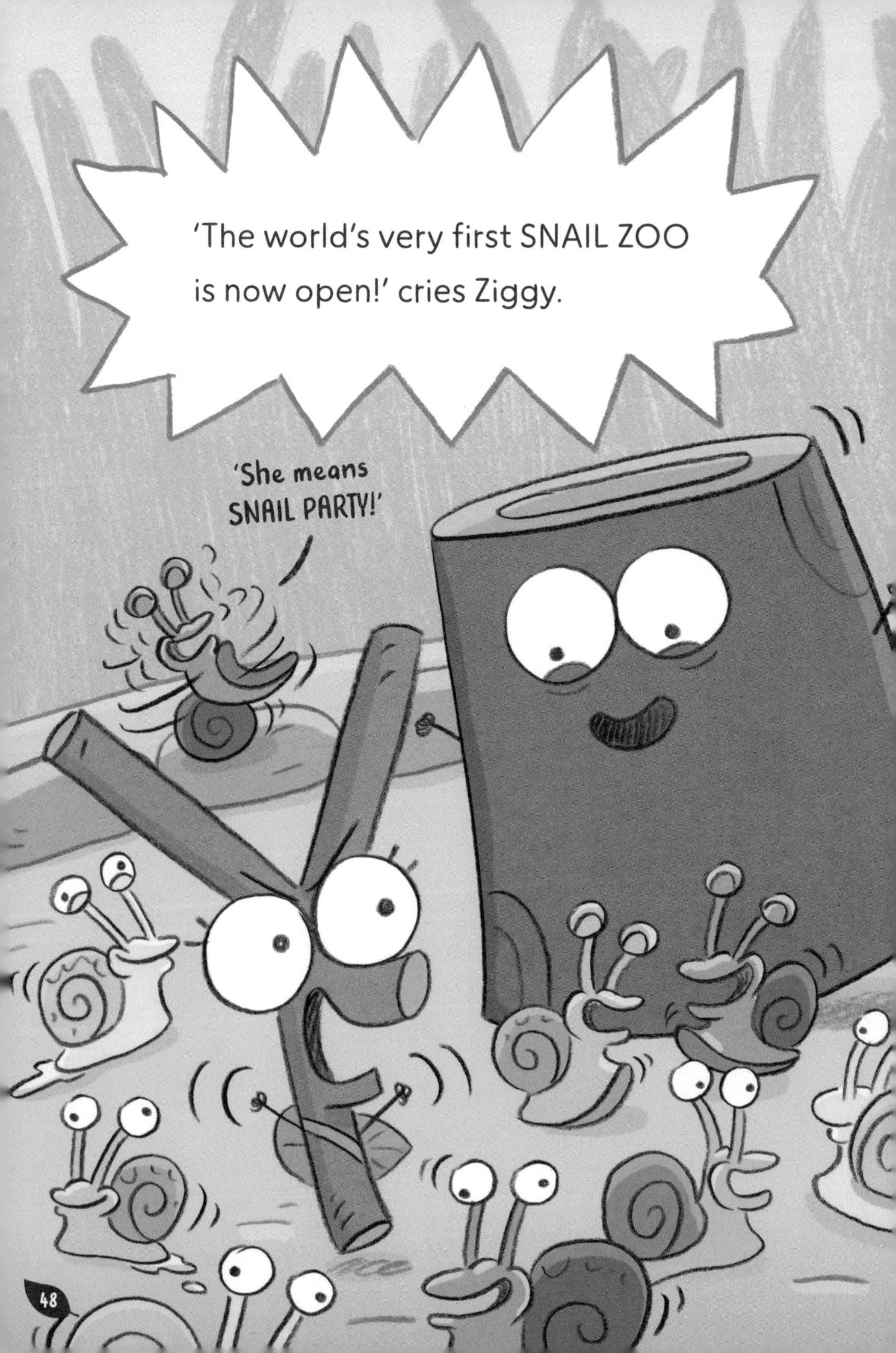
'The world's very first SNAIL ZOO is now open!' cries Ziggy.
'She means SNAIL PARTY!'

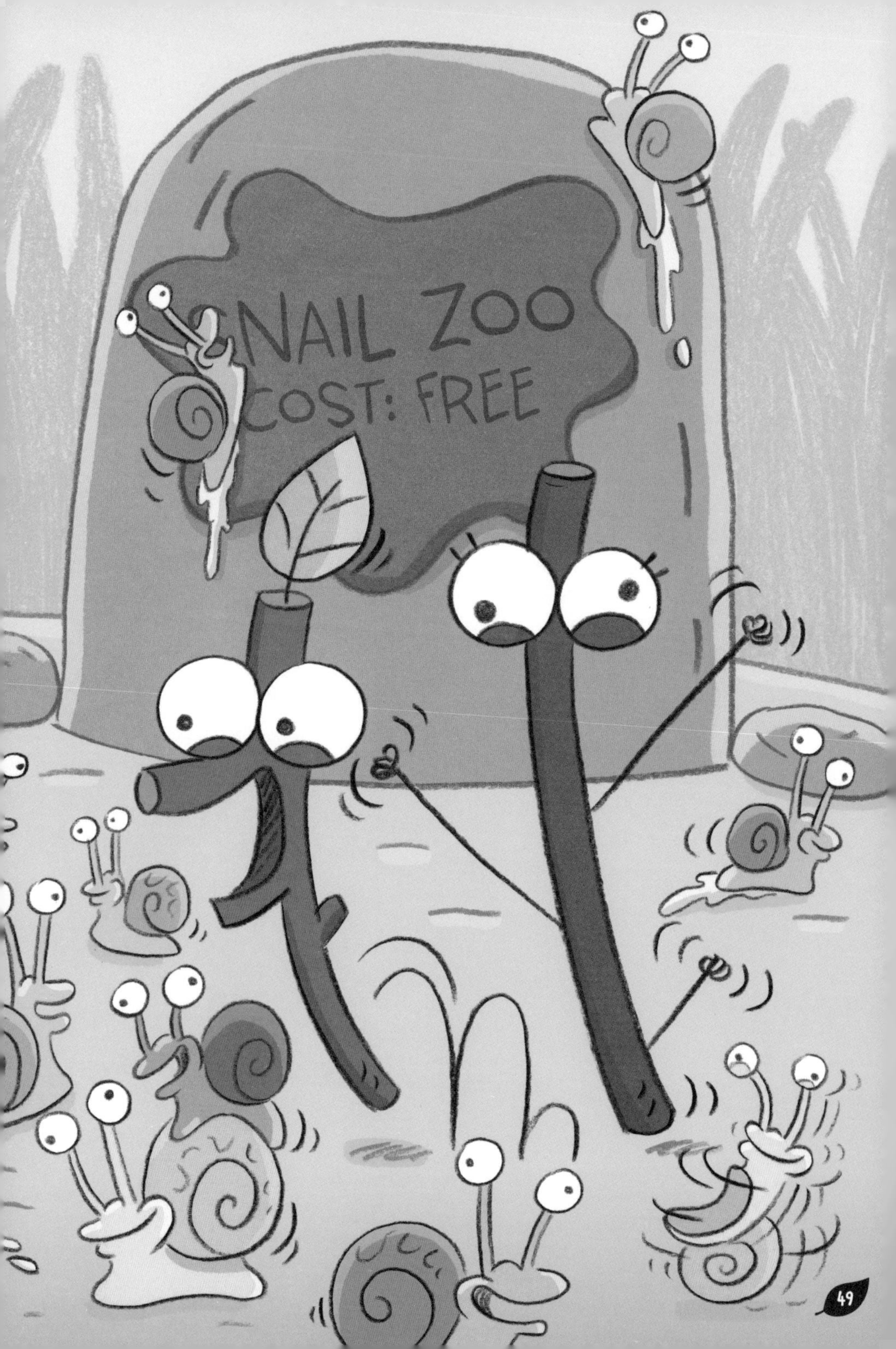
SNAIL ZOO
COST: FREE

Go, Red, go!

You might be a WILD TWIG.

But you're also a NICE TWIG!

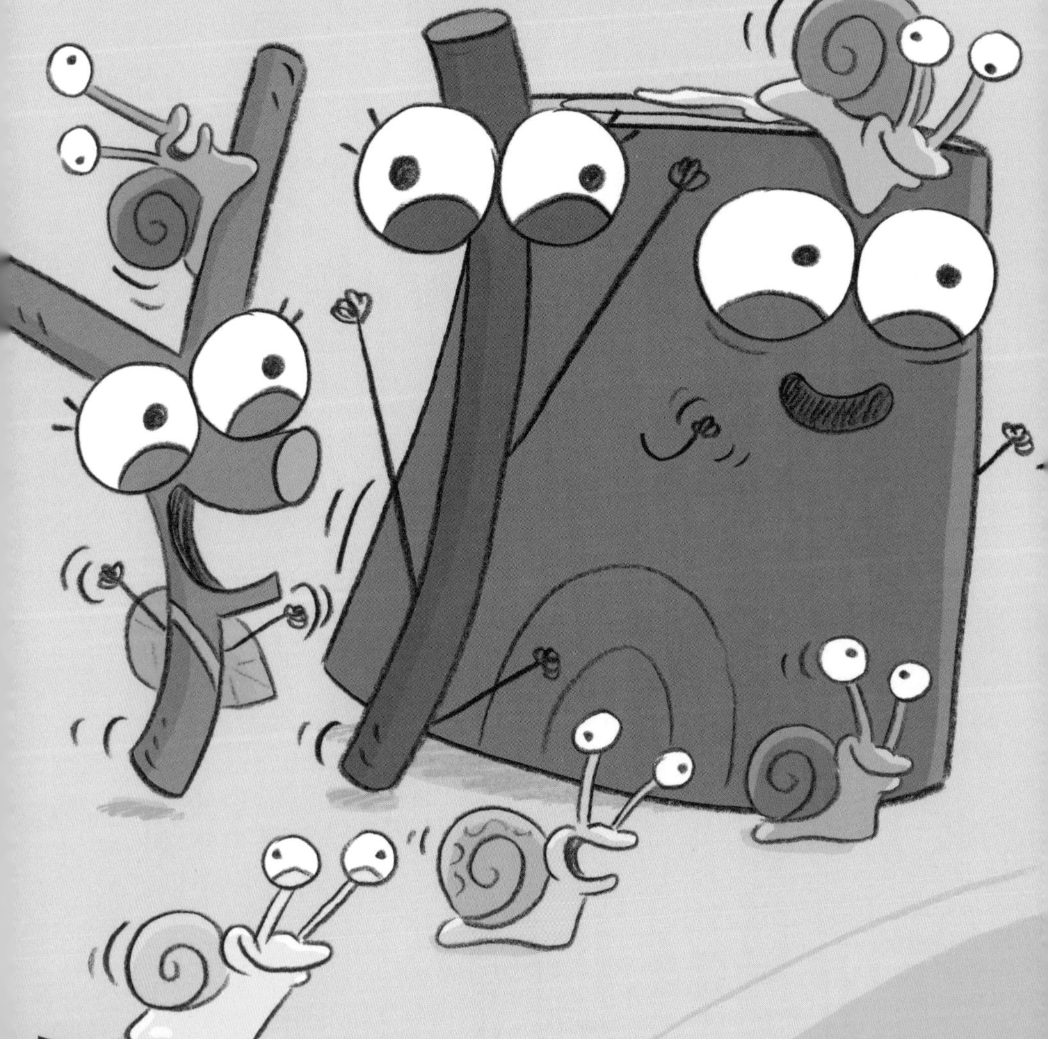

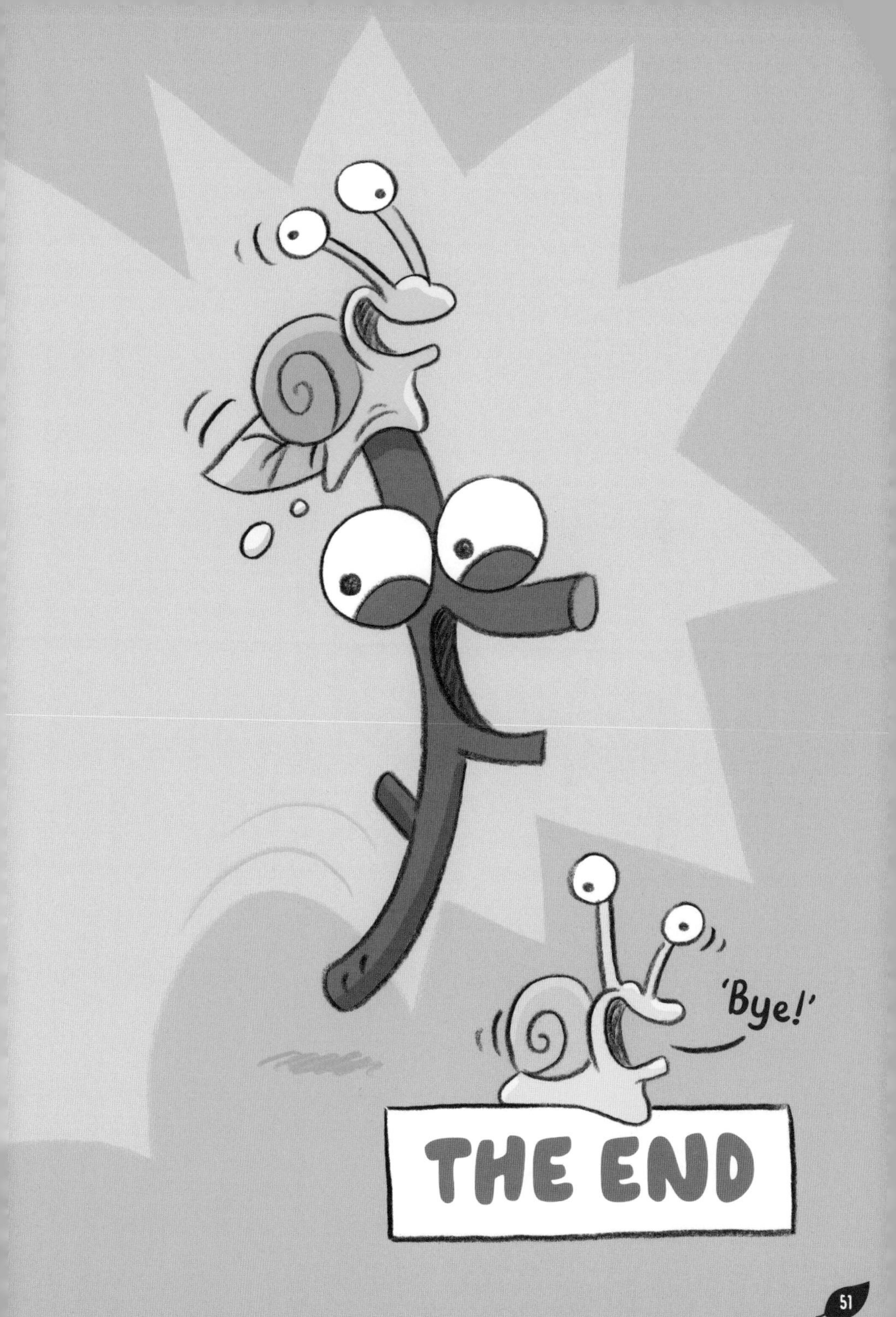
'Bye!'
THE END

2. ZIGGY AND THE VOLCANO

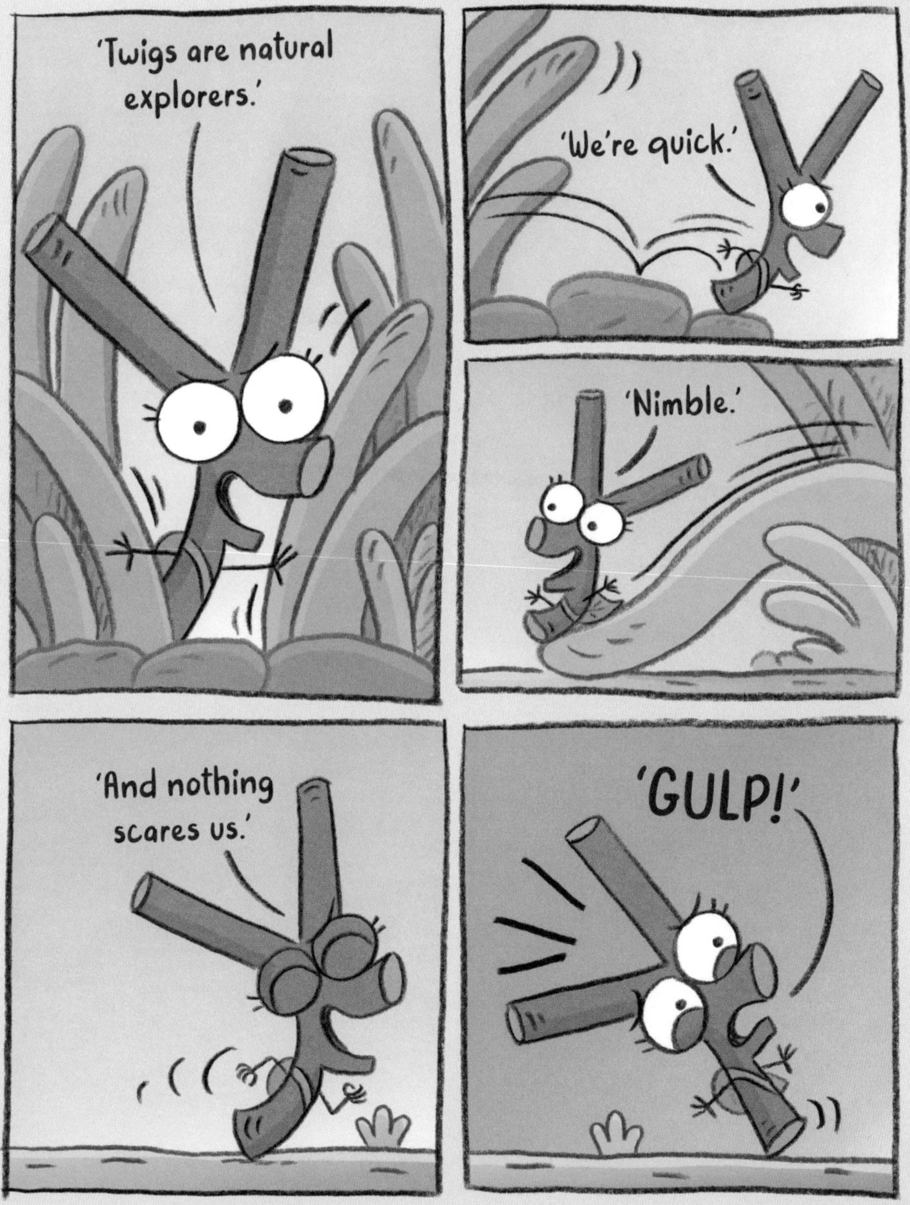

'Twigs are natural explorers.'
'We're quick.'
'Nimble.'
'And nothing scares us.'
'GULP!'

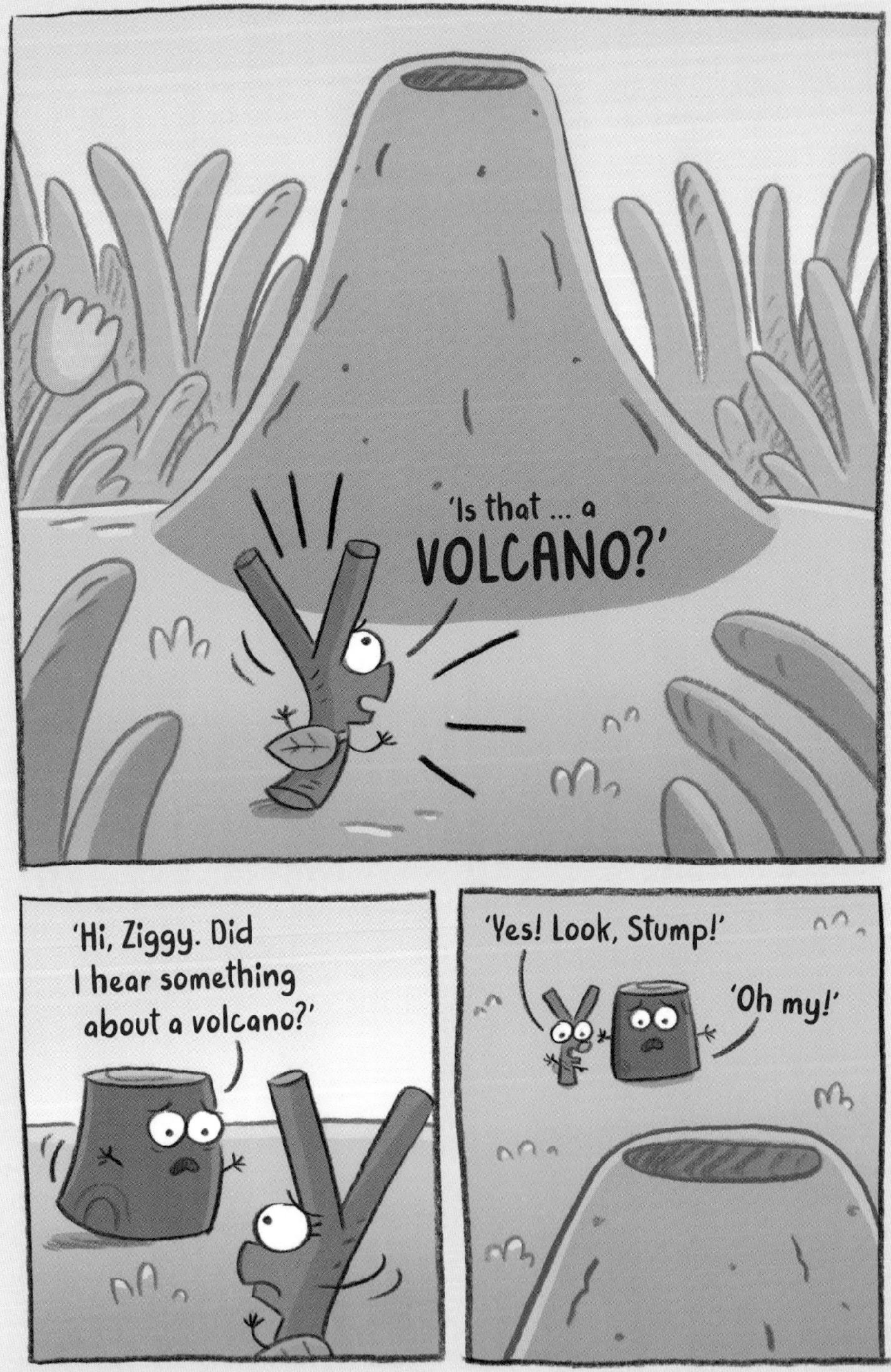
'Is that ... a
VOLCANO?'
'Hi, Ziggy. Did
I hear something
about a volcano?'
'Yes! Look, Stump!'
'Oh my!'

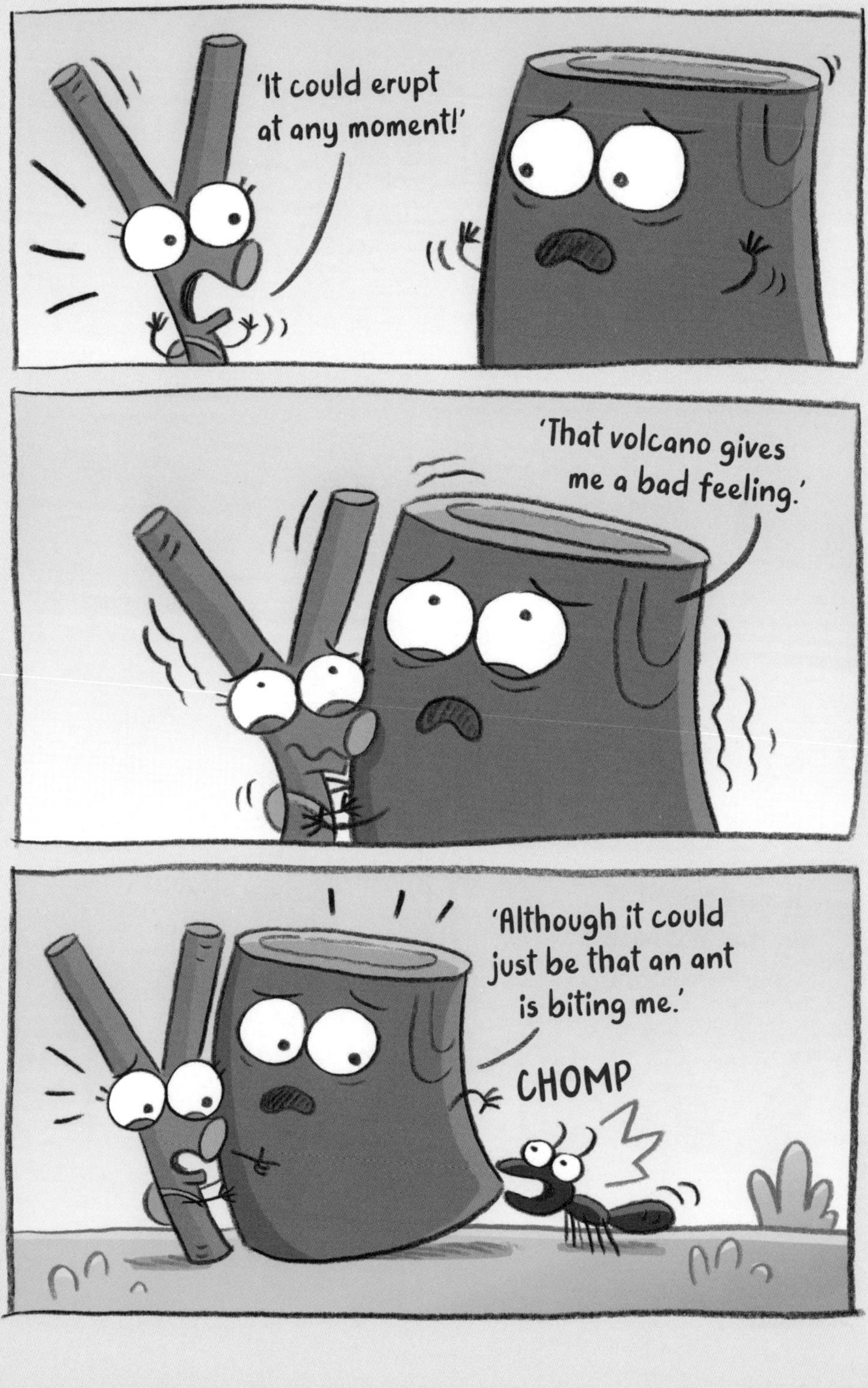
'It could erupt at any moment!'
'That volcano gives me a bad feeling.'
'Although it could just be that an ant is biting me.'
CHOMP

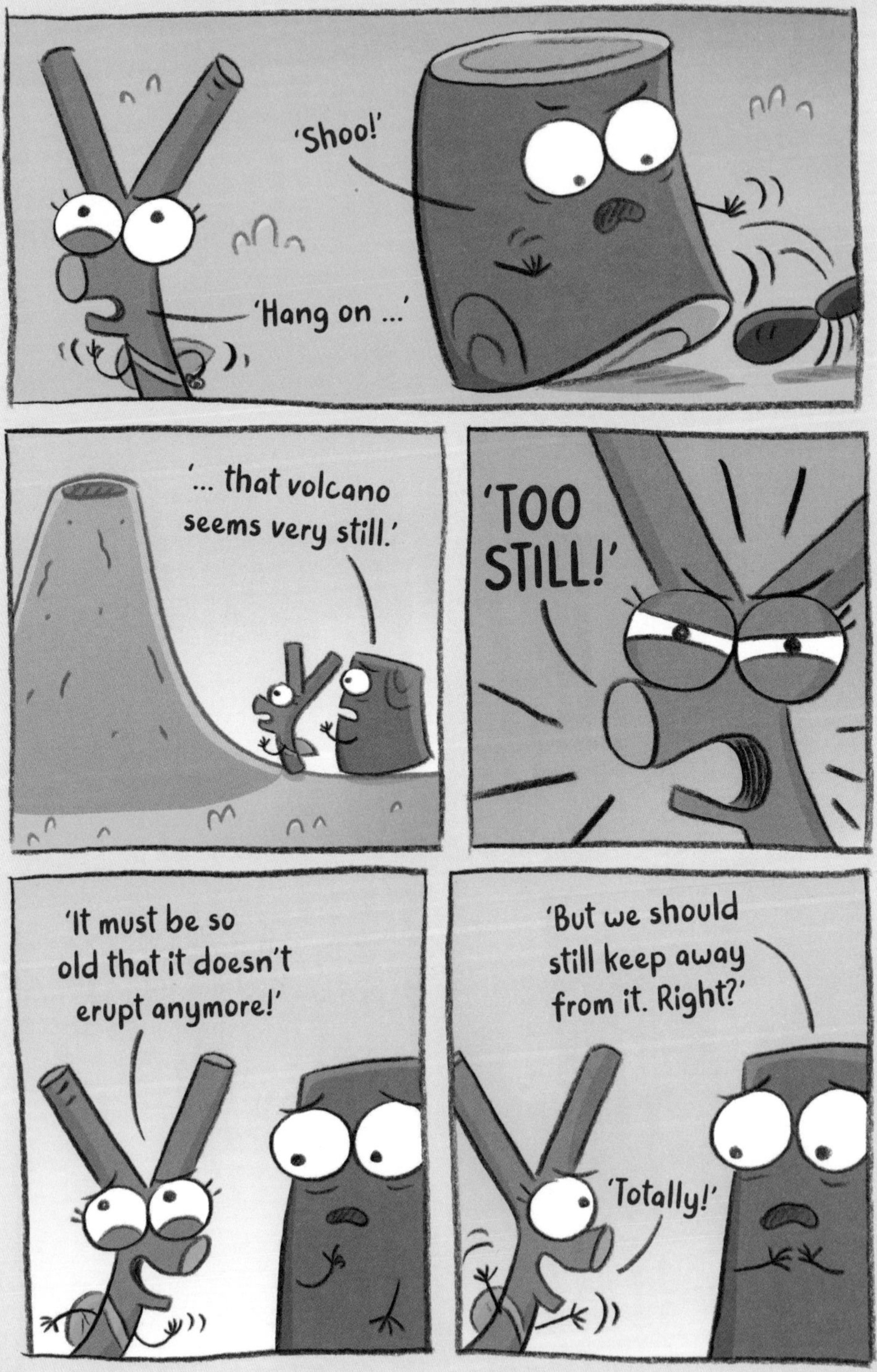
'Shoo!'
'Hang on ...'
'... that volcano seems very still.'
'TOO STILL!'
'It must be so old that it doesn't erupt anymore!'
'But we should still keep away from it. Right?'
'Totally!'

10 SECONDS LATER ...
VOLCANO TOURS HERE
'Who wants to explore a volcano with me?'
'Us! Us! Us!'
'Hello, Noodle! Hello, Red!'

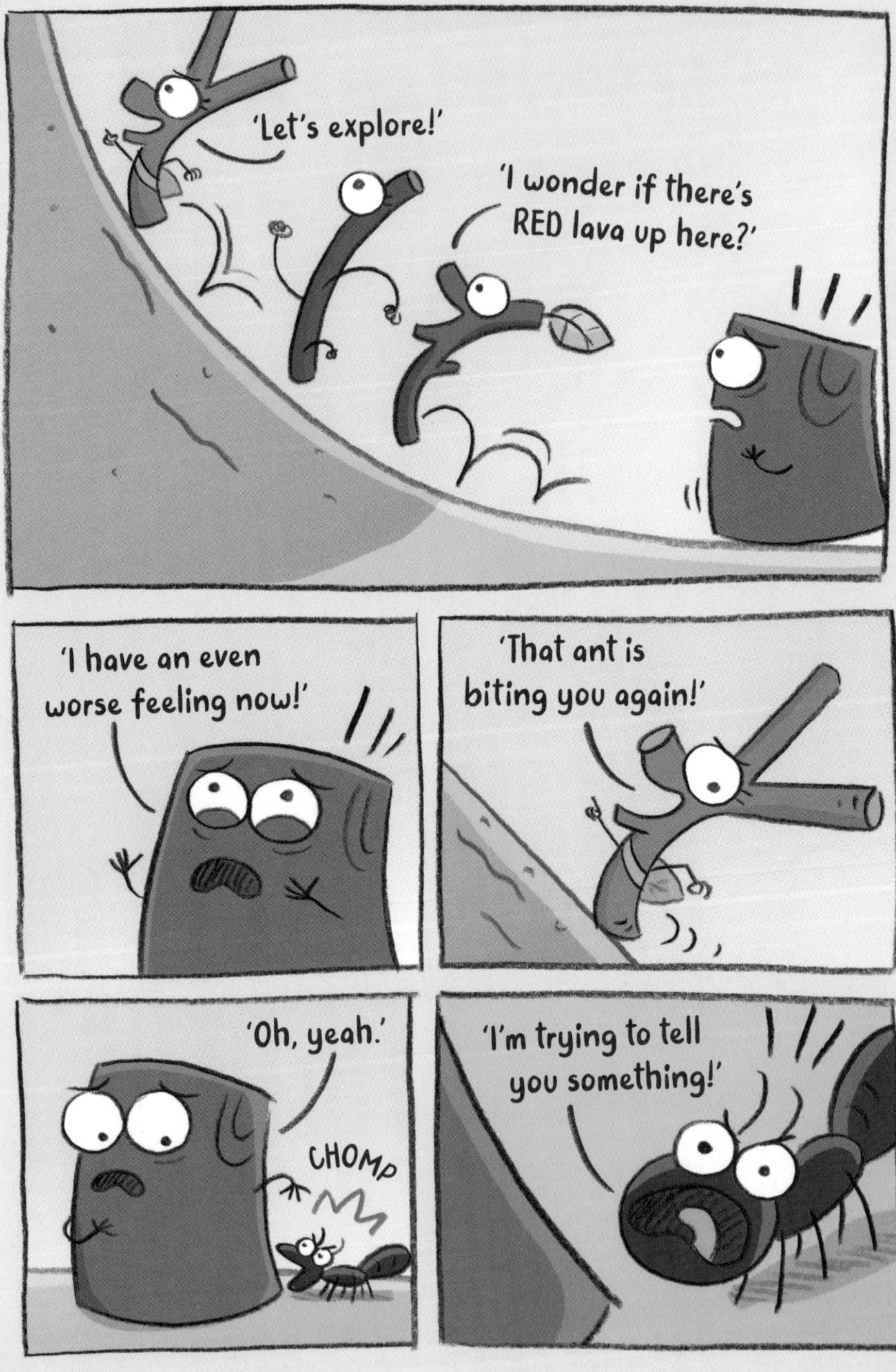
'Let's explore!'
'I wonder if there's RED lava up here?'
'I have an even worse feeling now!'
'That ant is biting you again!'
'Oh, yeah.'
CHOMP
'I'm trying to tell you something!'

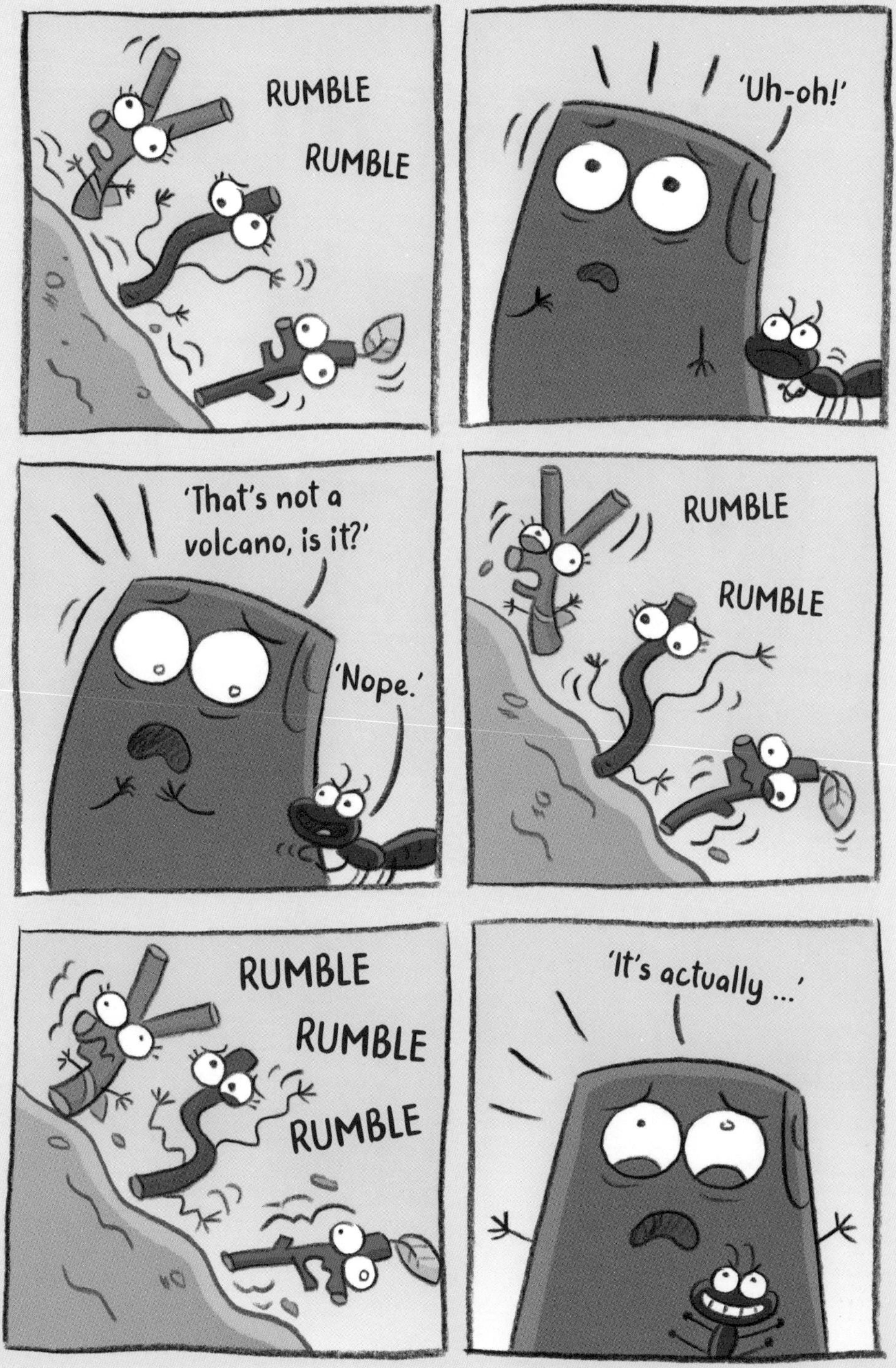
RUMBLE
RUMBLE
'Uh-oh!'
'That's not a volcano, is it?'
'Nope.'
RUMBLE
RUMBLE
RUMBLE
RUMBLE
RUMBLE
'It's actually ...'

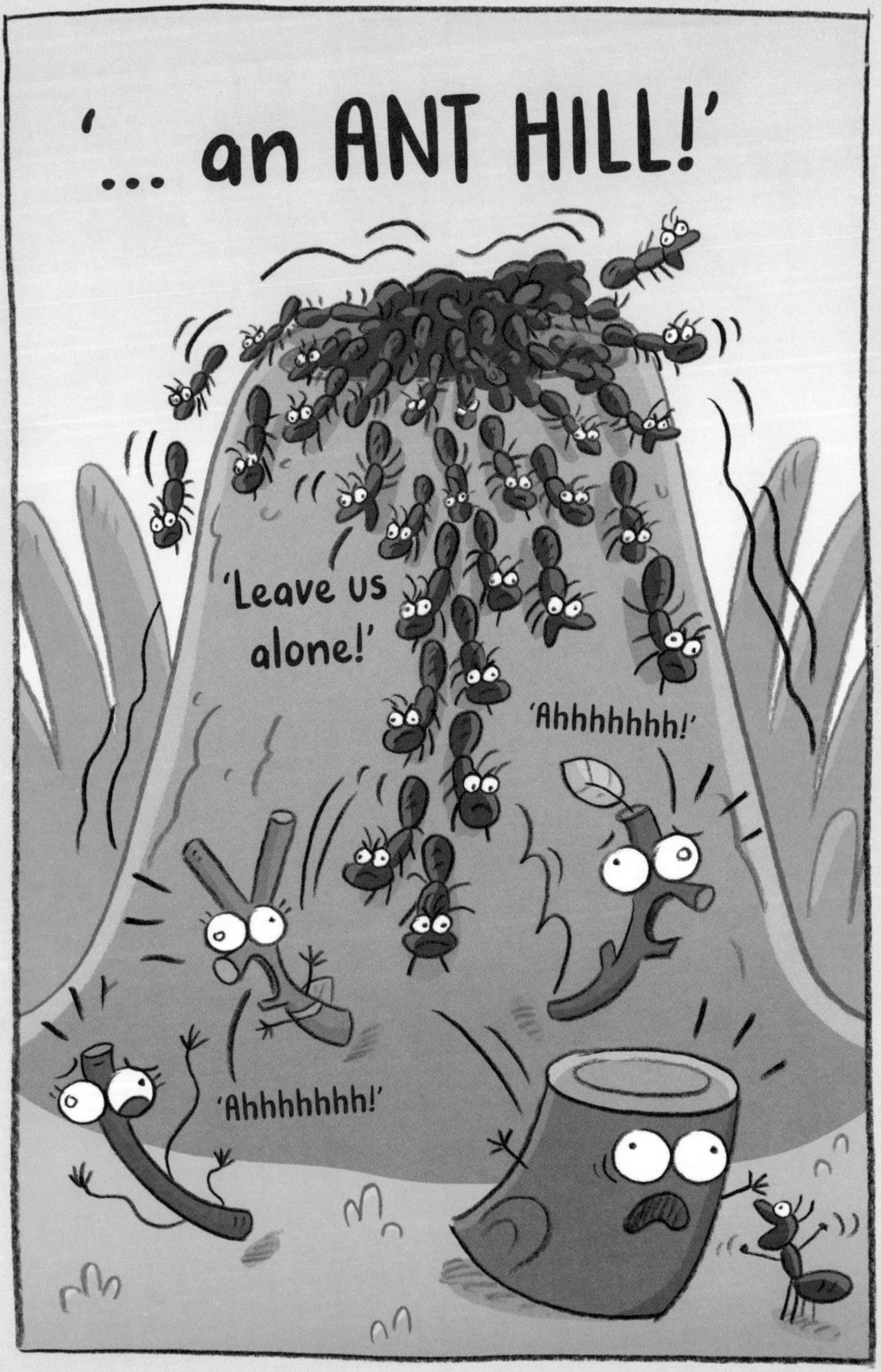
'... an ANT HILL!'
'Leave us alone!'
'Ahhhhhhh!'
'Ahhhhhhh!'

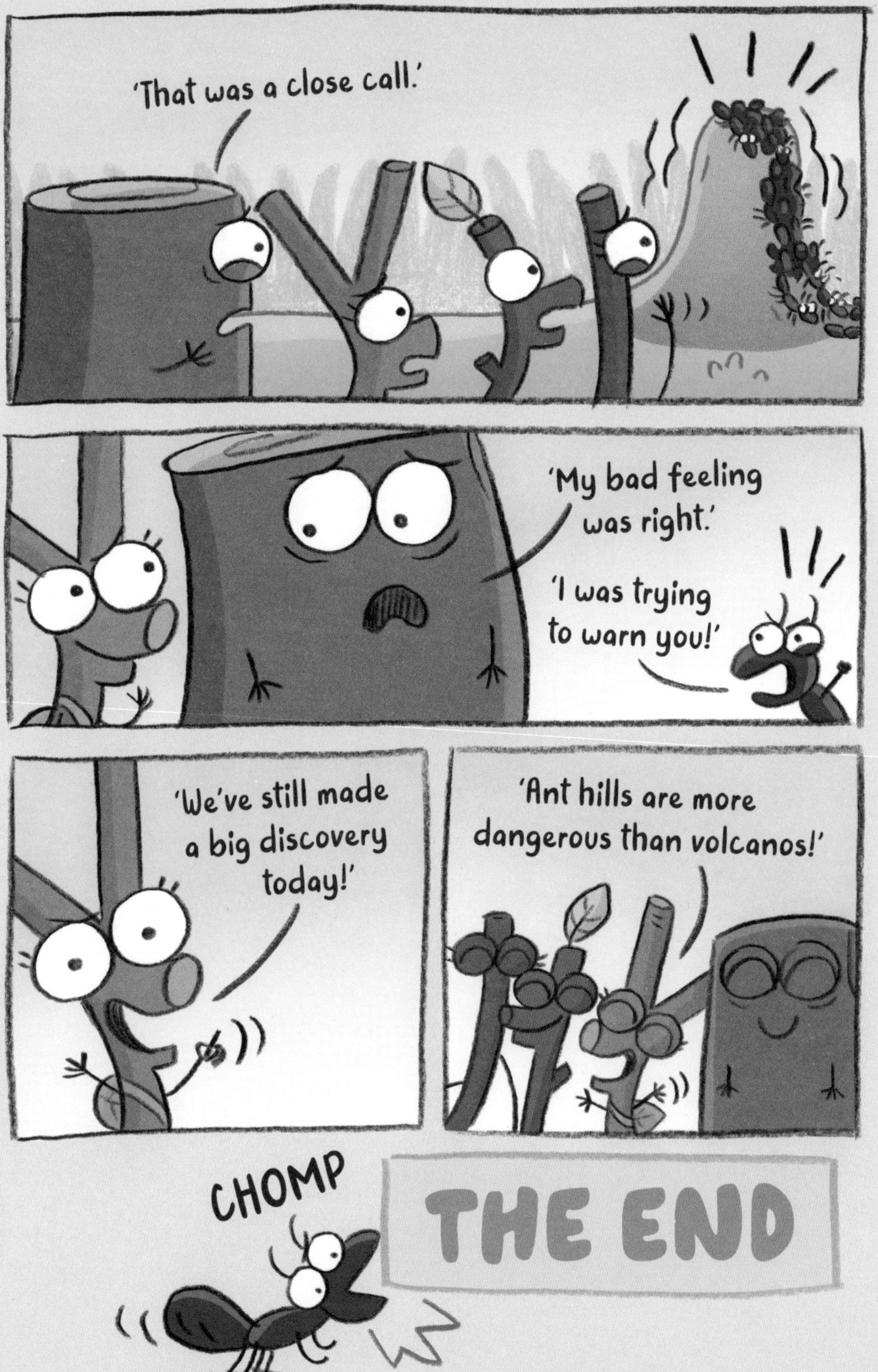
'That was a close call.'
'My bad feeling was right.'
'I was trying to warn you!'
'We've still made a big discovery today!'
'Ant hills are more dangerous than volcanos!'
CHOMP
THE END

3. TWIG ART

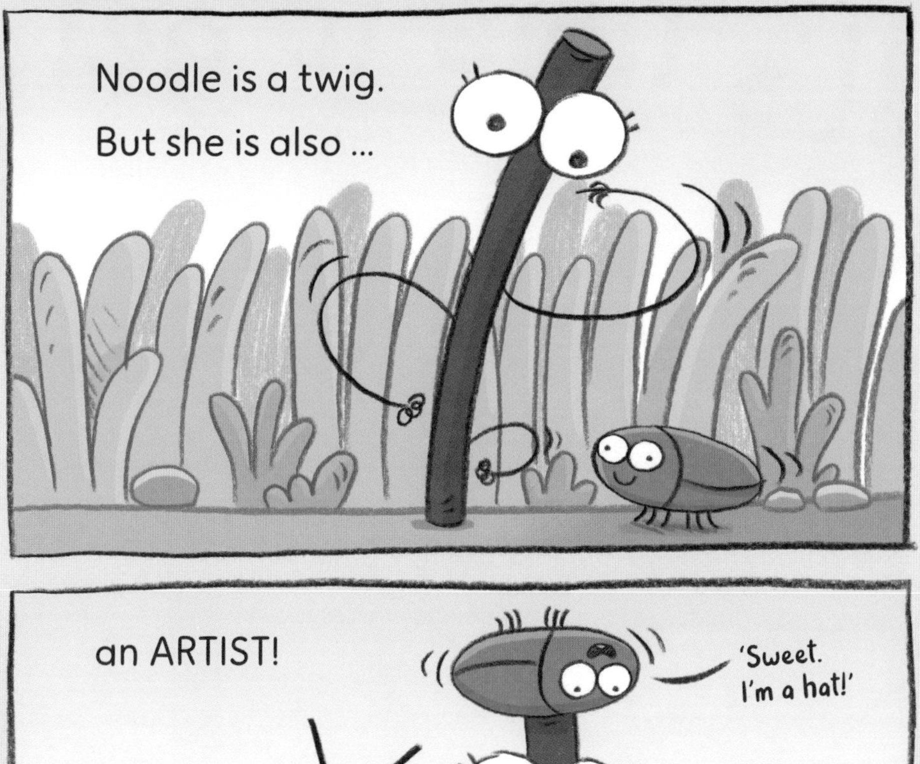
Noodle is a twig.
But she is also ...

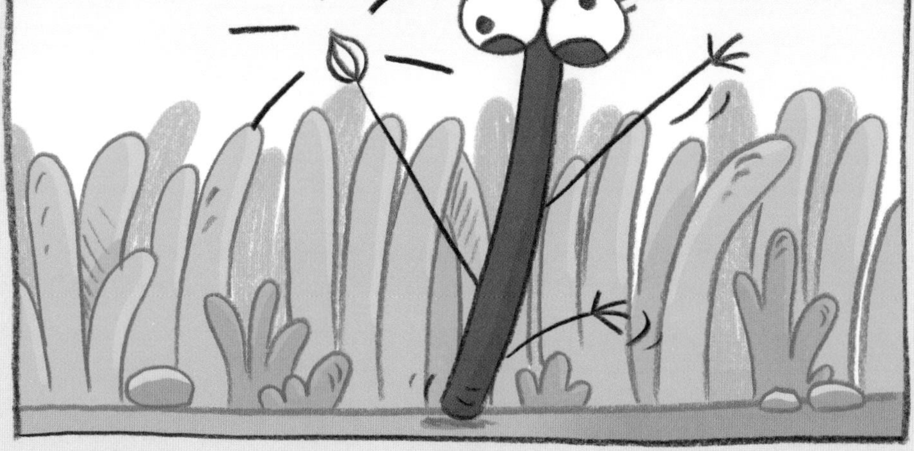
an ARTIST!
'Sweet. I'm a hat!'

It's time to get

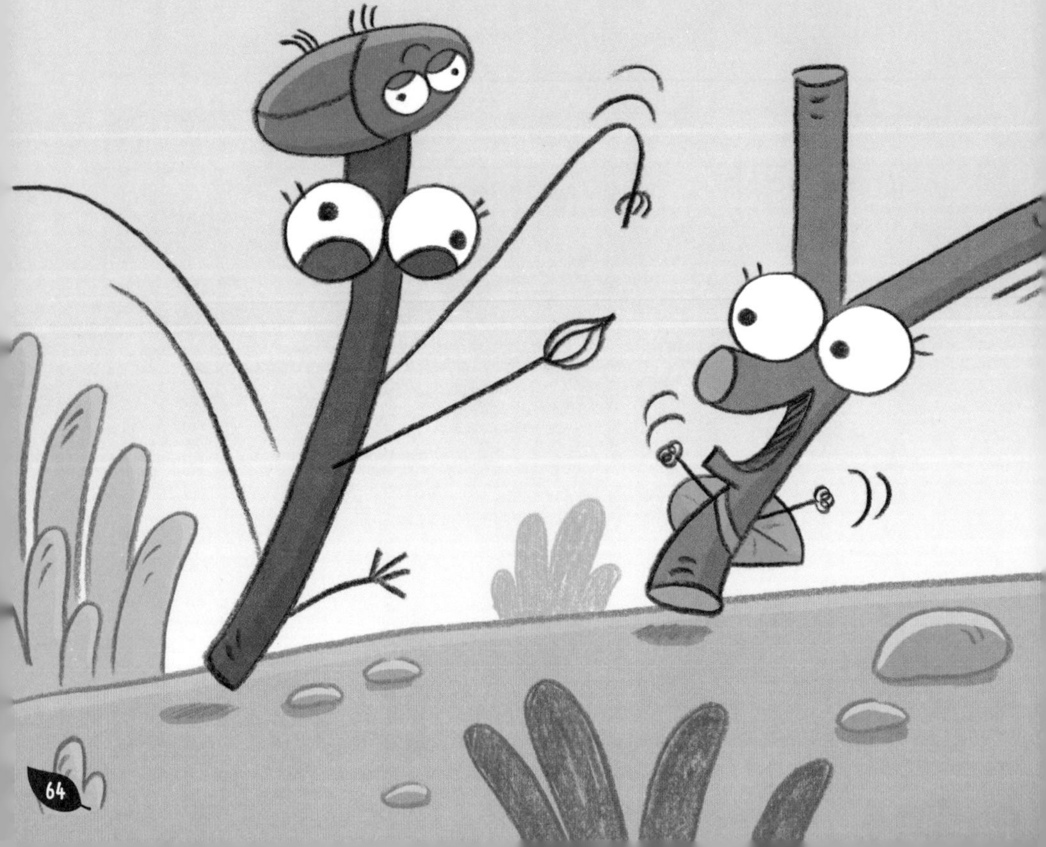

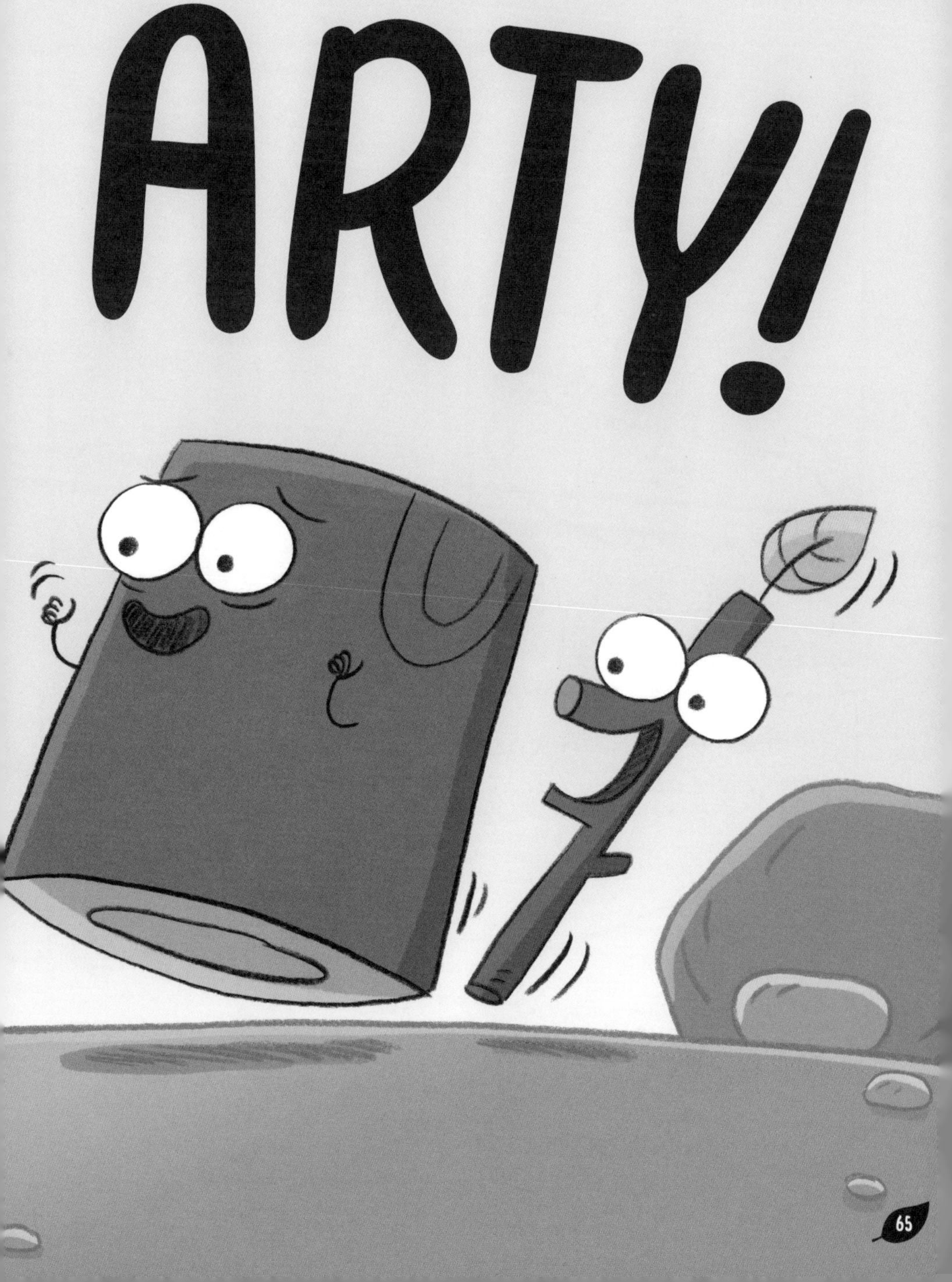
ARTY!

Today, Noodle is going to paint something.

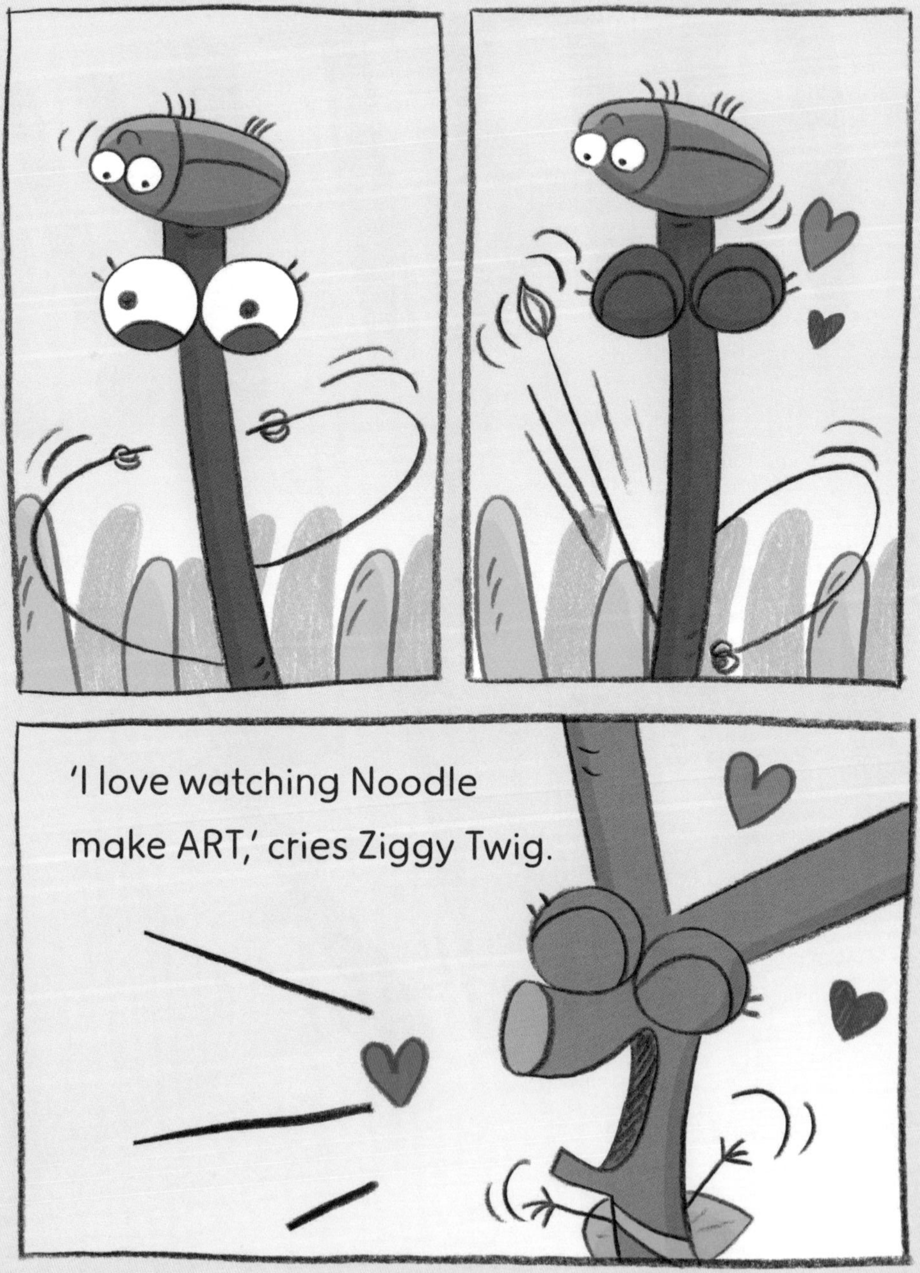
'I love watching Noodle
make ART,' cries Ziggy Twig.

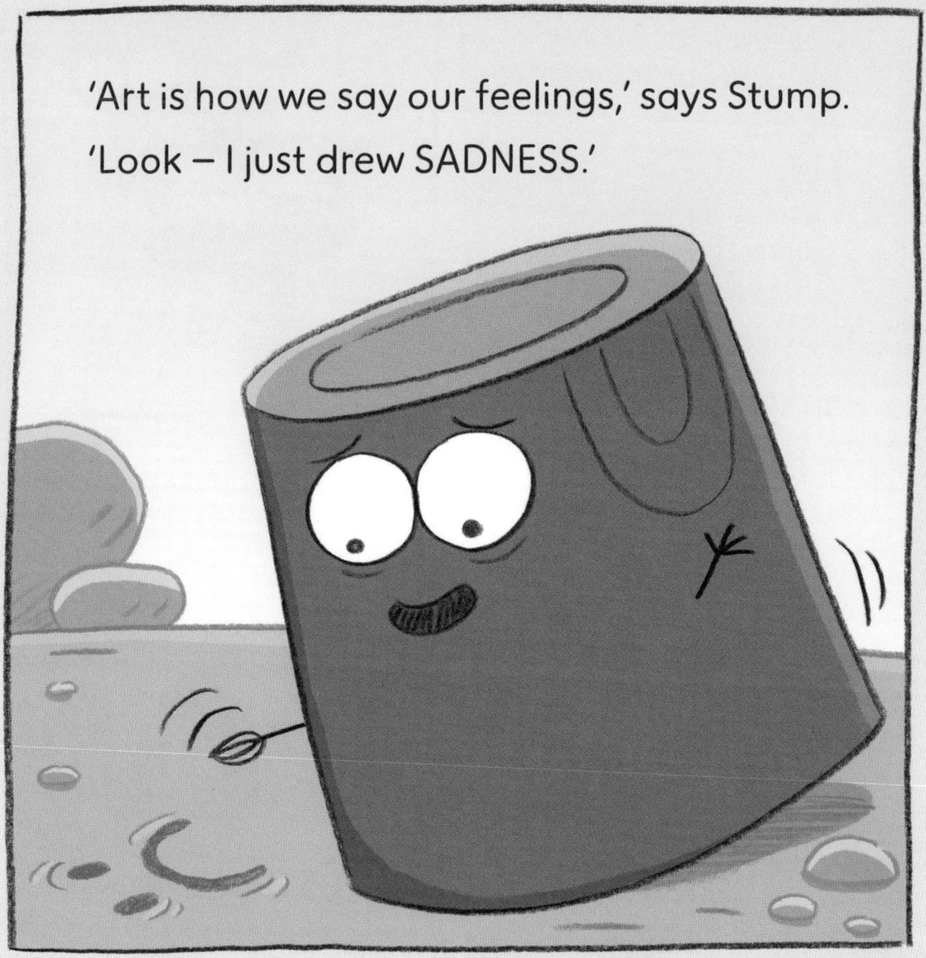
'Art is how we say our feelings,' says Stump.
'Look – I just drew SADNESS.'

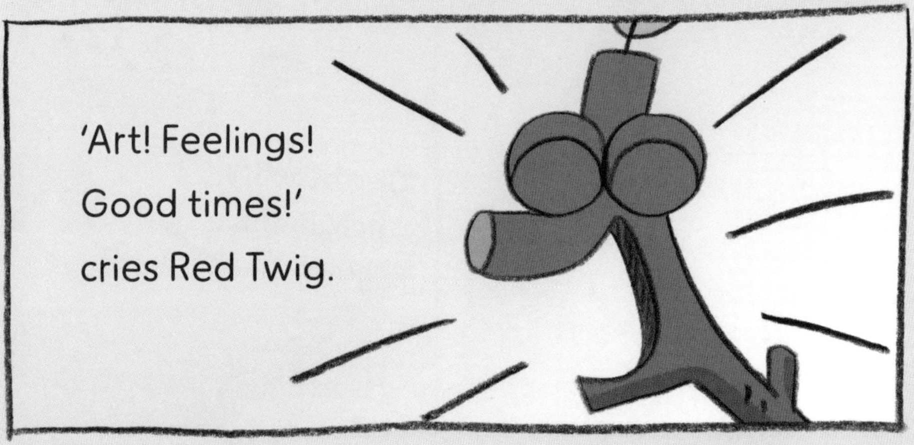
'Art! Feelings!
Good times!'
cries Red Twig.

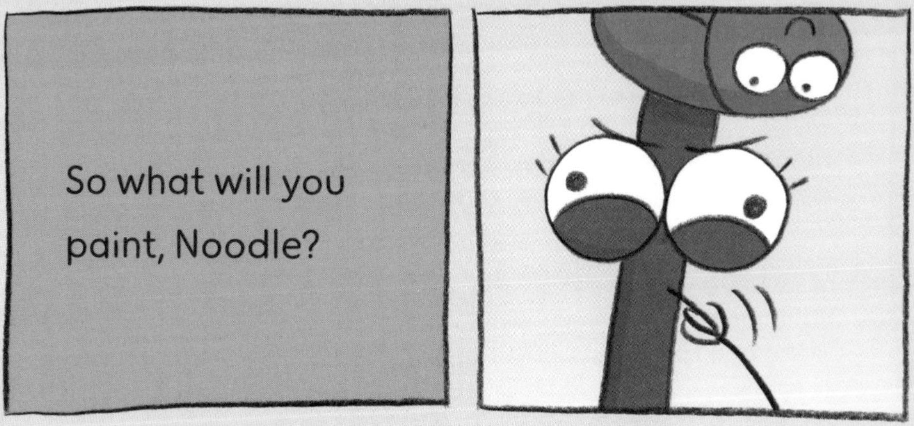
So what will you paint, Noodle?

Ziggy has some ideas.

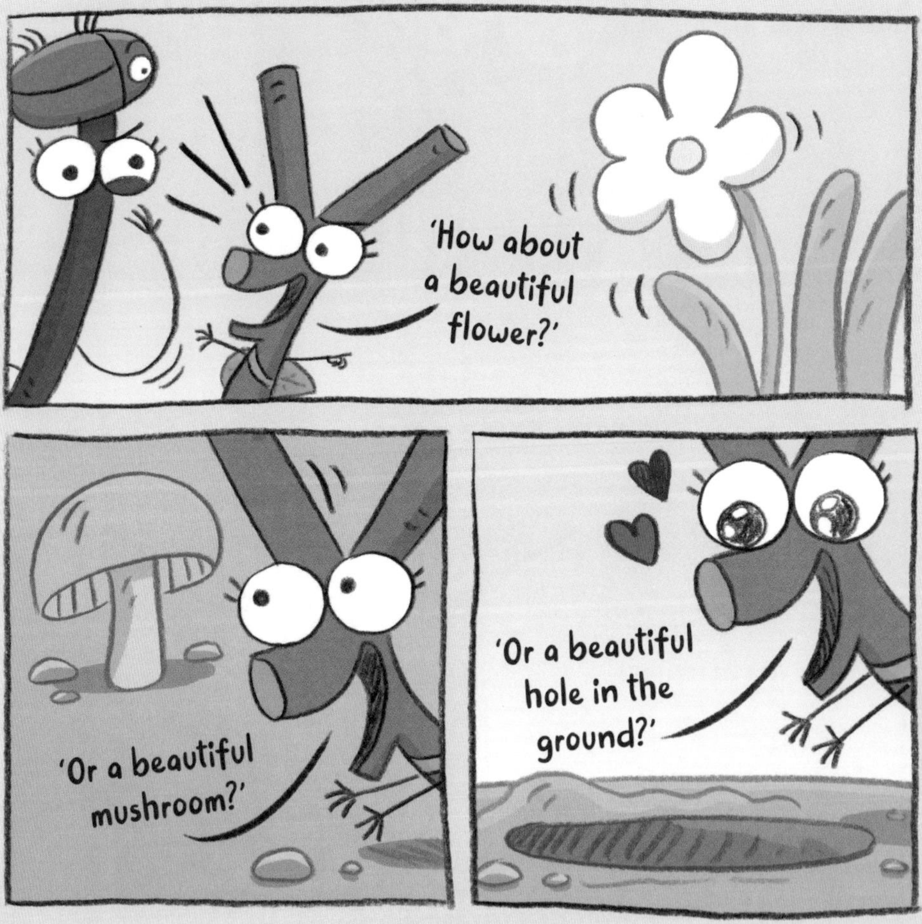
'How about a beautiful flower?'
'Or a beautiful mushroom?'
'Or a beautiful hole in the ground?'

Noodle knows EXACTLY what she wants to paint. But first — she needs all the right art stuff.

'We'll help you get ready!' cries Ziggy.

Stump helps by turning nature into PAINT!

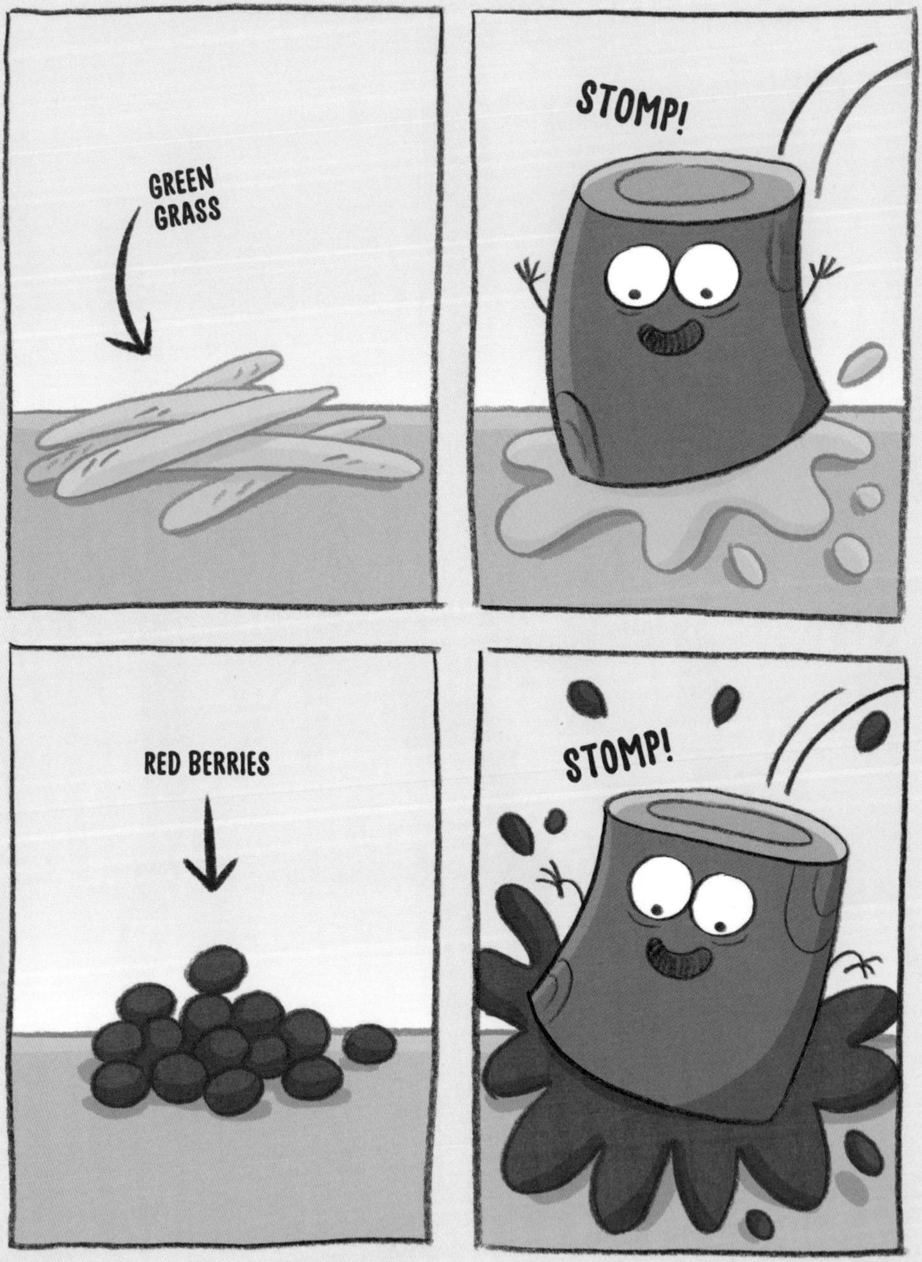

GREEN GRASS
STOMP!
RED BERRIES
STOMP!

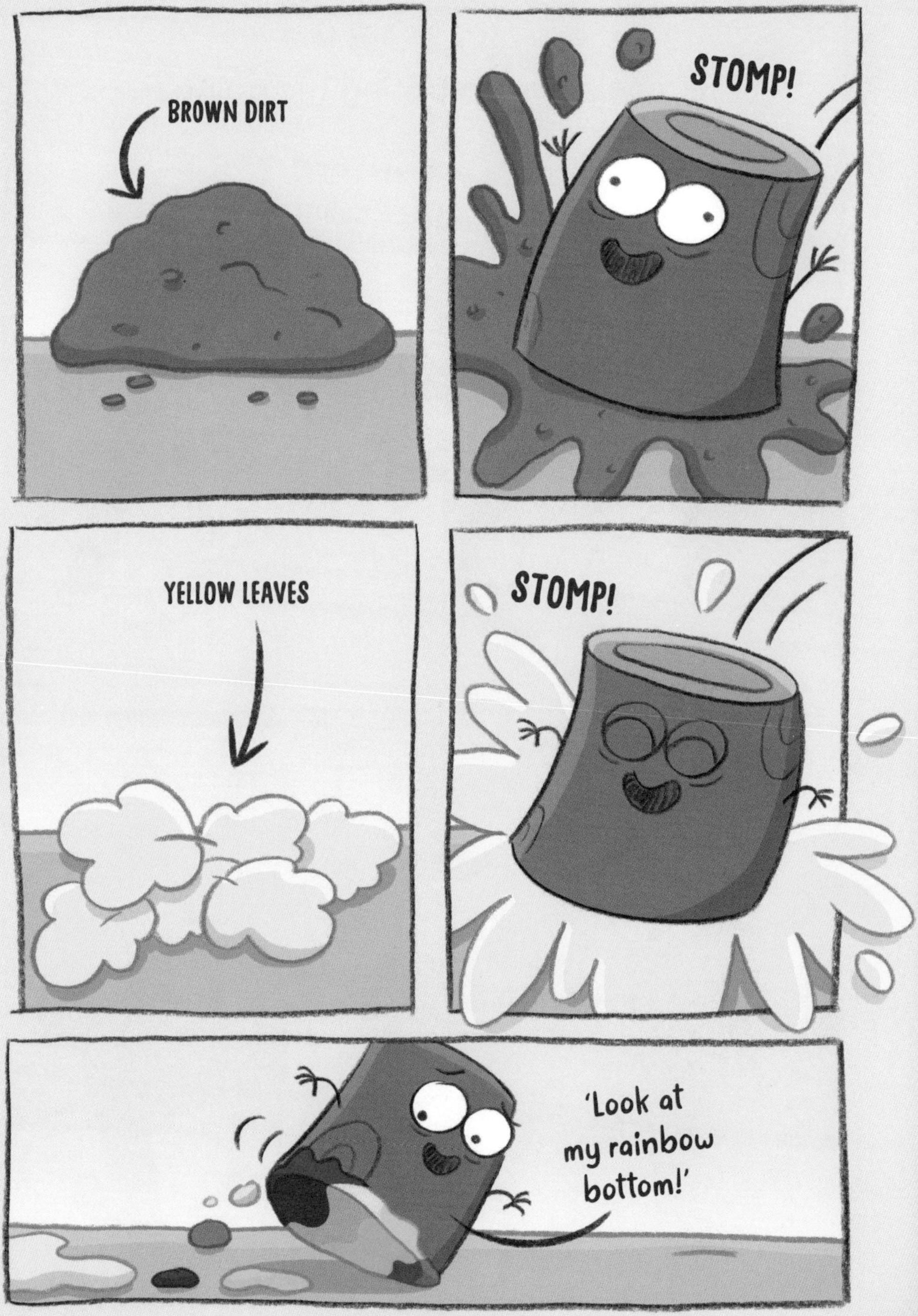
BROWN DIRT
STOMP!
YELLOW LEAVES
STOMP!
'Look at my rainbow bottom!'

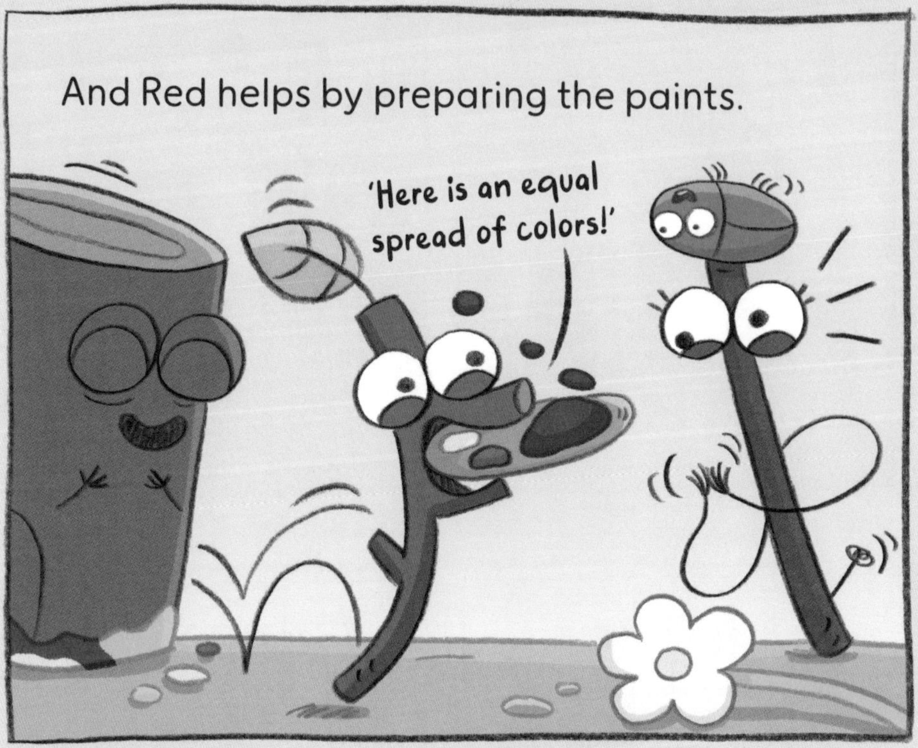
And Red helps by preparing the paints.
'Here is an equal spread of colors!'

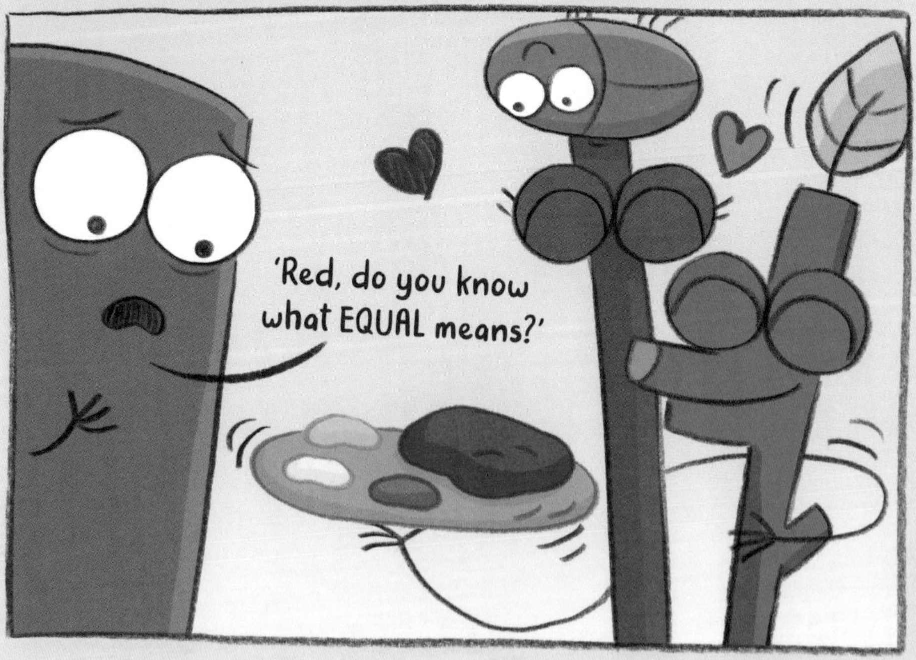
'Red, do you know what EQUAL means?'

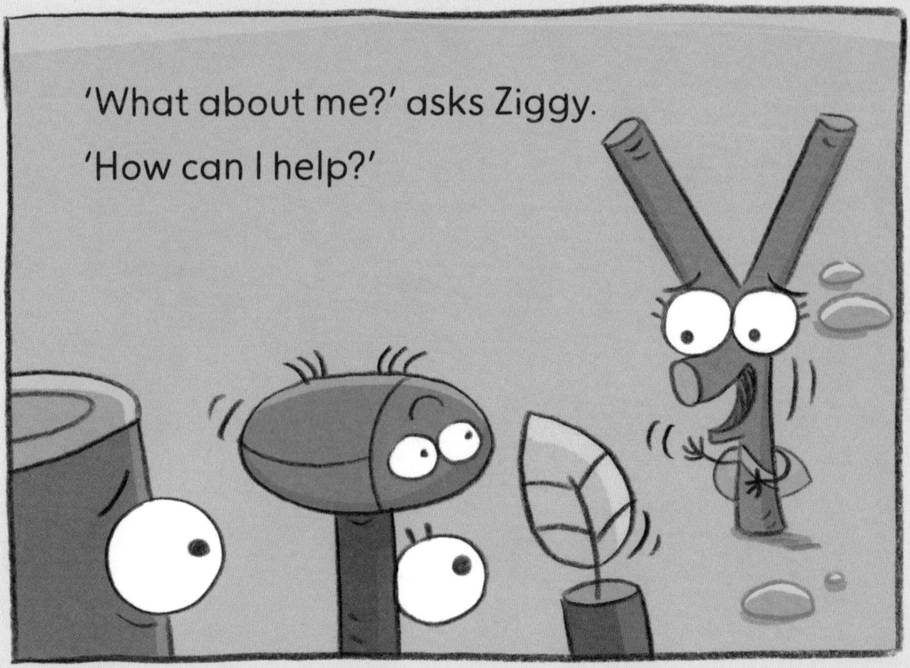
'What about me?' asks Ziggy.
'How can I help?'

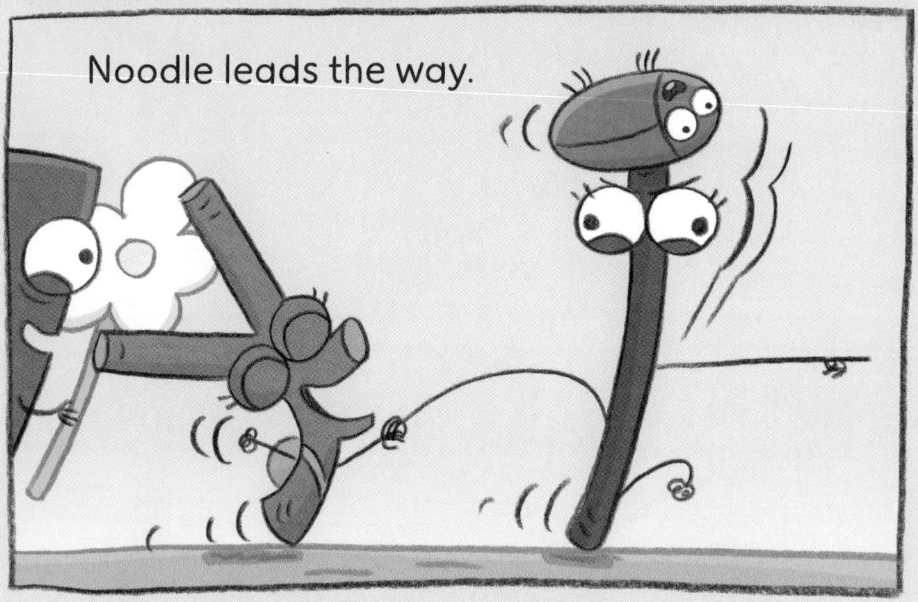
Noodle leads the way.

She has an important job for her friend.

Noodle gives Ziggy a large leaf. It will be the paper.

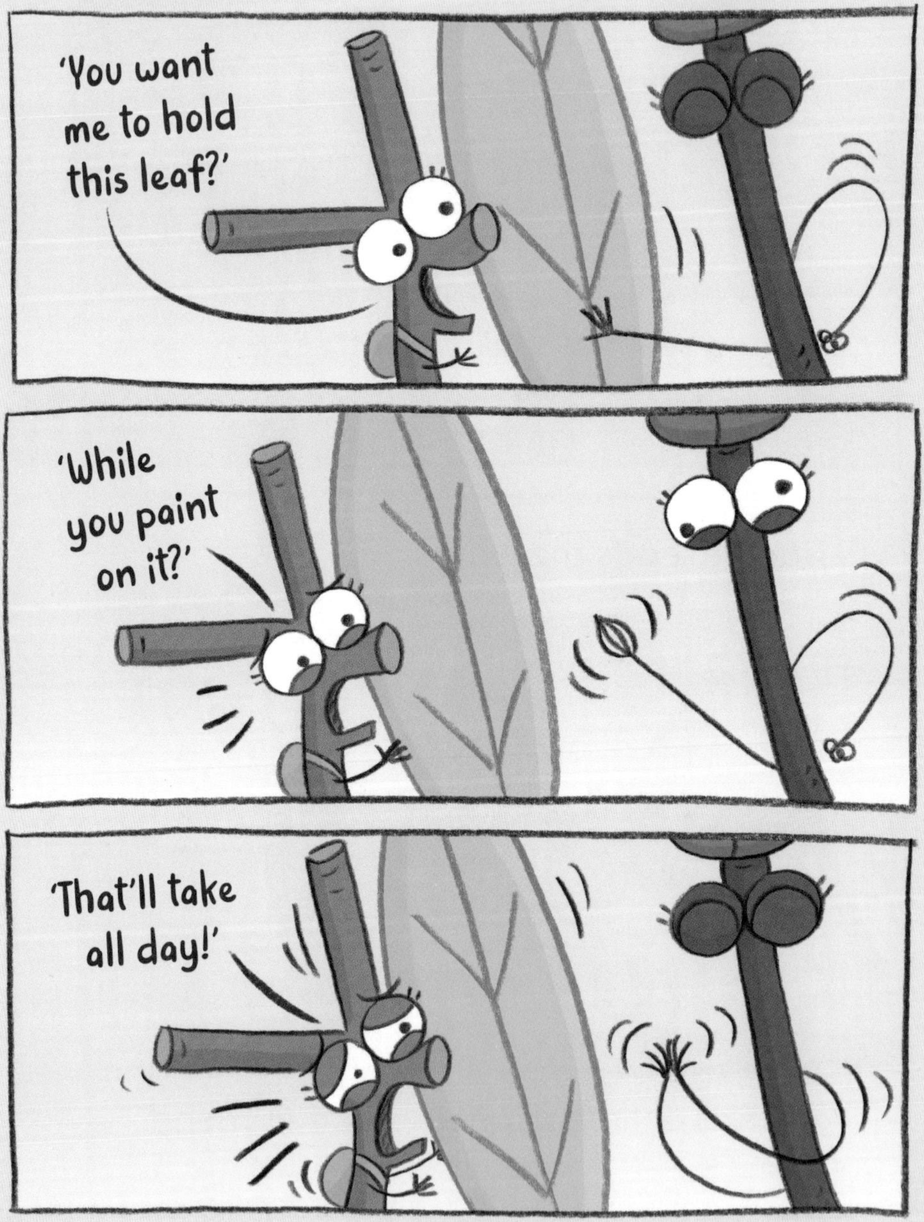
'You want me to hold this leaf?'
'While you paint on it?'
'That'll take all day!'

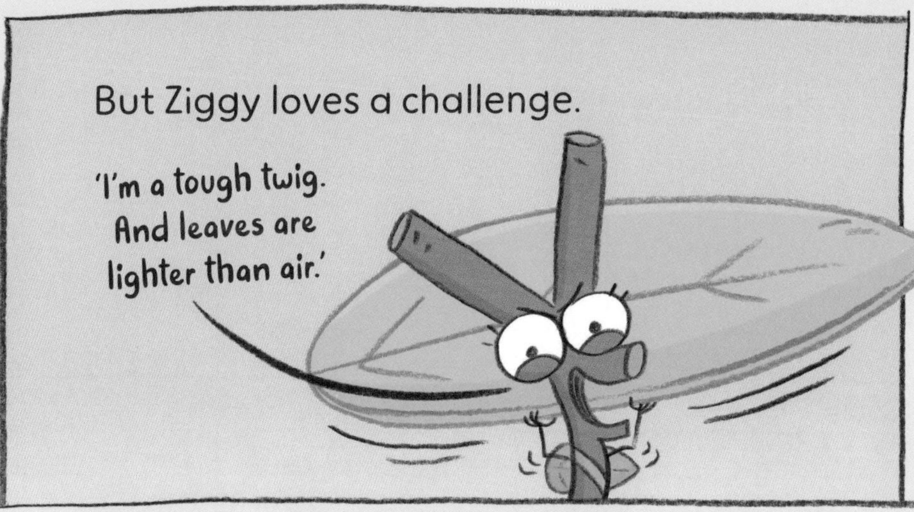
But Ziggy loves a challenge.
'I'm a tough twig. And leaves are lighter than air.'

Leaves are NOT lighter than air, Ziggy.

But we get it – they are very light.

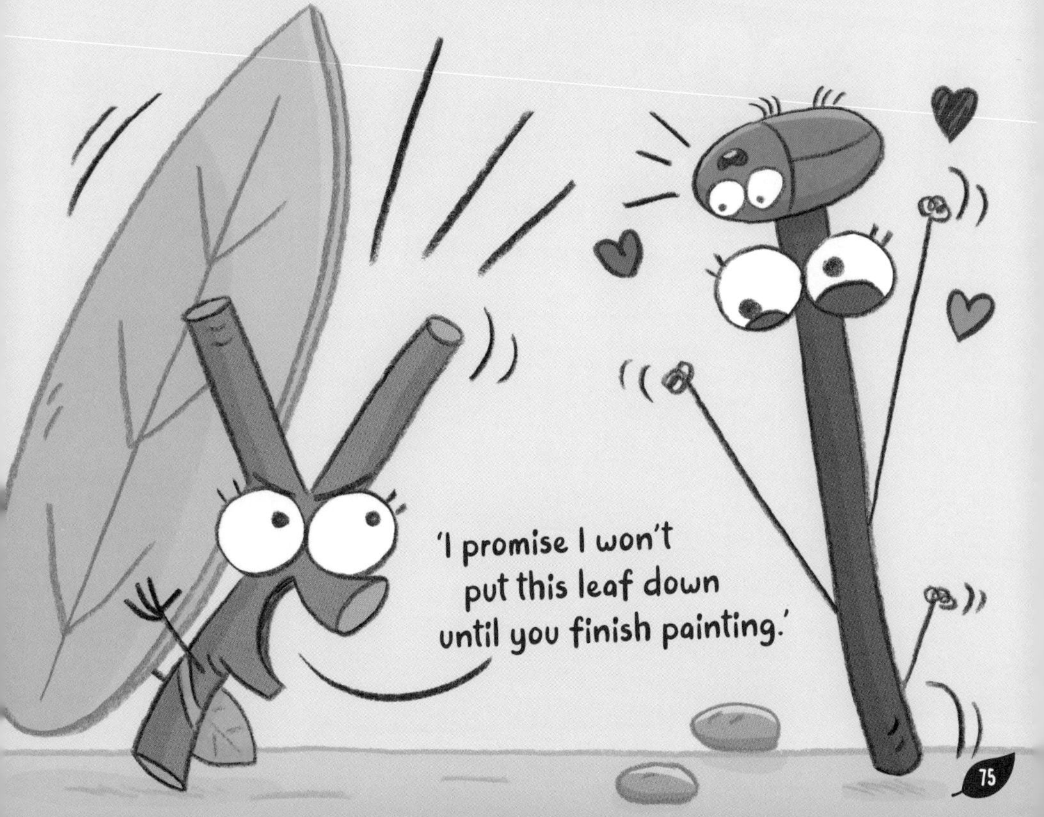
'I promise I won't put this leaf down until you finish painting.'

Ziggy is very kind.

And Noodle thanks her.

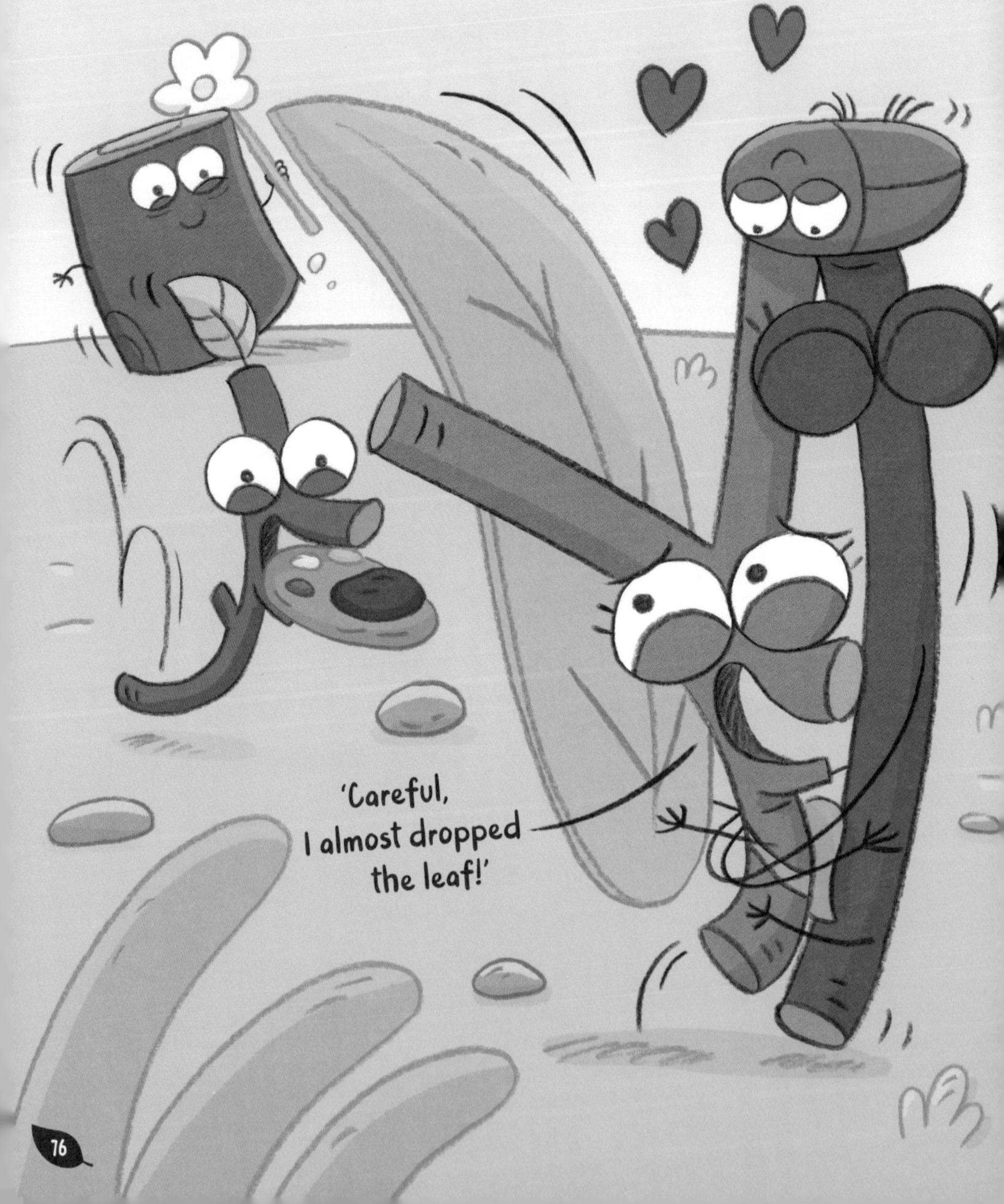
'Careful,
I almost dropped
the leaf!'

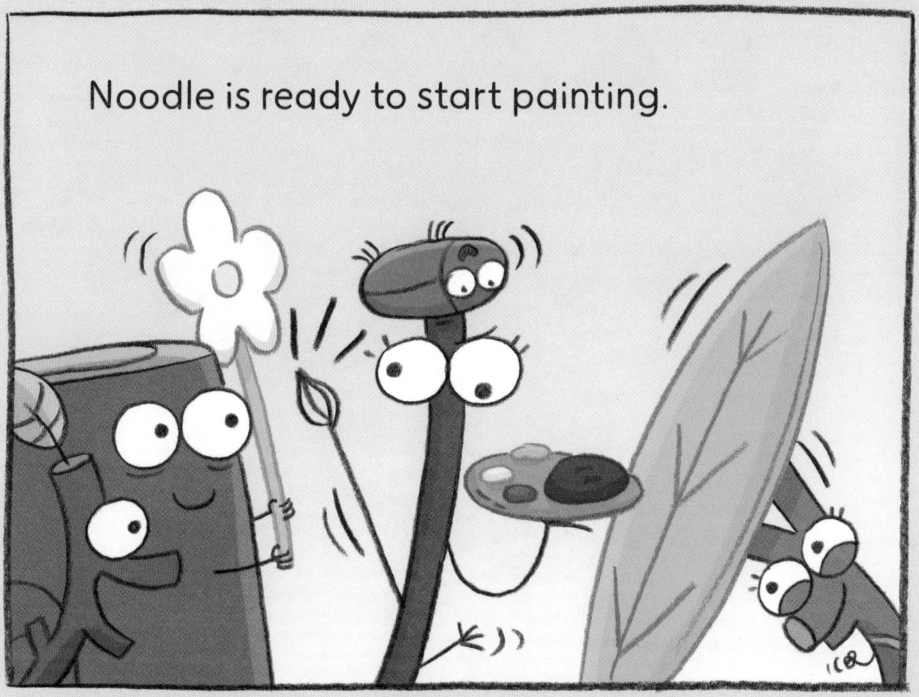
Noodle is ready to start painting.

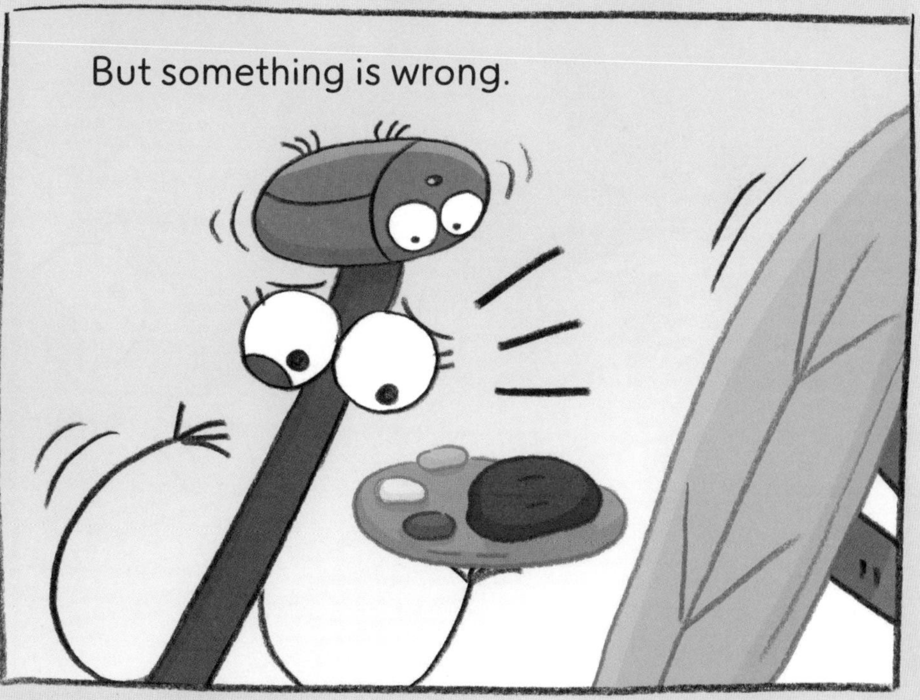
But something is wrong.

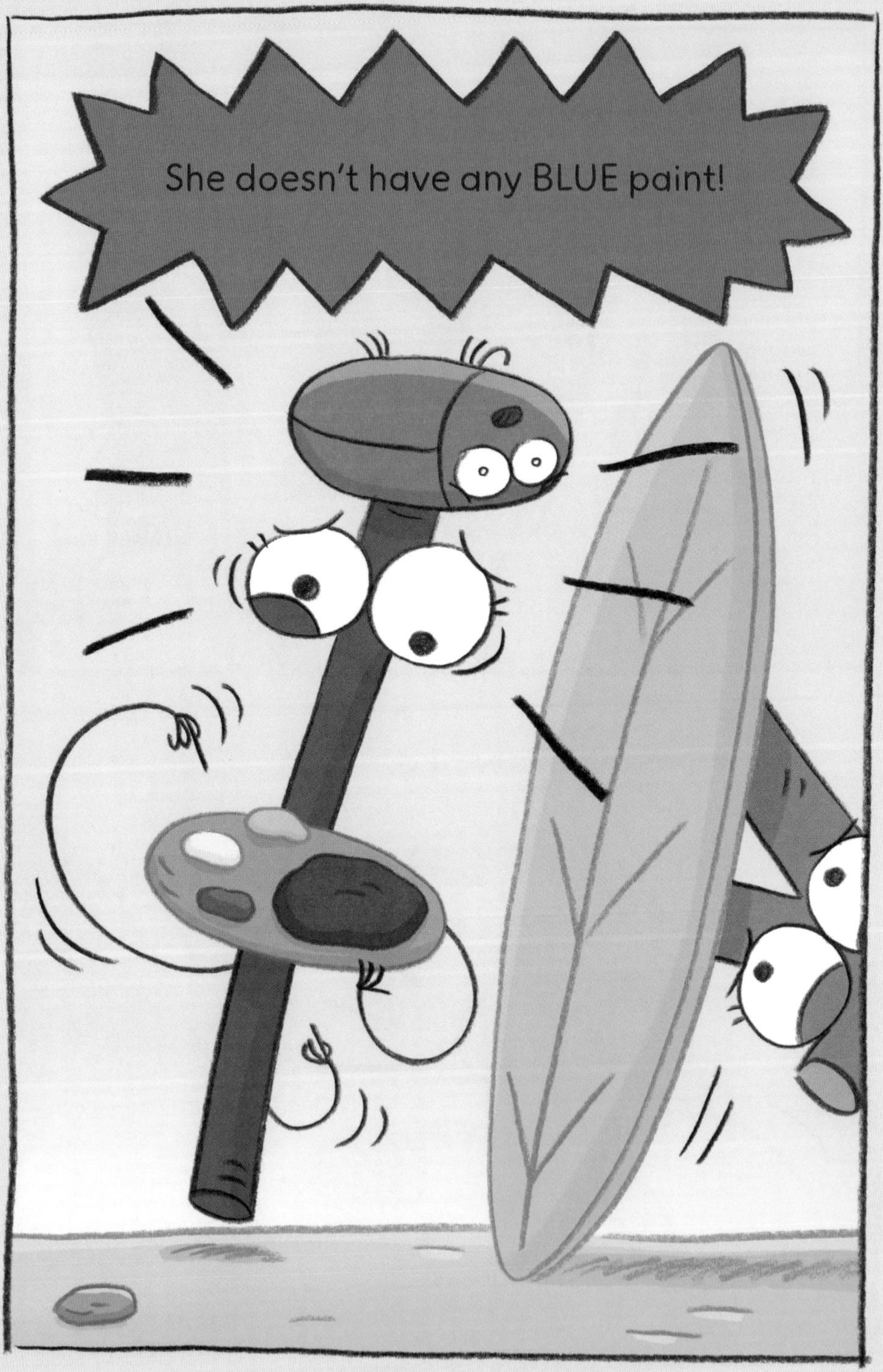
She doesn't have any BLUE paint!

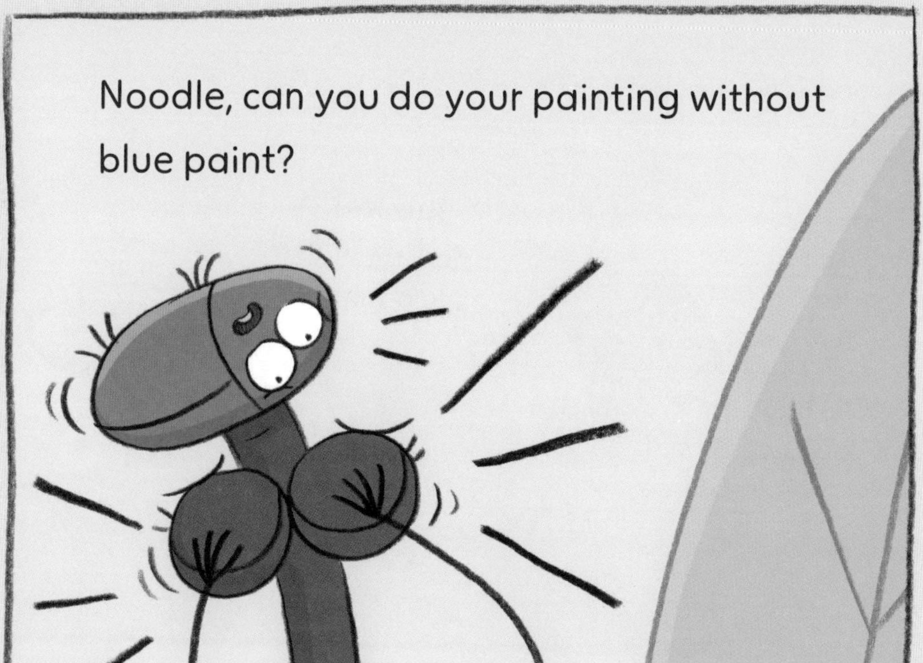
Noodle, can you do your painting without blue paint?

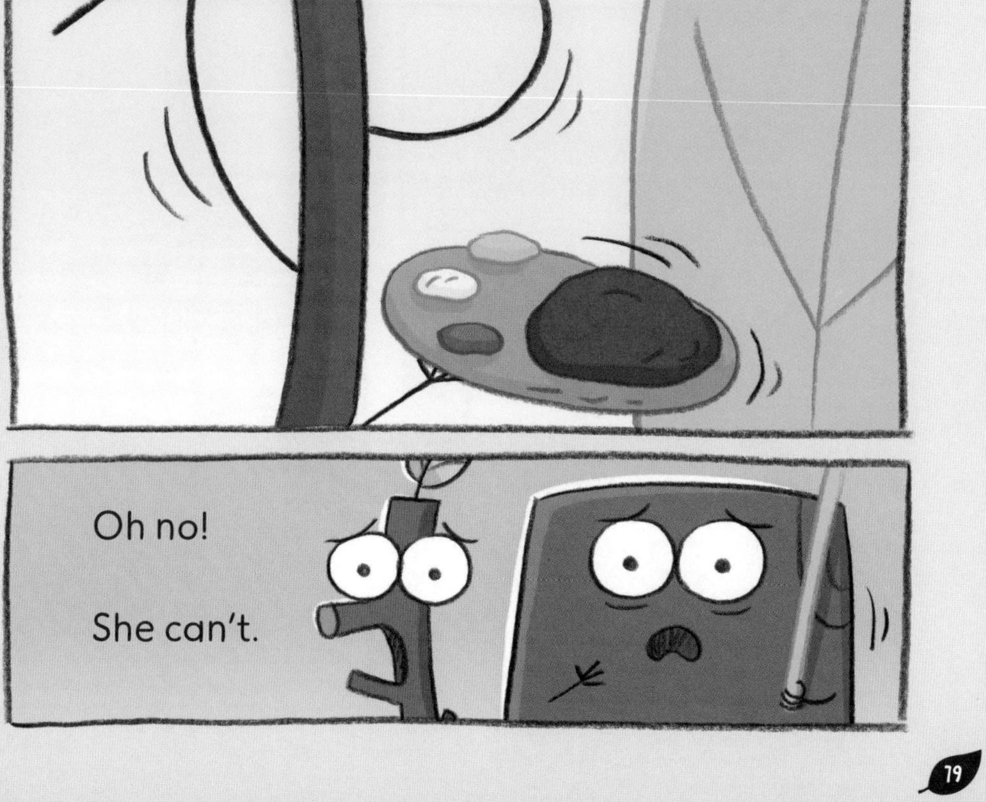
Oh no!
She can't.

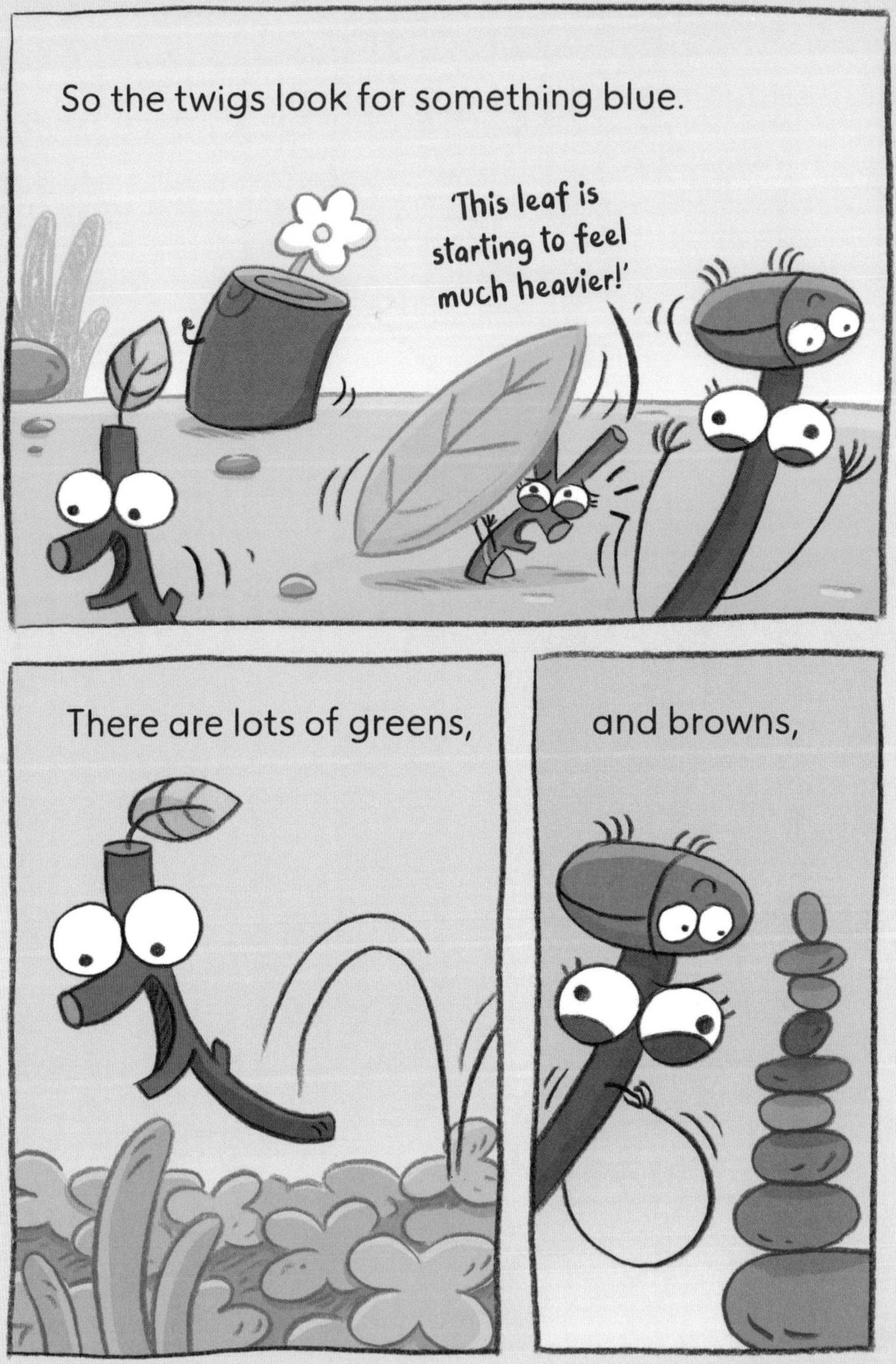
So the twigs look for something blue.
'This leaf is starting to feel much heavier!'
There are lots of greens,
and browns,

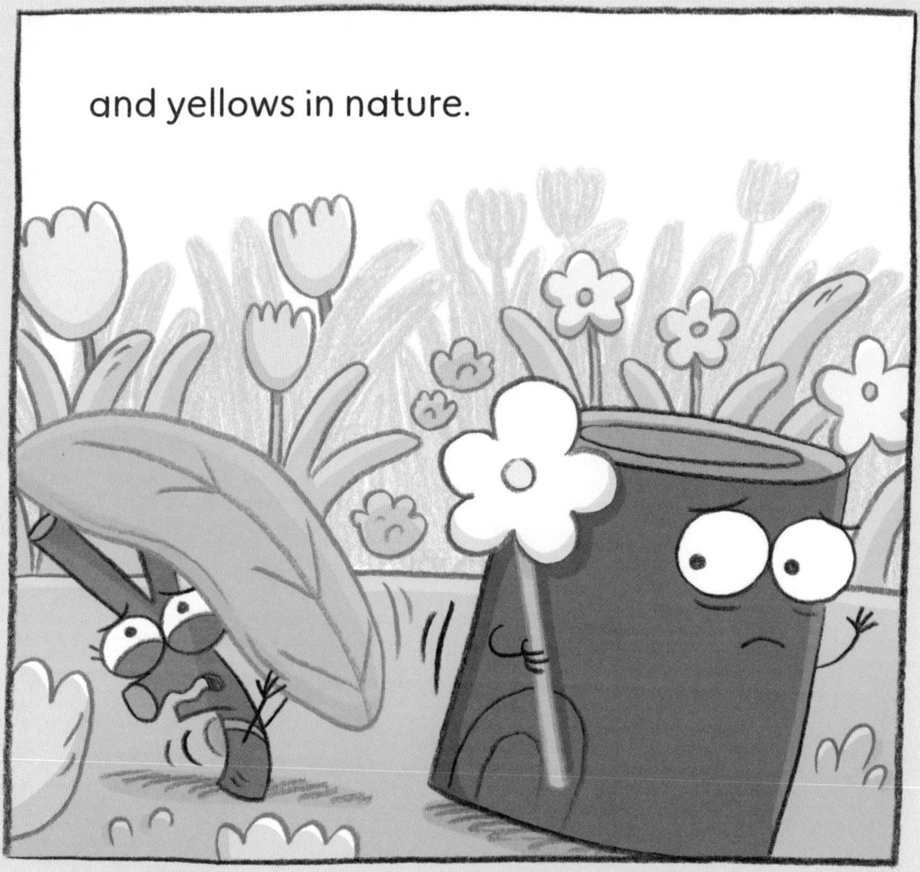
and yellows in nature.

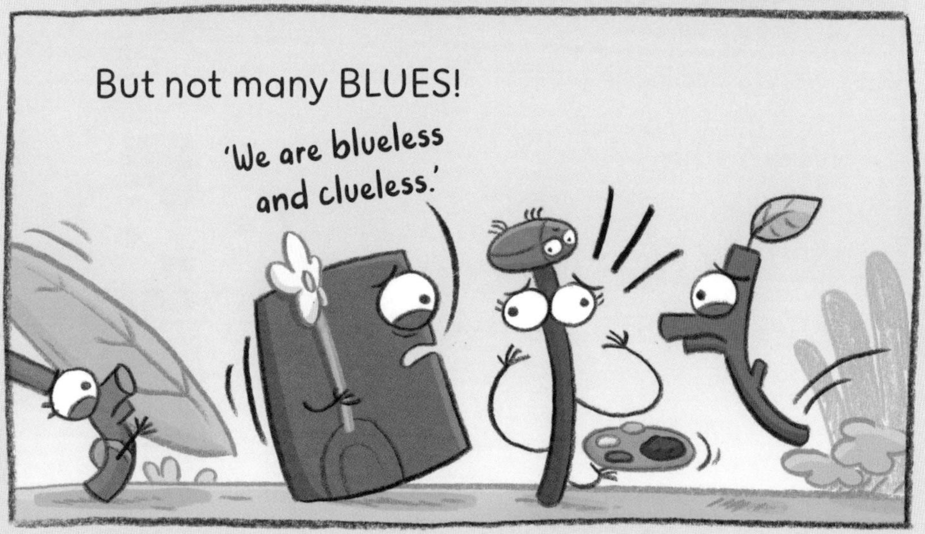
But not many BLUES!
'We are blueless and clueless.'

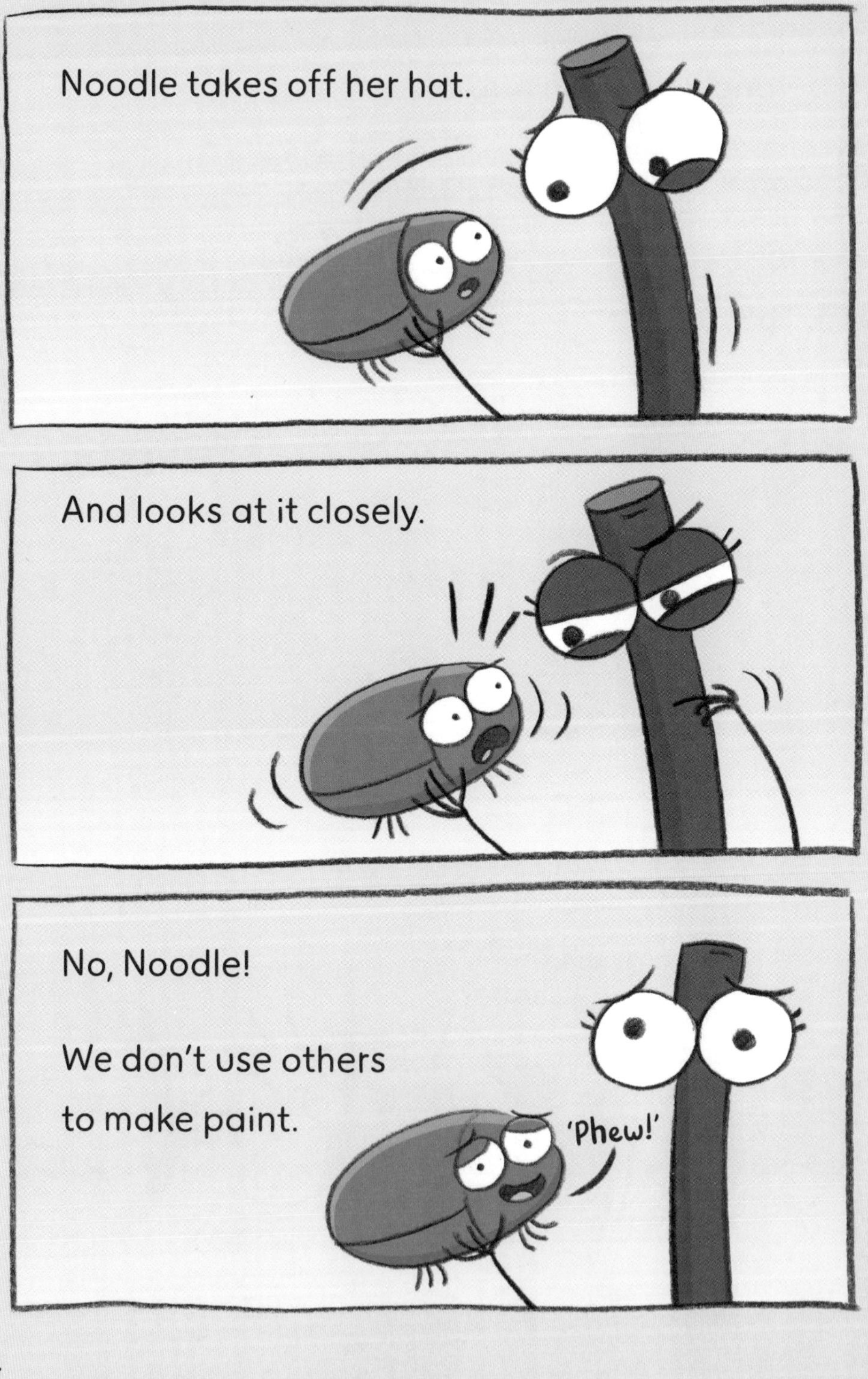
Noodle takes off her hat.
And looks at it closely.
No, Noodle!
We don't use others
to make paint.
'Phew!'

Noodle starts to worry.

She knows what she wants to paint.

But it HAS to have blue in it. Or else!

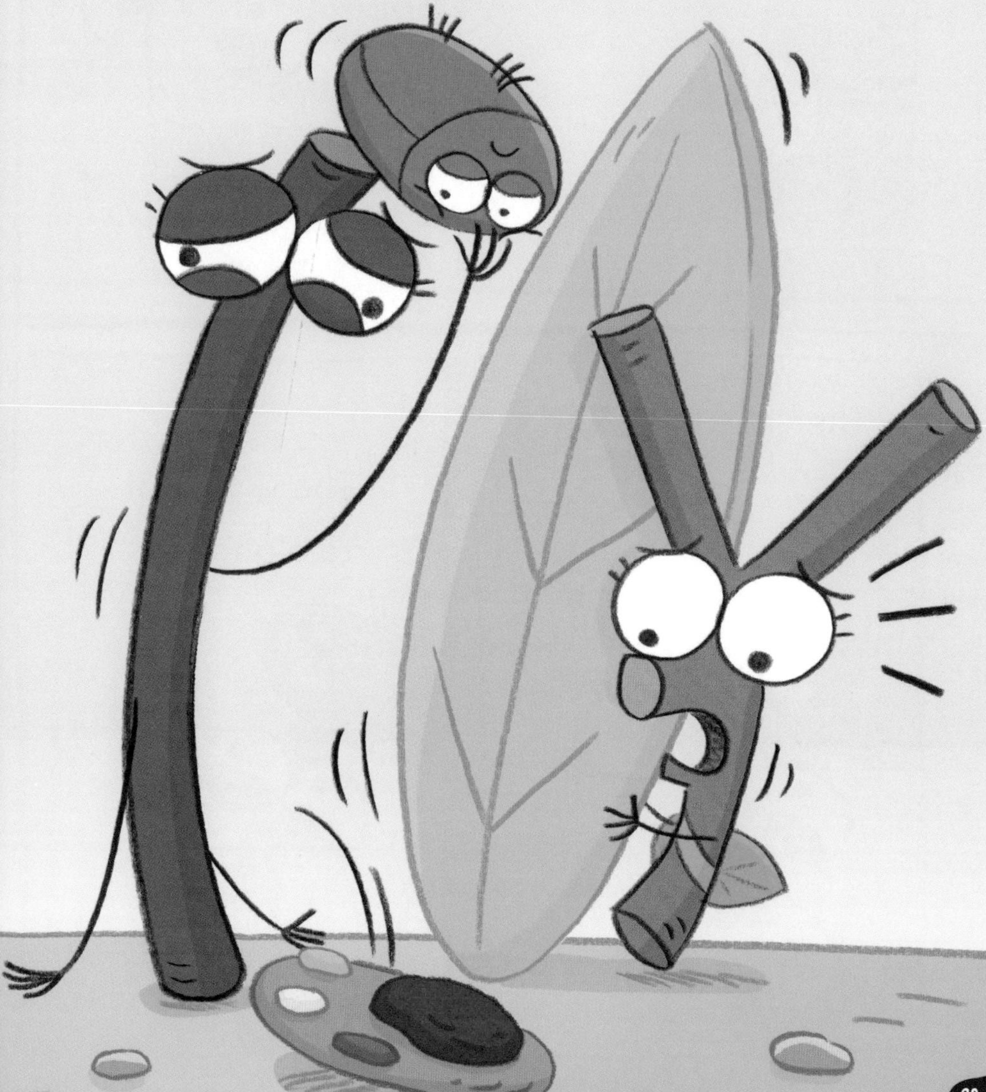

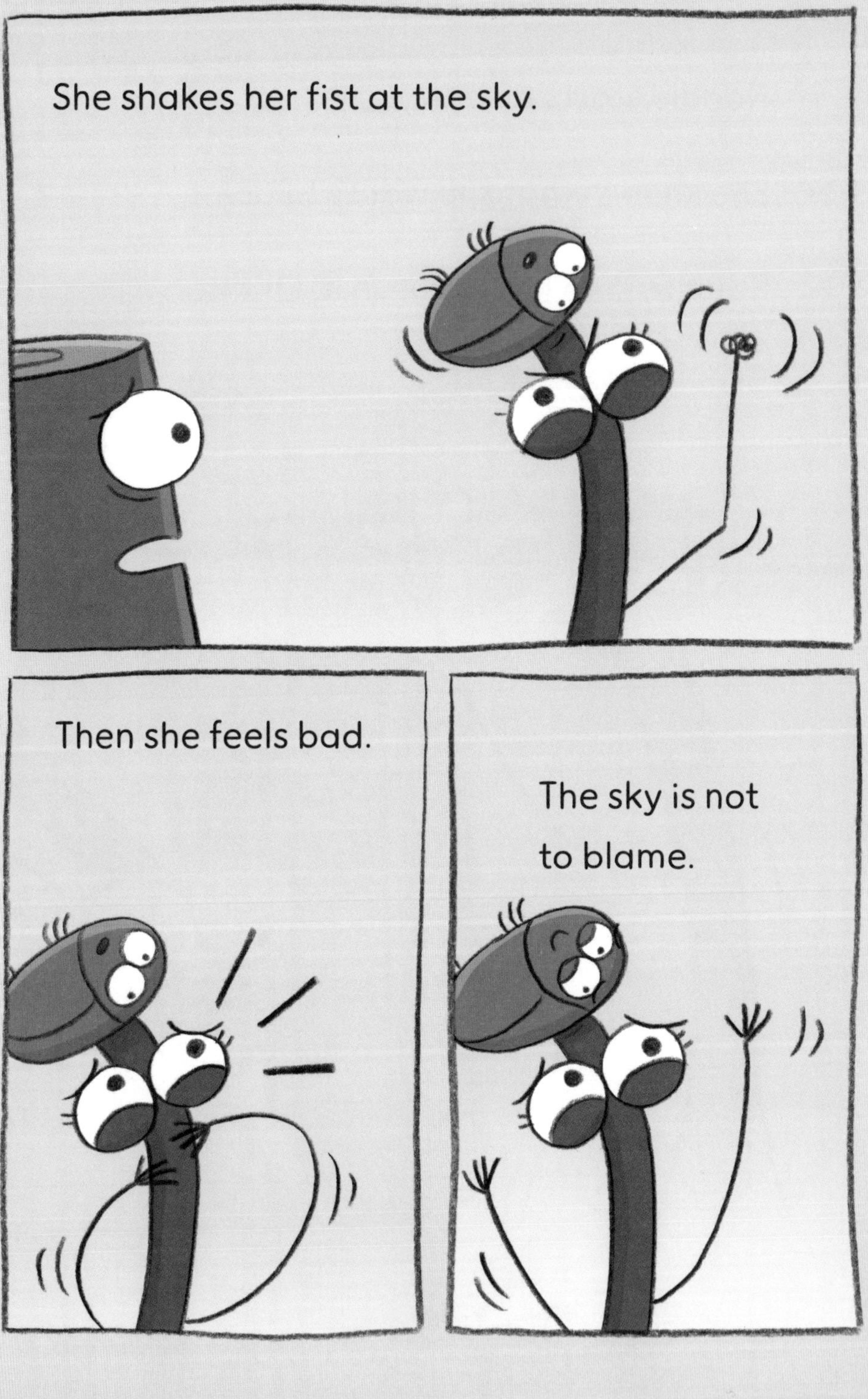
She shakes her fist at the sky.
Then she feels bad.
The sky is not
to blame.

Although, the sky is ... **BLUE!**

Clever Noodle!

There's plenty of blue in nature ... if you just look up.

She climbs
onto Stump.

But the sky
is still too high.

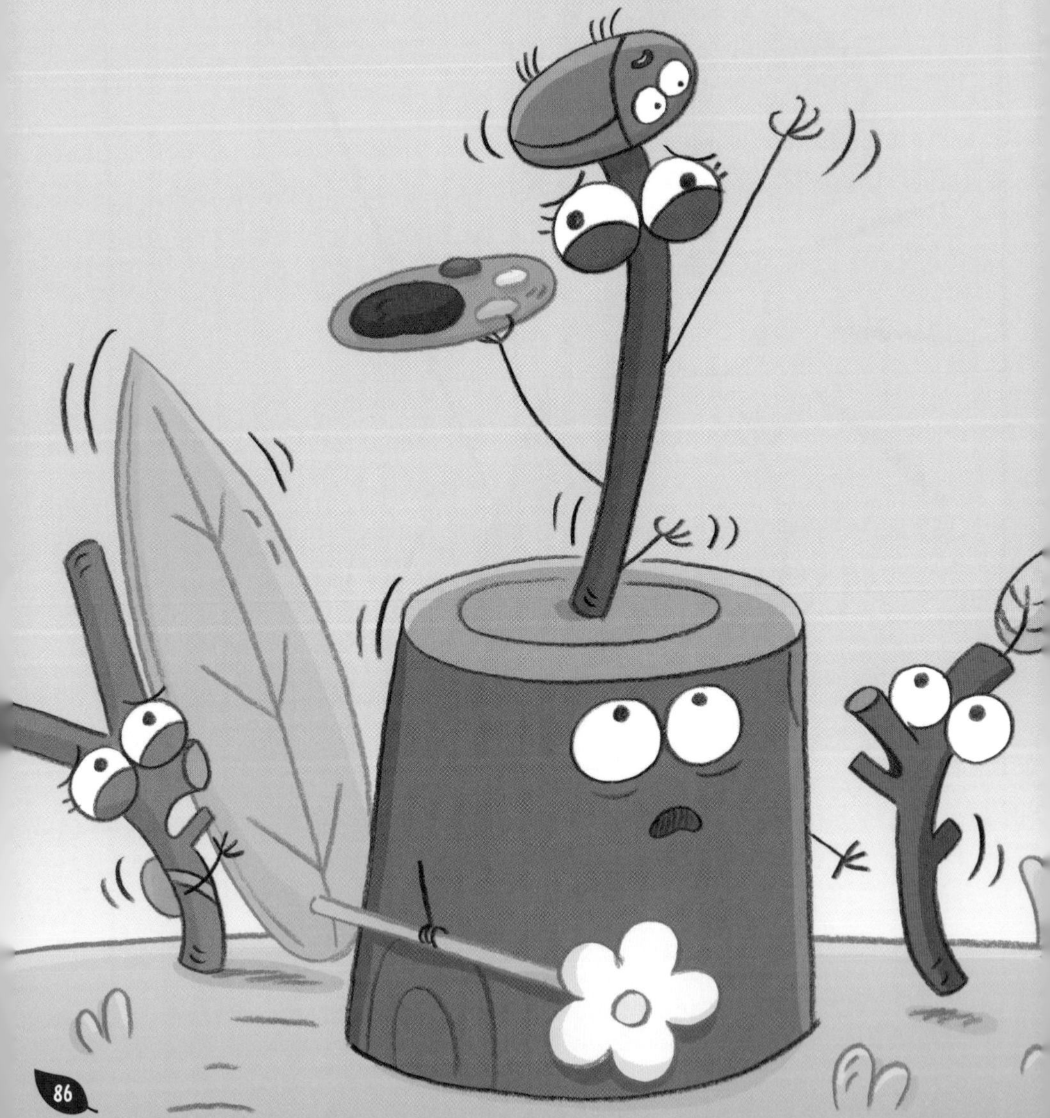

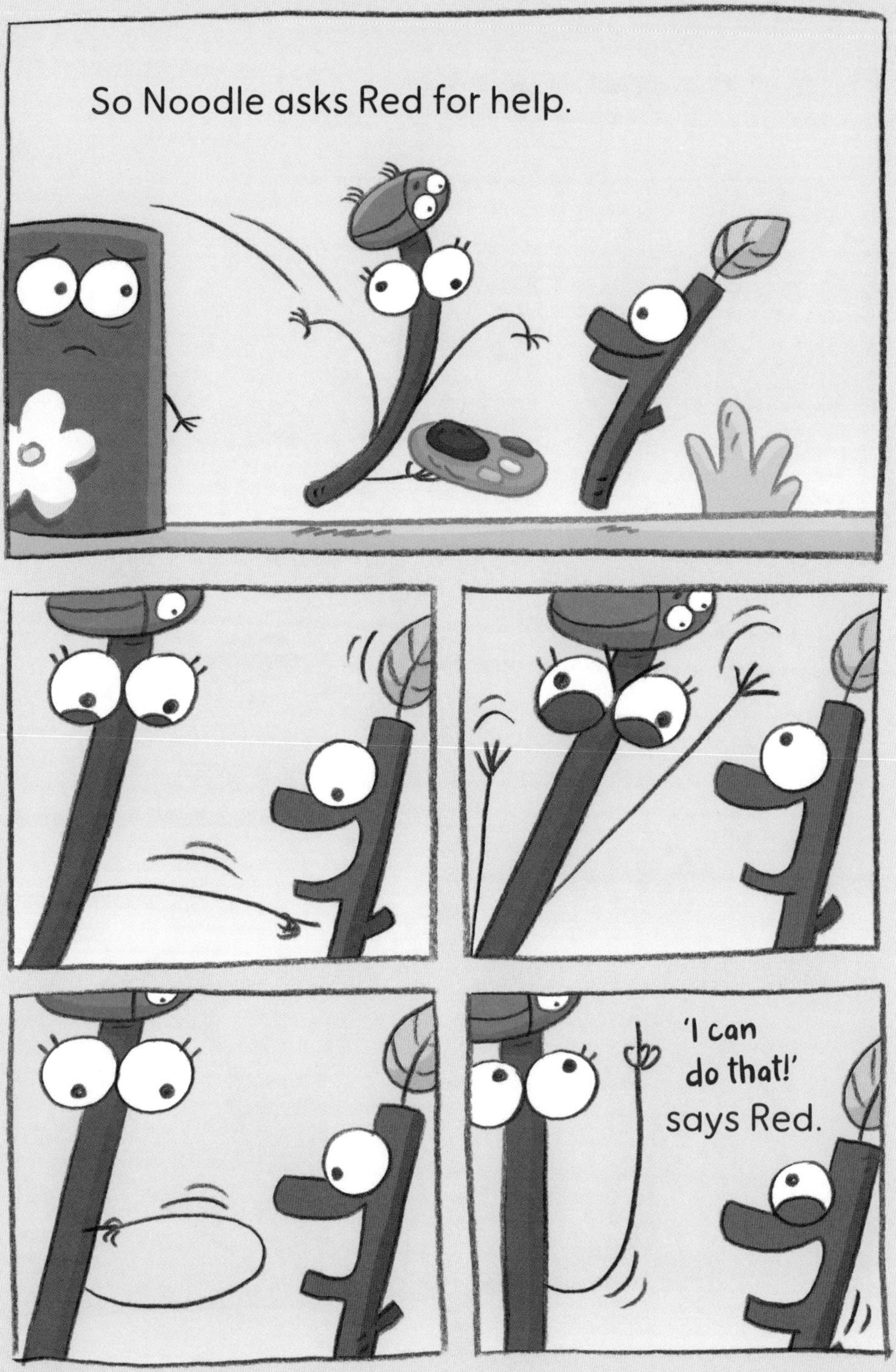
So Noodle asks Red for help.
'I can do that!'
says Red.

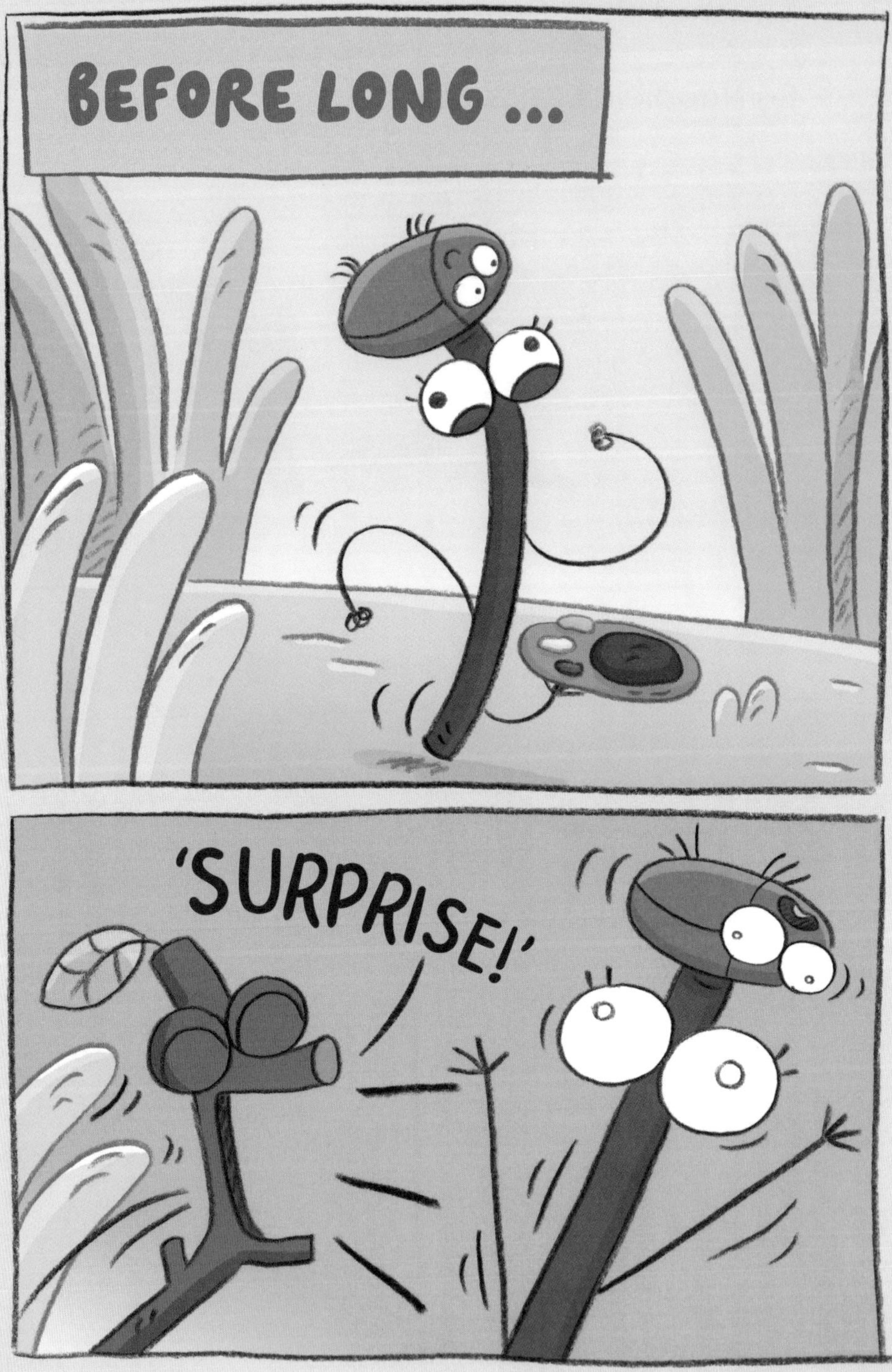
BEFORE LONG ...
'SURPRISE!'

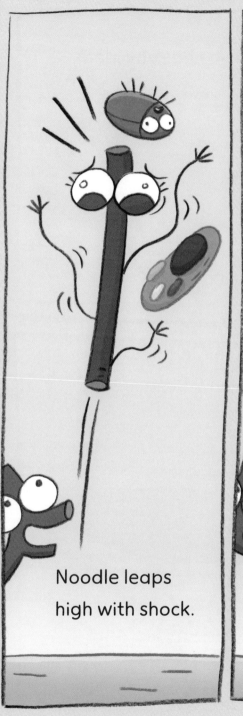

Noodle leaps
high with shock.

But not high
enough to reach
the sky.

So Noodle asks Ziggy if she has any ideas.

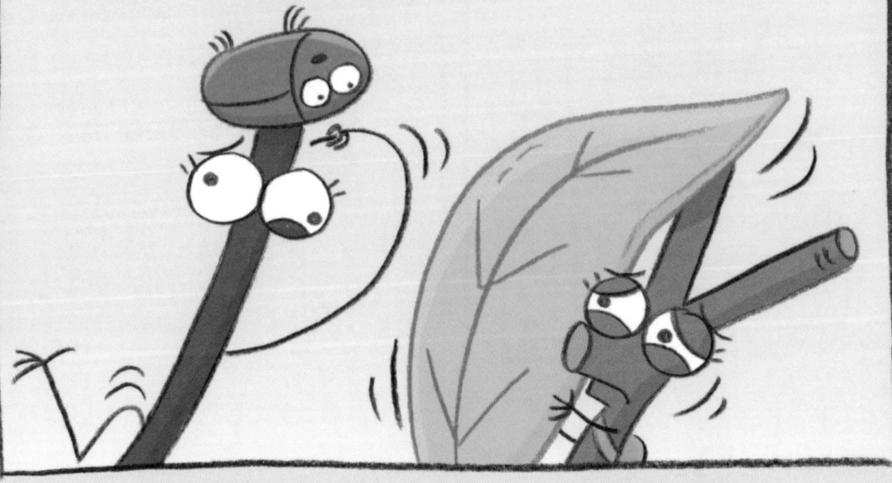

'I just want to LAUNCH this leaf into the sky,' says Ziggy. 'But I won't. Because I promised to hold it.'

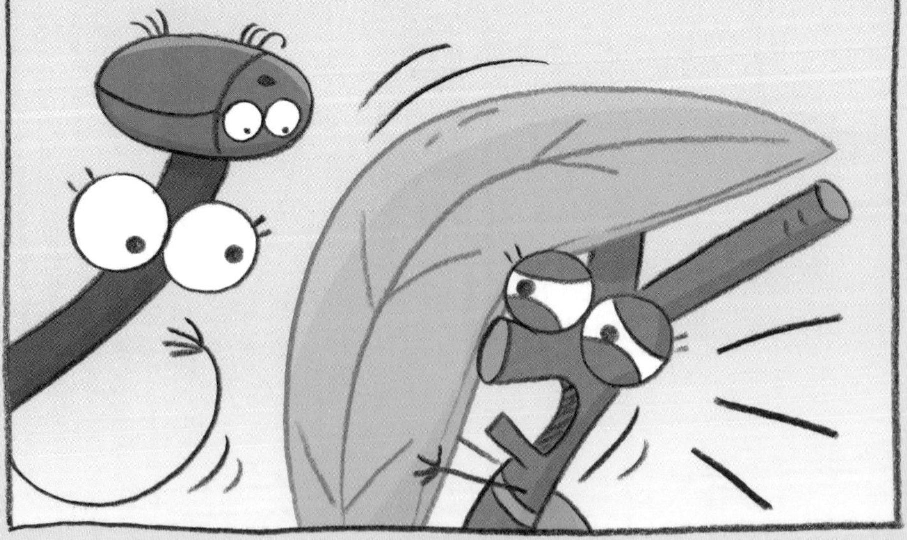

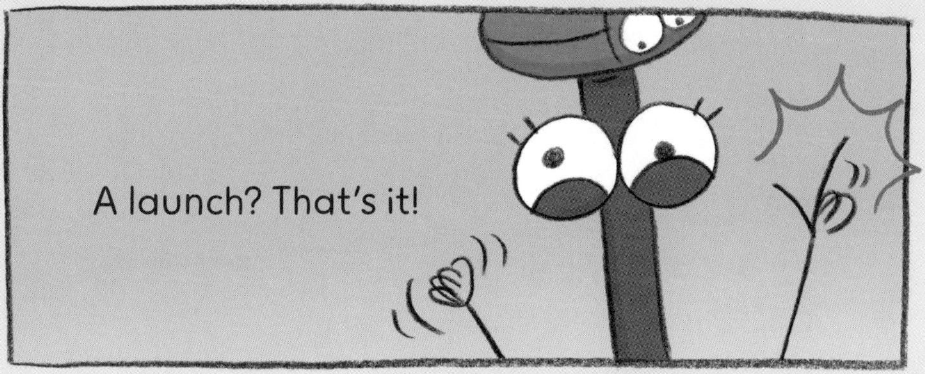
A launch? That's it!

Noodle points out her idea. She's going to need help from all the twigs.

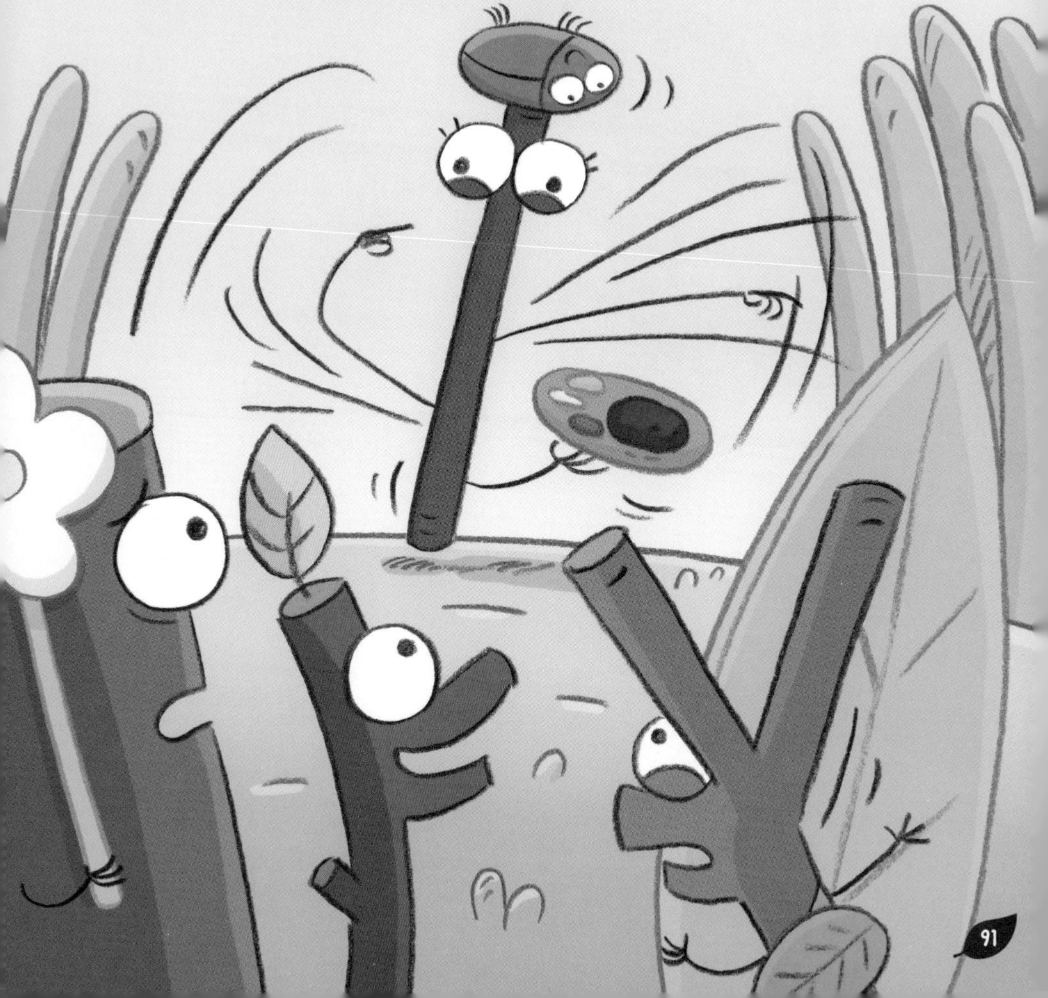

TEN SECONDS LATER ...

They are all in position.

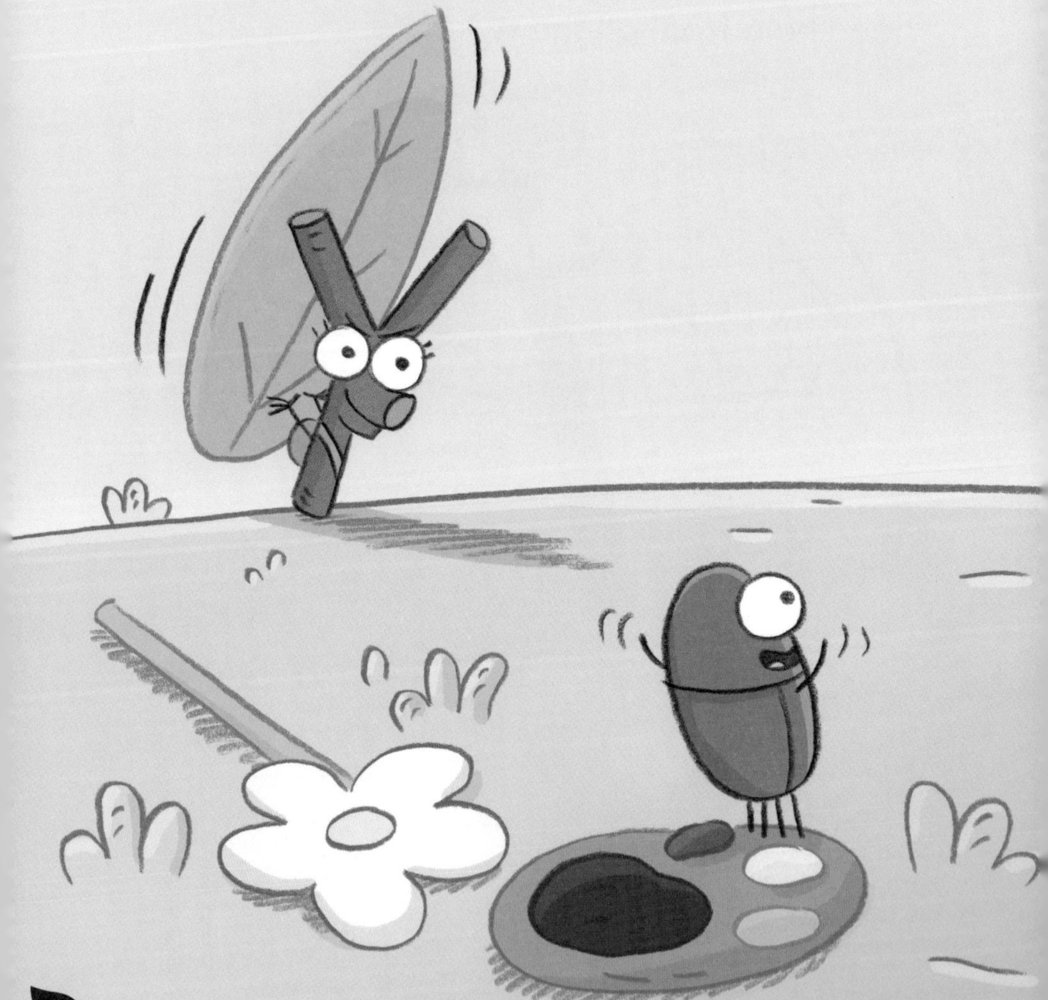

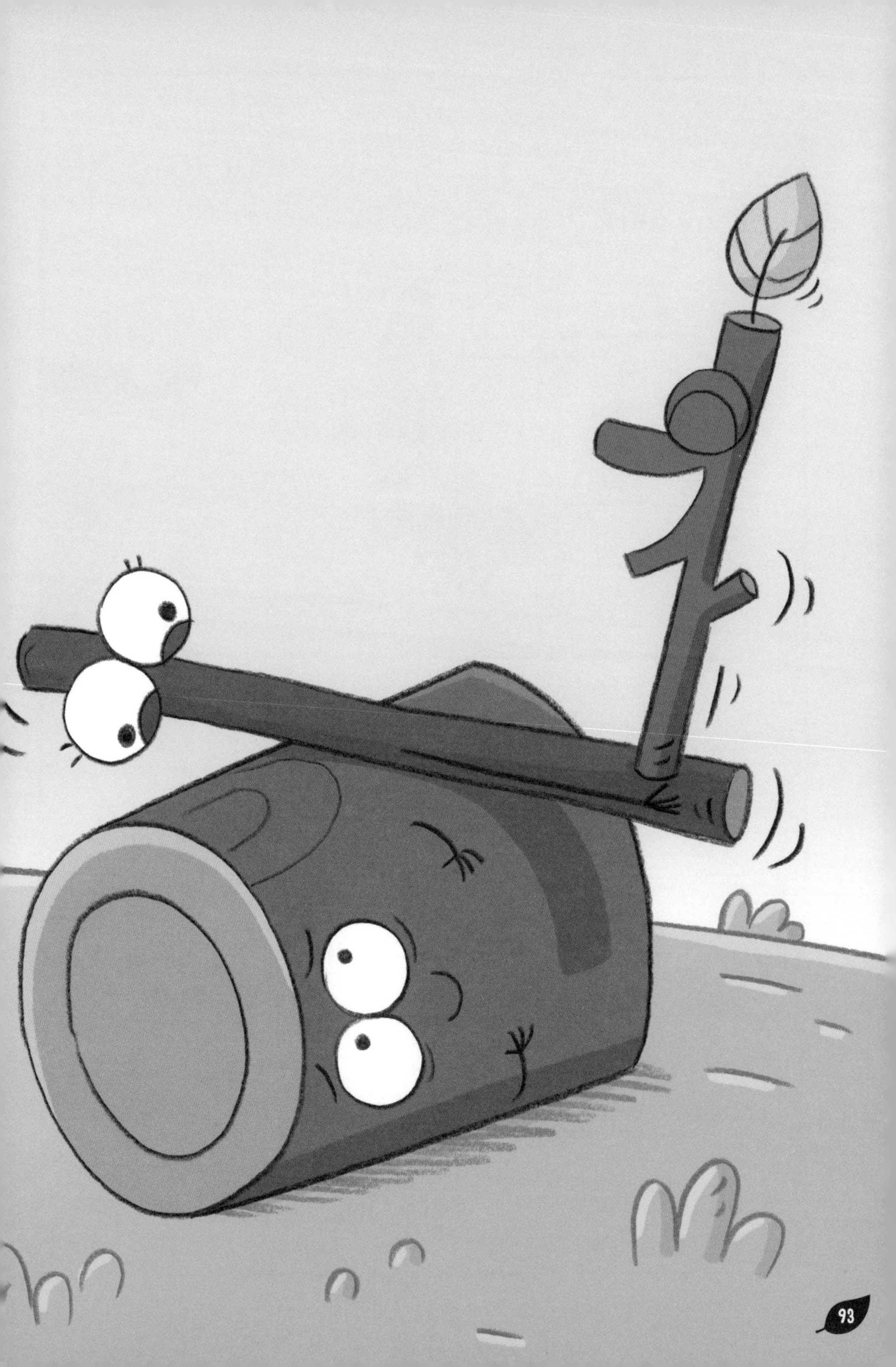

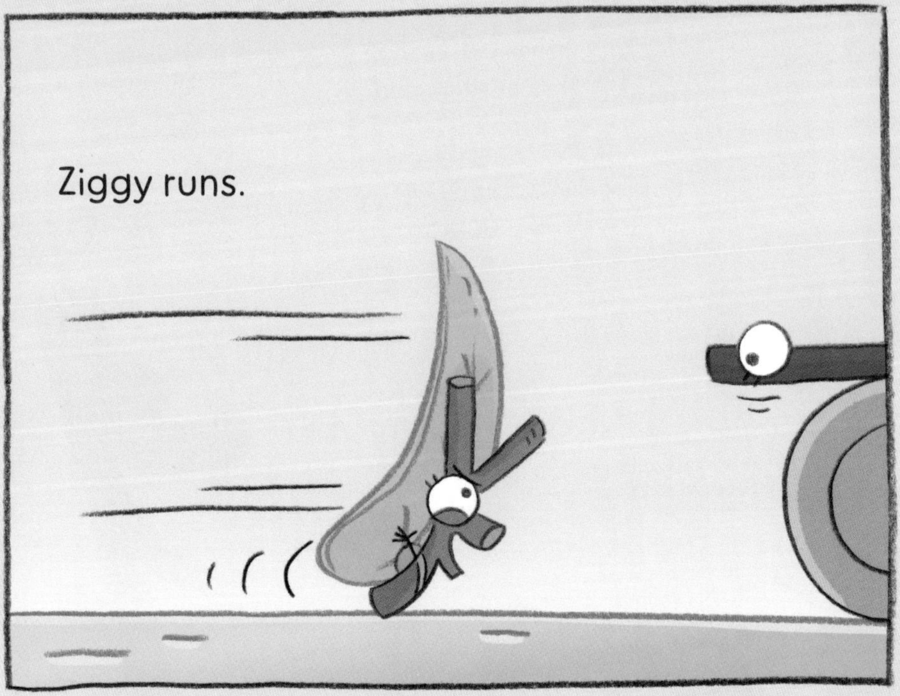
Ziggy runs.

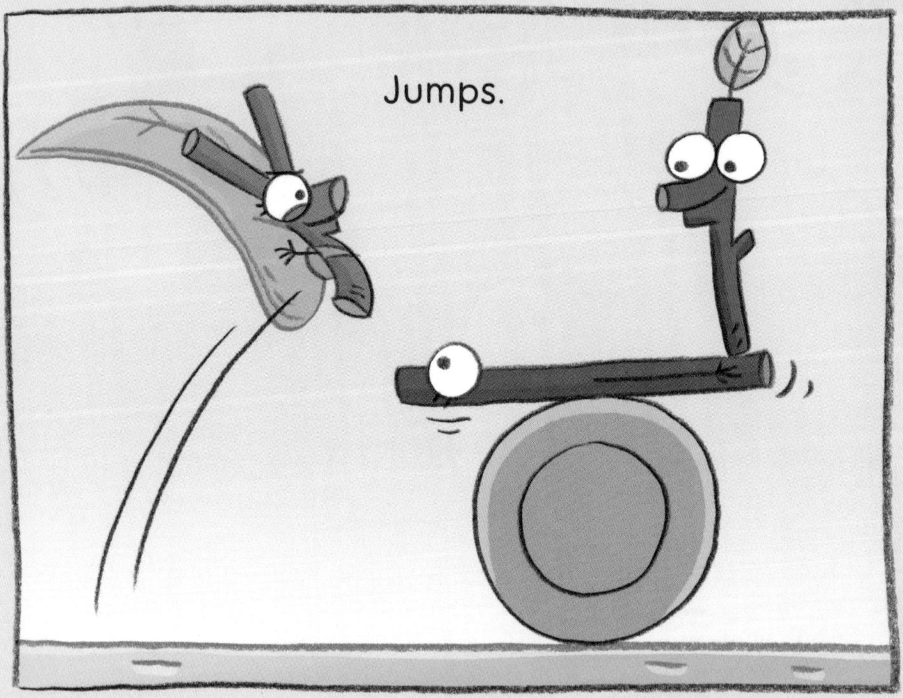
Jumps.

And sends Red up.
'Red
Red
Red!'
'Red
Red
Red
Red
Red
Red
Red!'

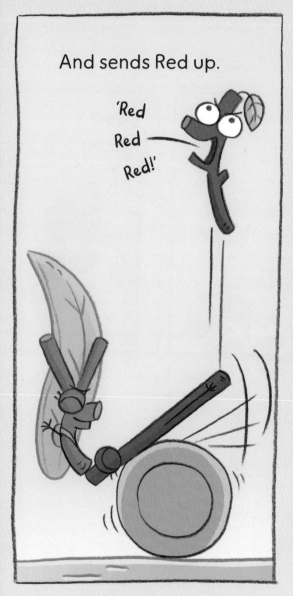

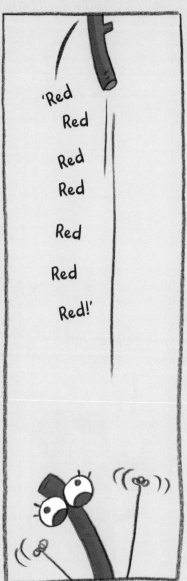

Great thinking, Noodle.

You've LAUNCHED Red high into the sky!

Red soars through the air.

'I'm a wild twig!'

'I will bite off some blue sky!'

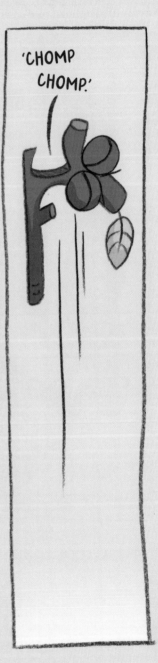

'CHOMP CHOMP.'

But he crashes into a bird.

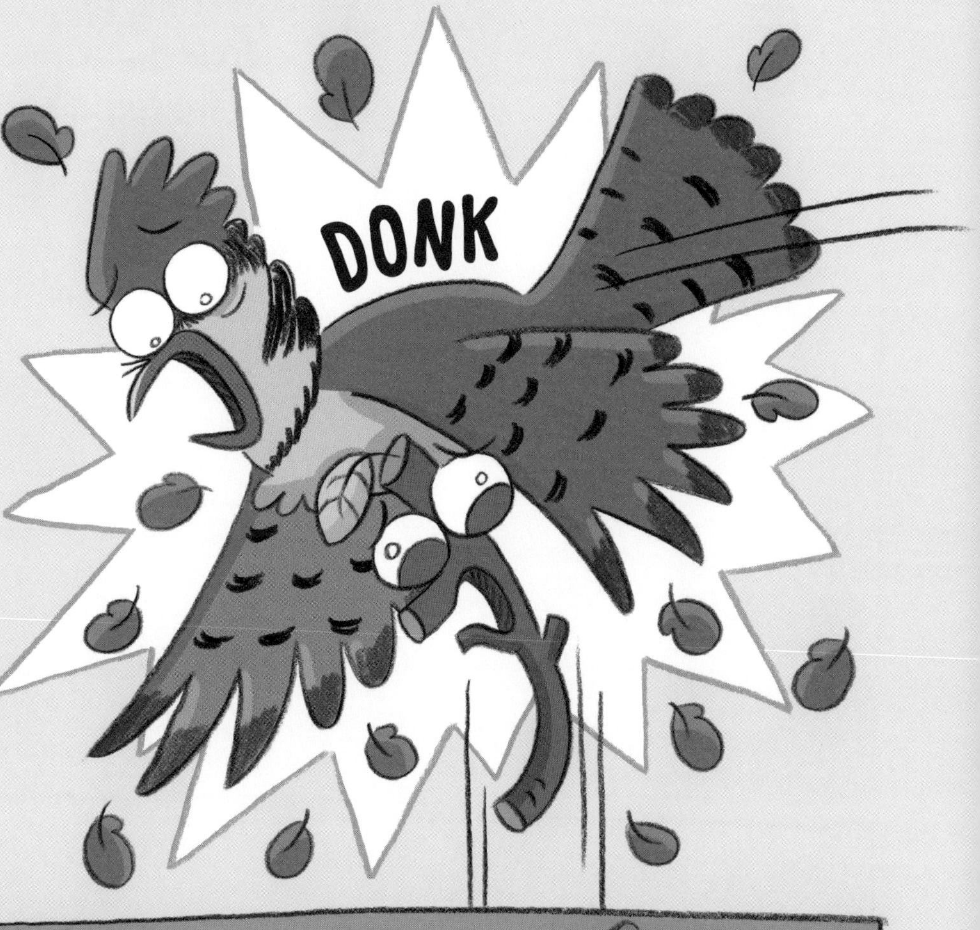
DONK

'Ow!' cries the bird.
'What are you? Some
kind of red rocket?
Get out of here!'

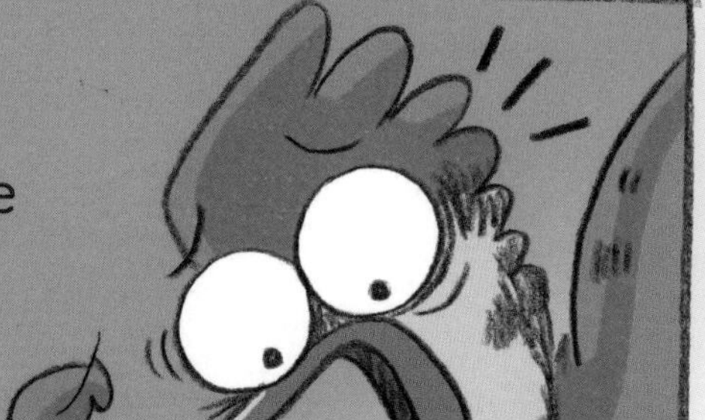

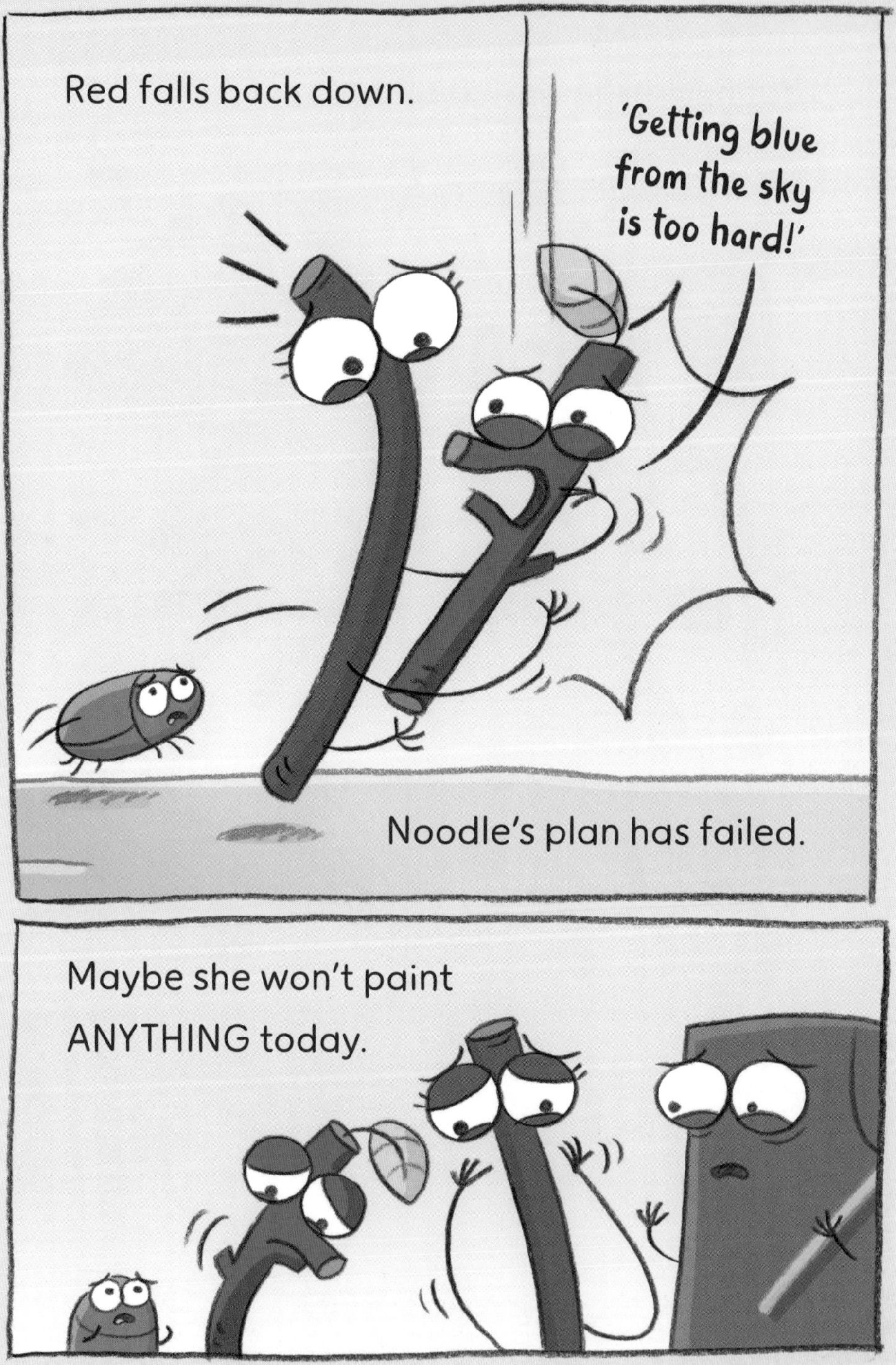
Red falls back down.
'Getting blue from the sky is too hard!'
Noodle's plan has failed.
Maybe she won't paint ANYTHING today.

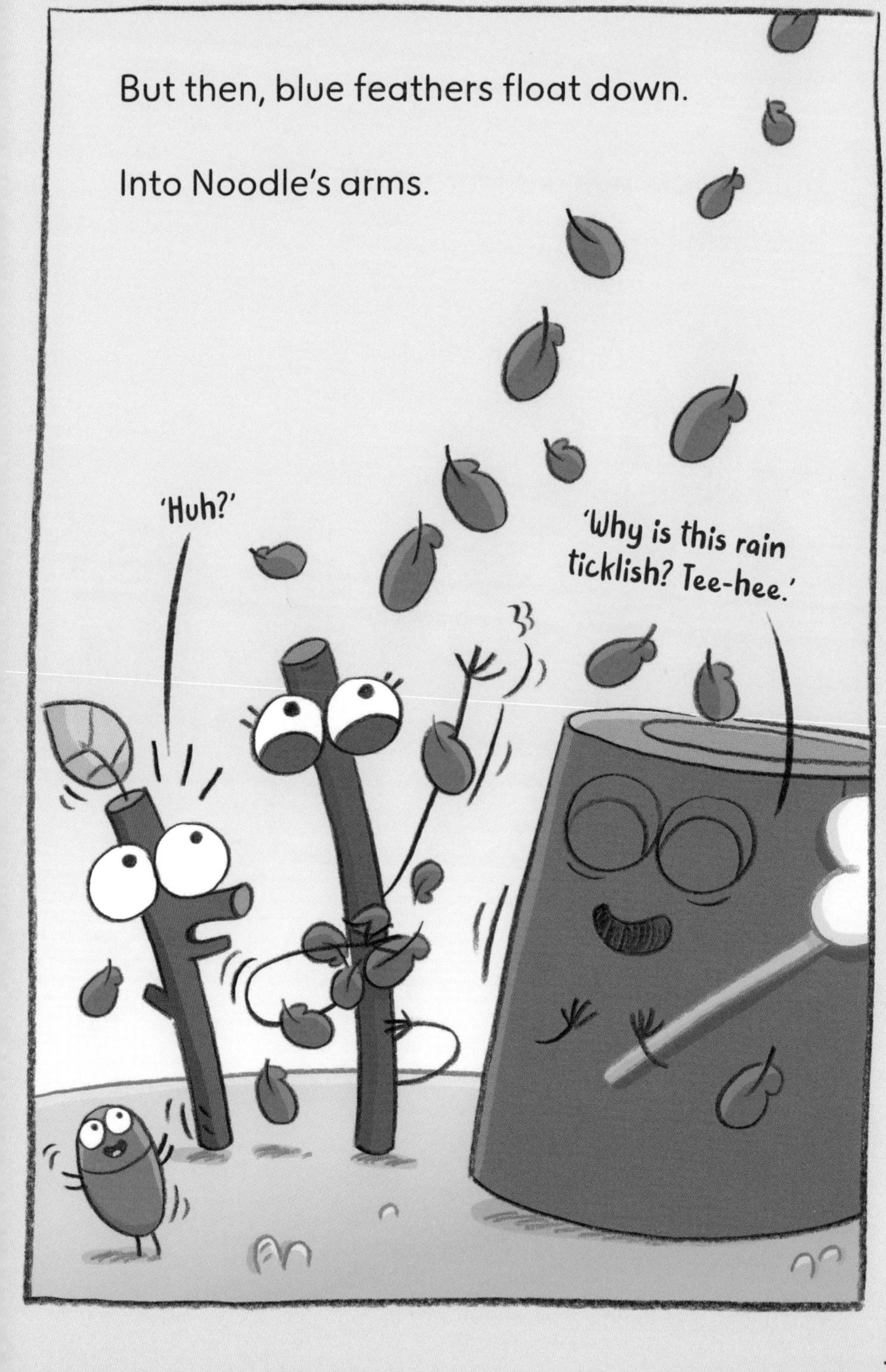
But then, blue feathers float down.
Into Noodle's arms.
'Huh?'
'Why is this rain ticklish? Tee-hee.'

You can't turn feathers into paint.

But Noodle has a different idea.

She leaps into action.

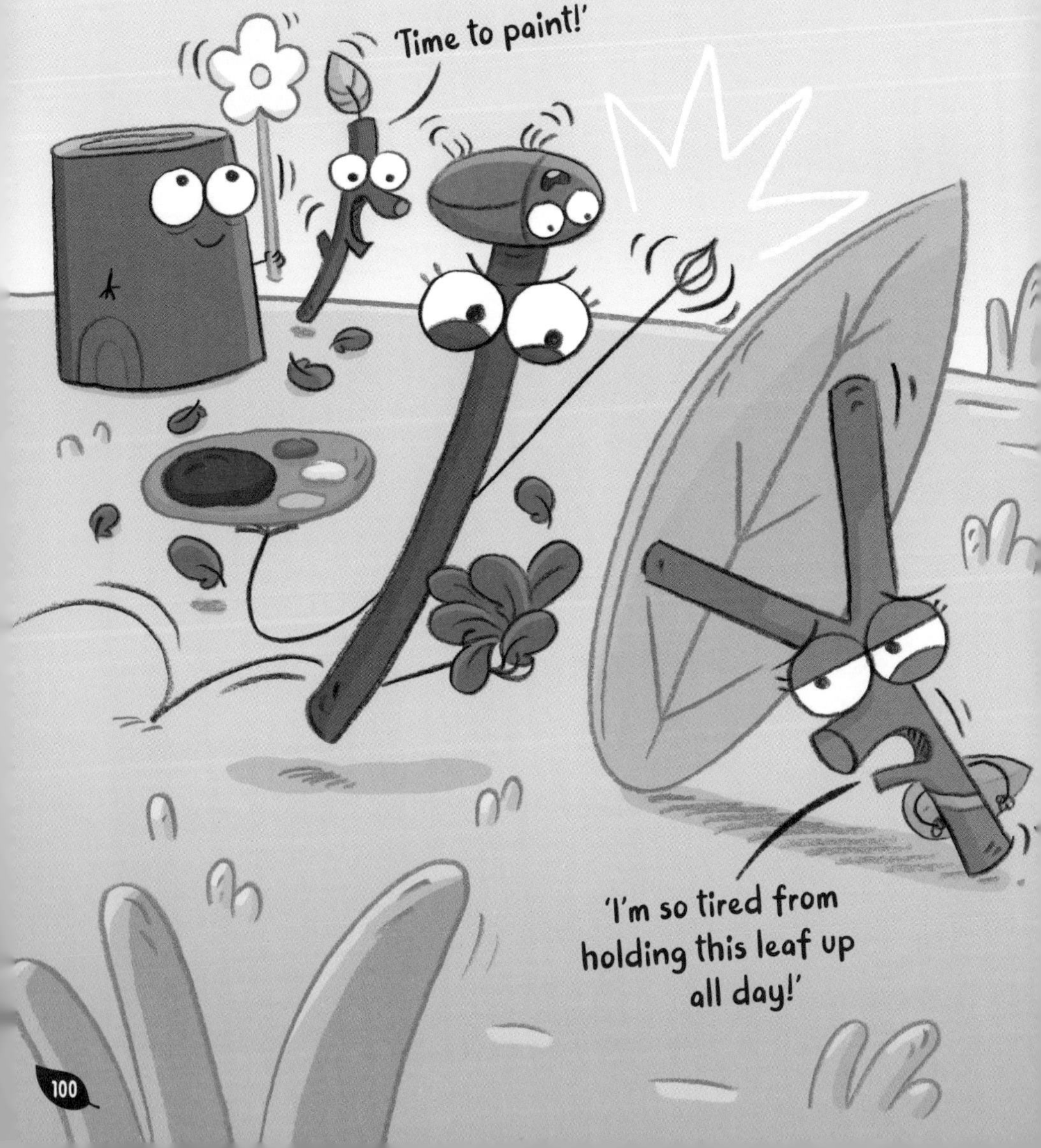
'Time to paint!'
'I'm so tired from holding this leaf up all day!'

Noodle paints.

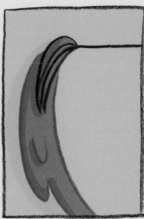

And paints.

And ...

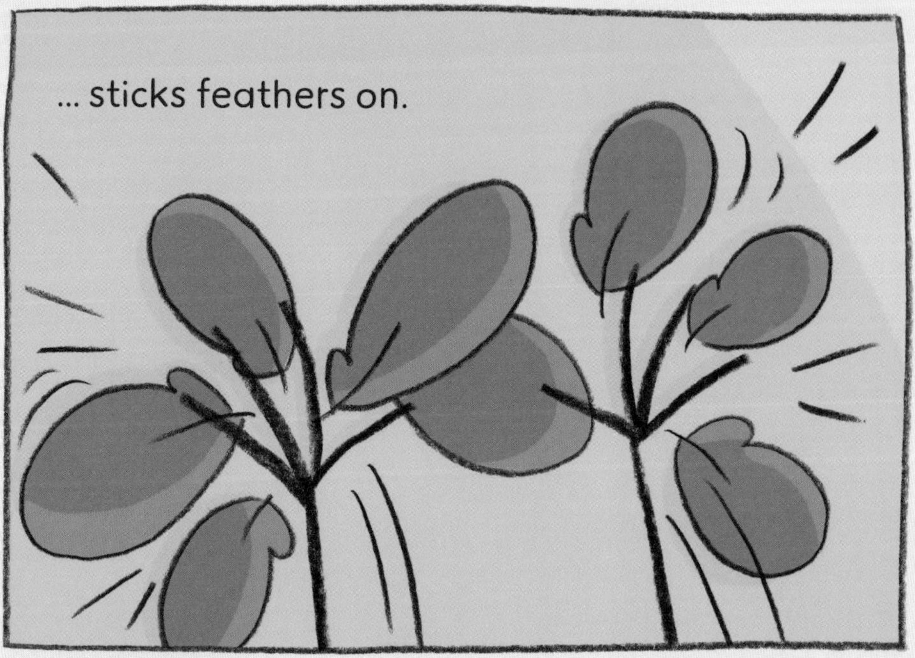
... sticks feathers on.

Because there are no rules with ART.

You can do whatever you want!

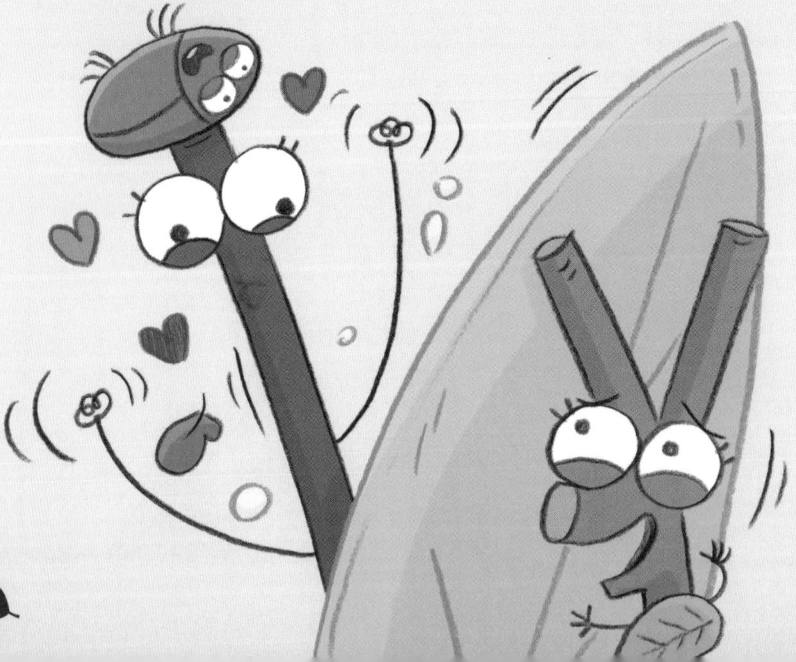

So, what have you made, Noodle?

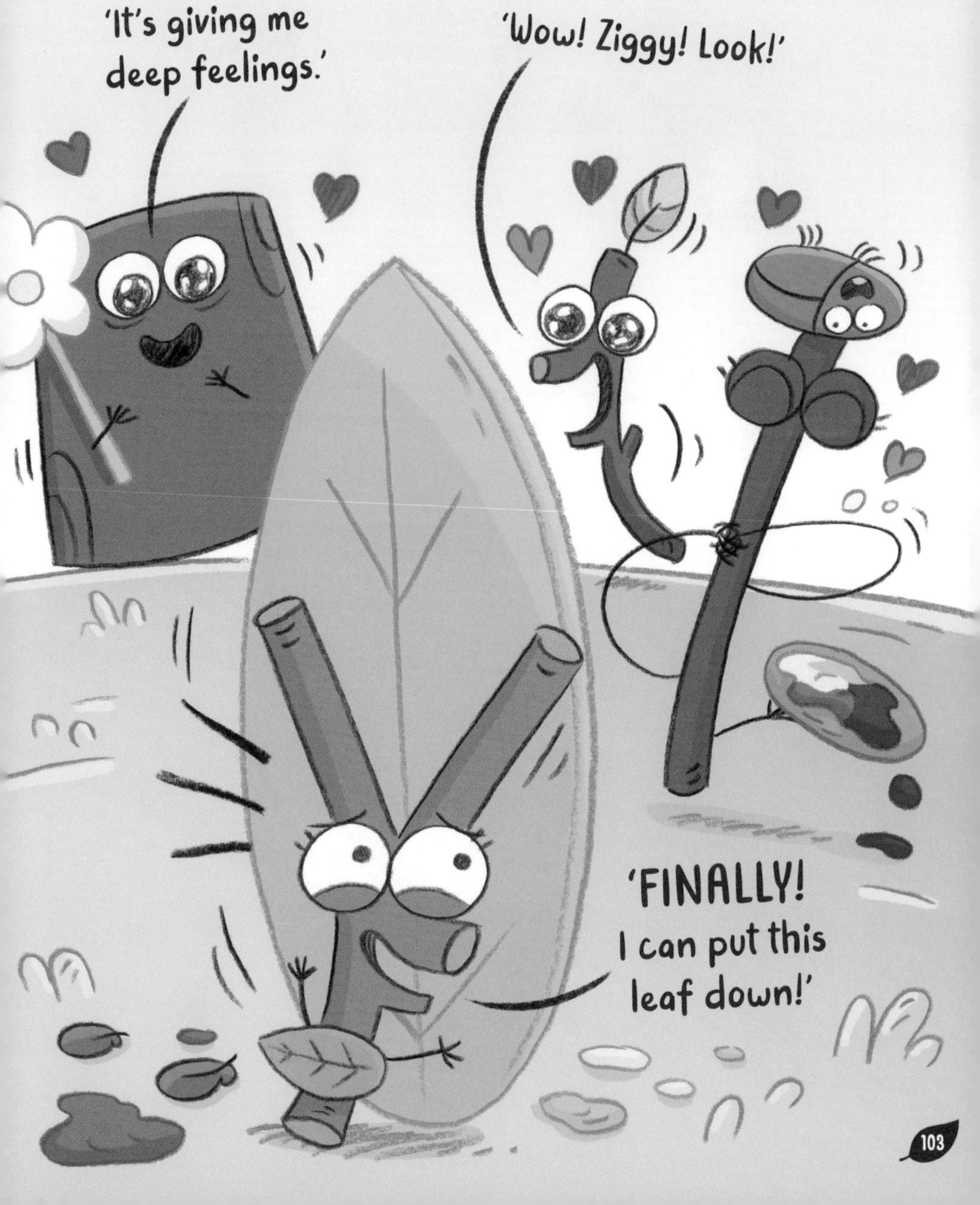
'It's giving me deep feelings.'
'Wow! Ziggy! Look!'
'FINALLY! I can put this leaf down!'

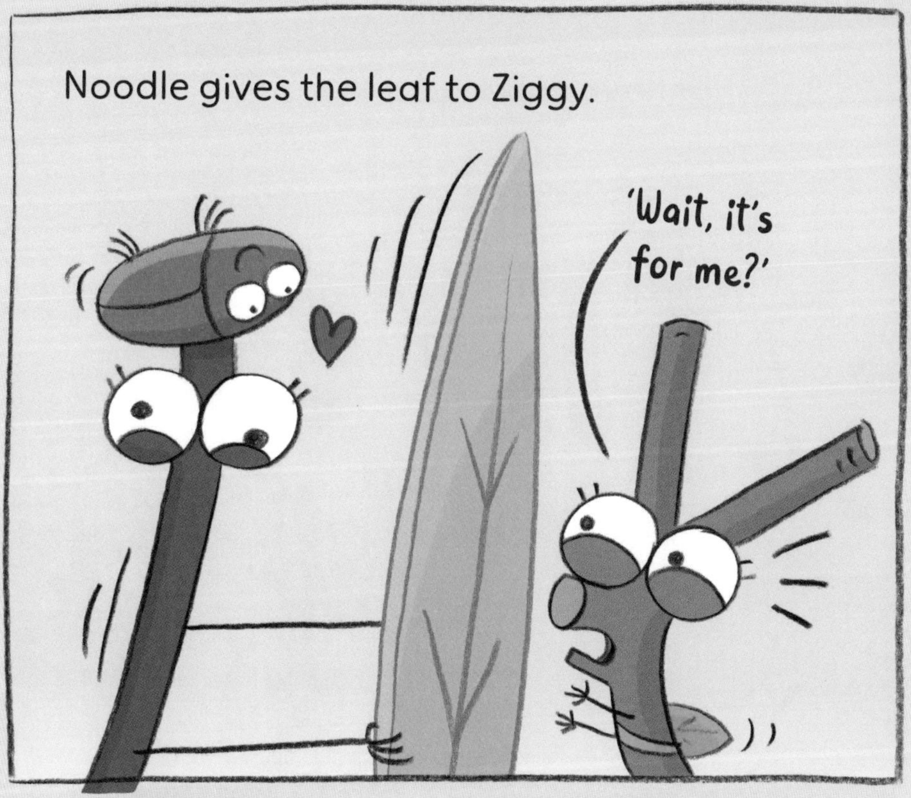
Noodle gives the leaf to Ziggy.
'Wait, it's for me?'

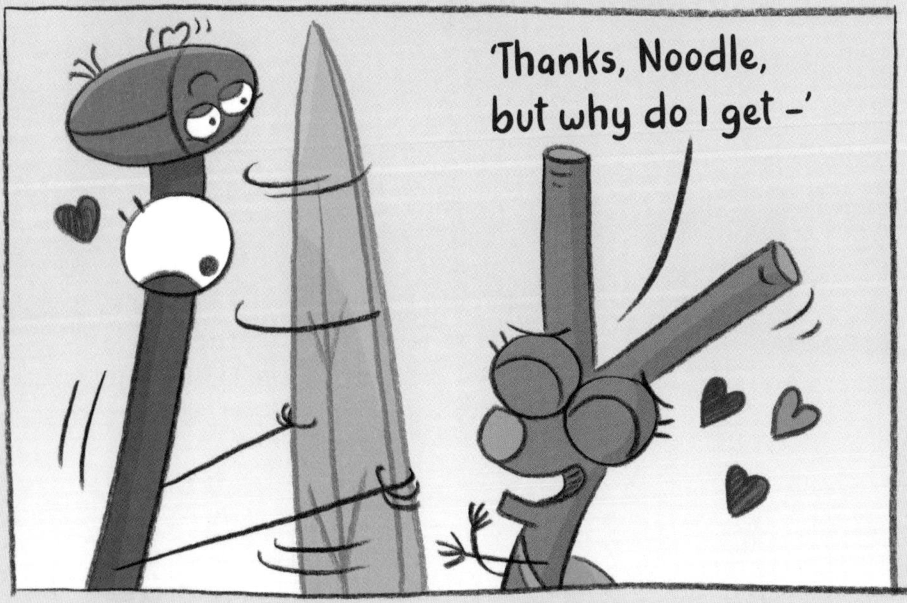
'Thanks, Noodle, but why do I get –'

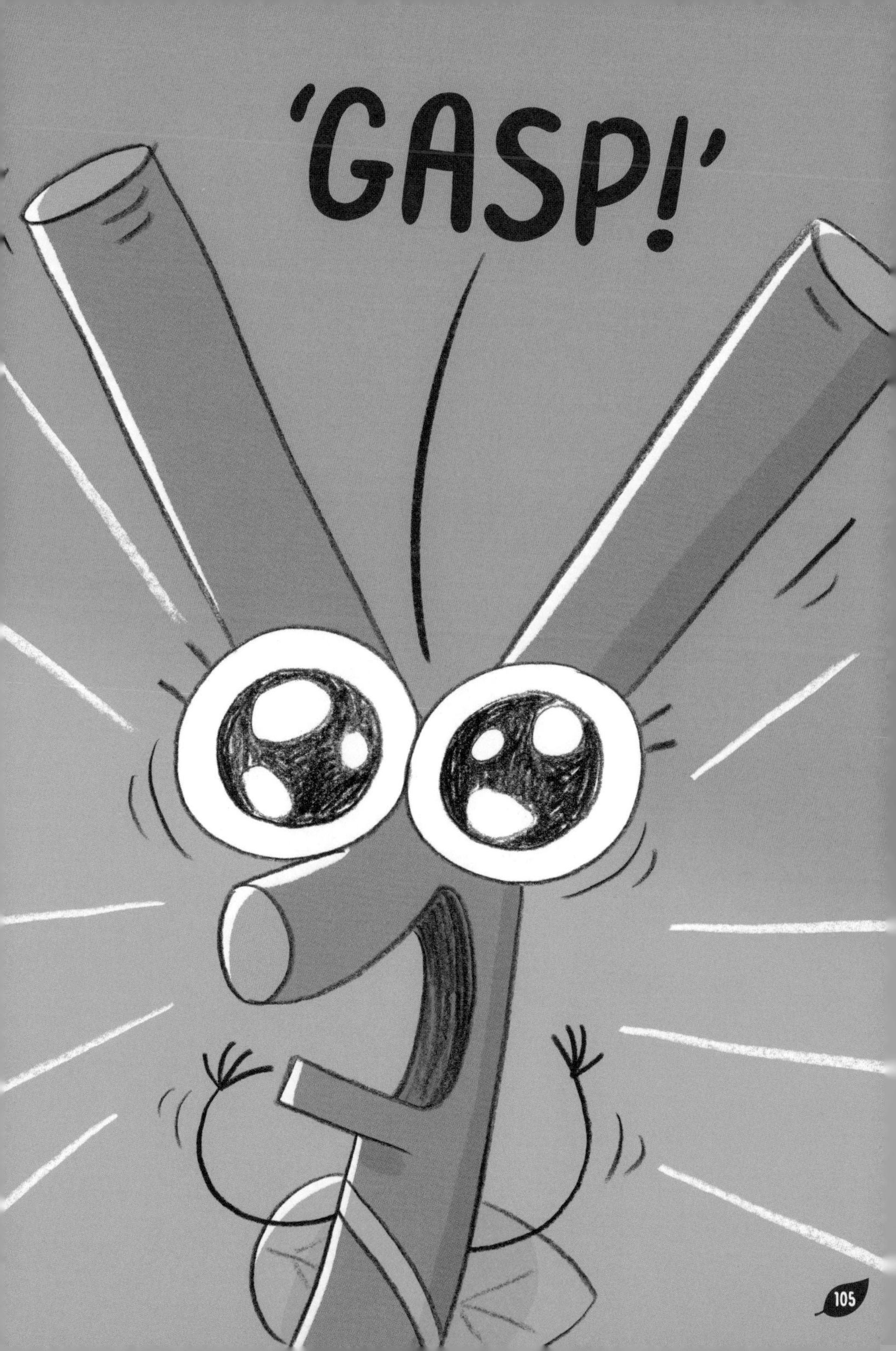
'GASP!'

It's a painting of Ziggy!

And the blue feathers are the big blue sky.

Very creative, Noodle!

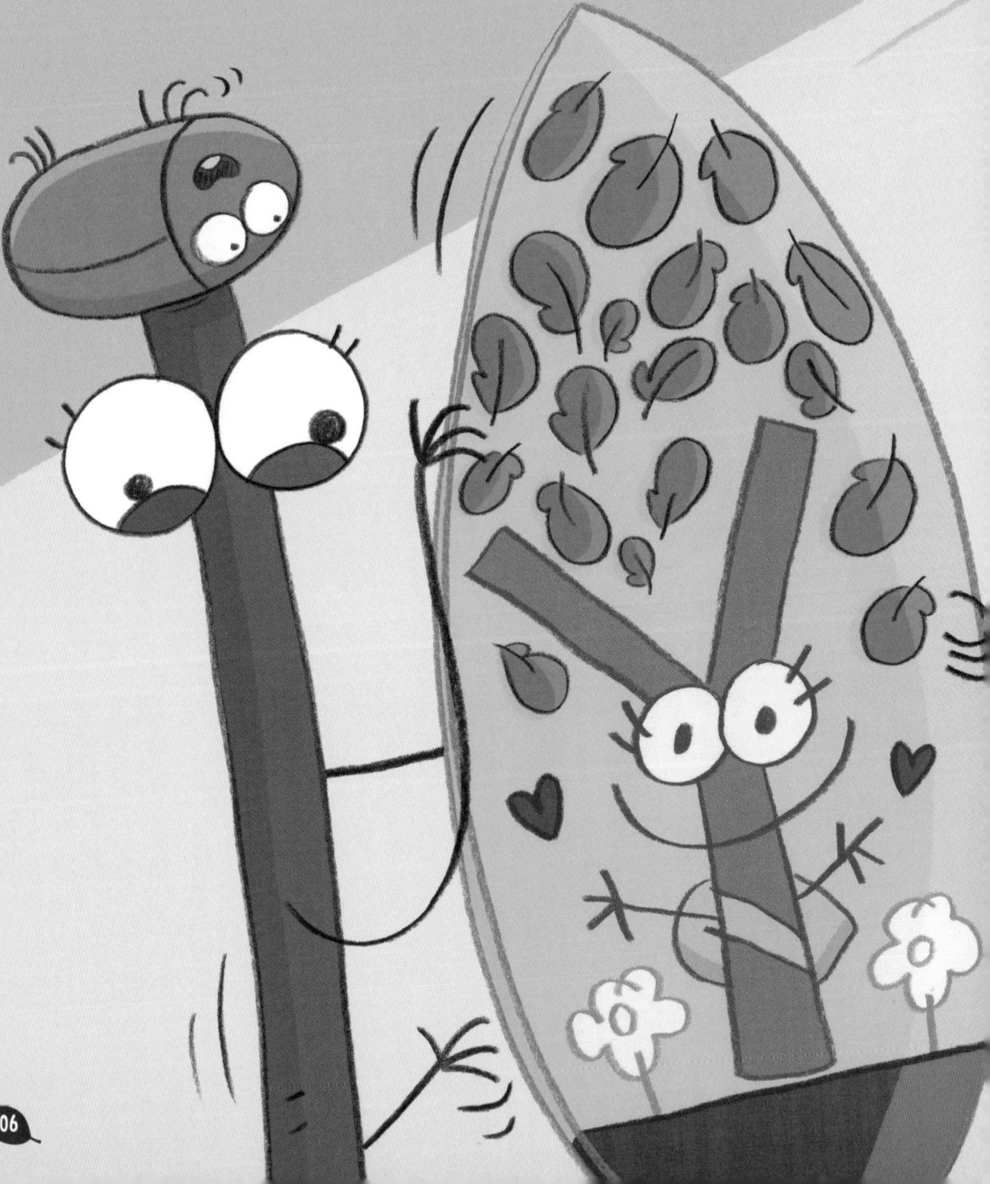

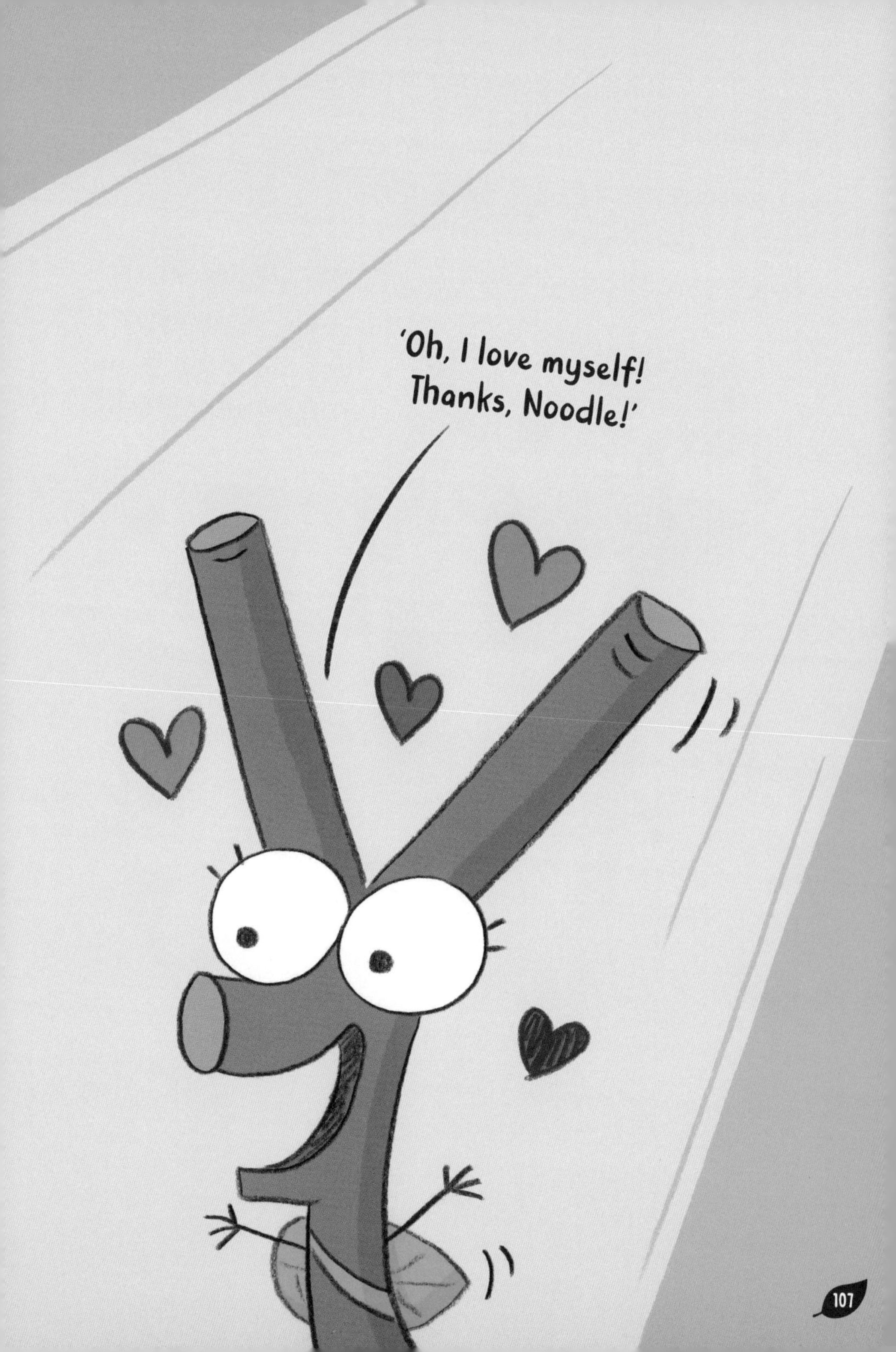
'Oh, I love myself! Thanks, Noodle!'

Noodle was planning on painting Ziggy all along. And Ziggy cheers.

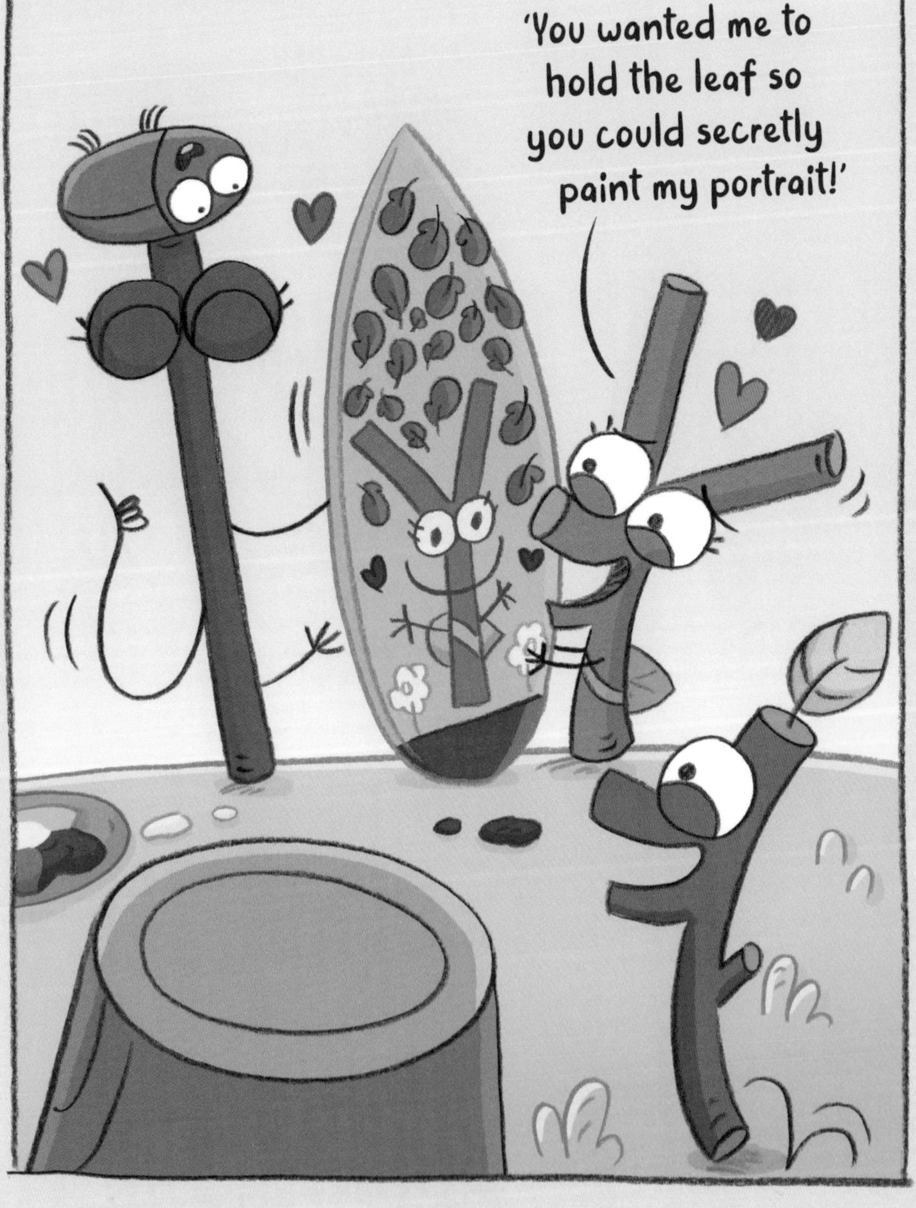
'You wanted me to hold the leaf so you could secretly paint my portrait!'

It turns out that Noodle is a twig.

And an artist.

But most of all ... she is a FRIEND!

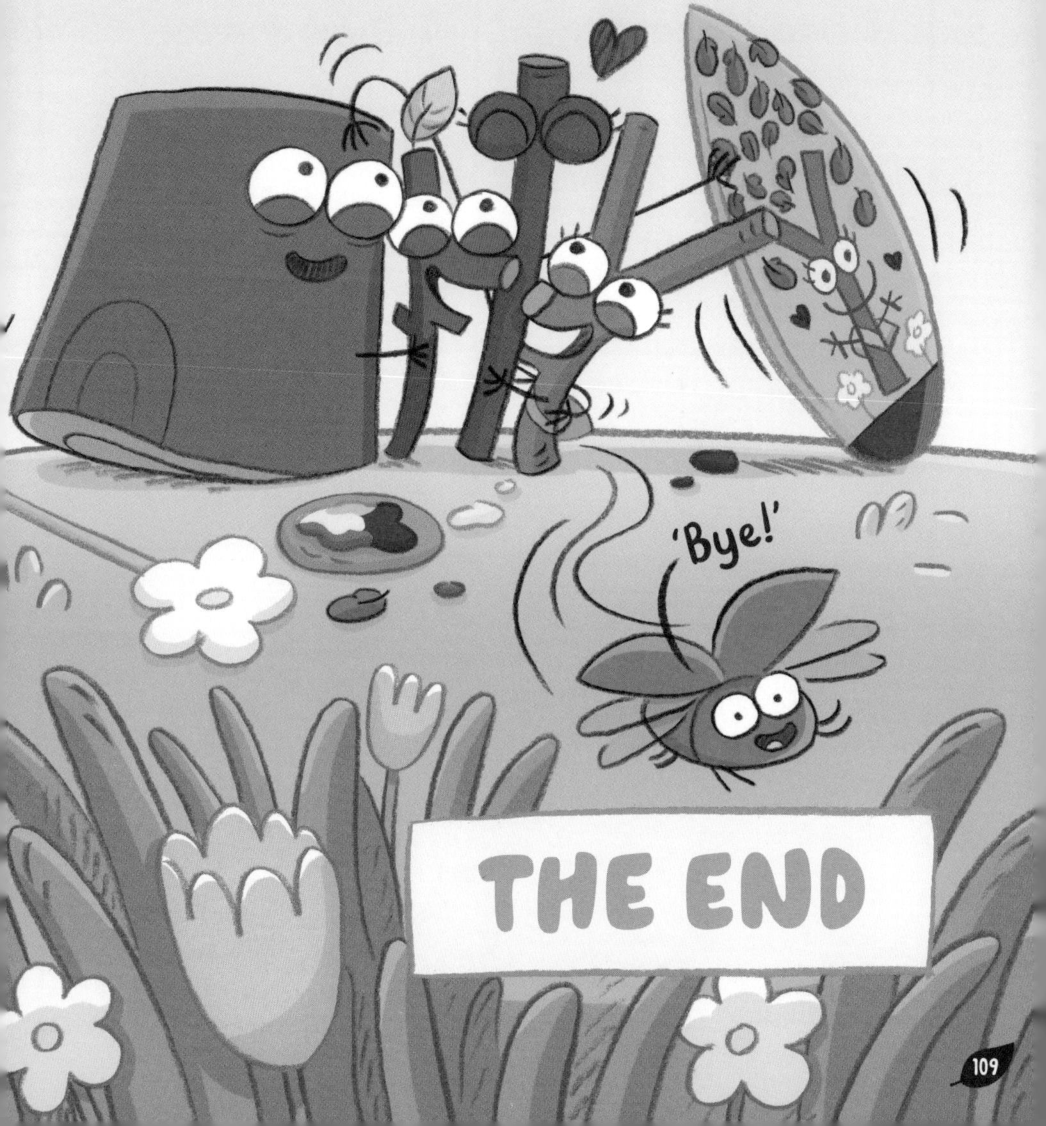
'Bye!'
THE END

MAKE YOUR OWN TWIG!

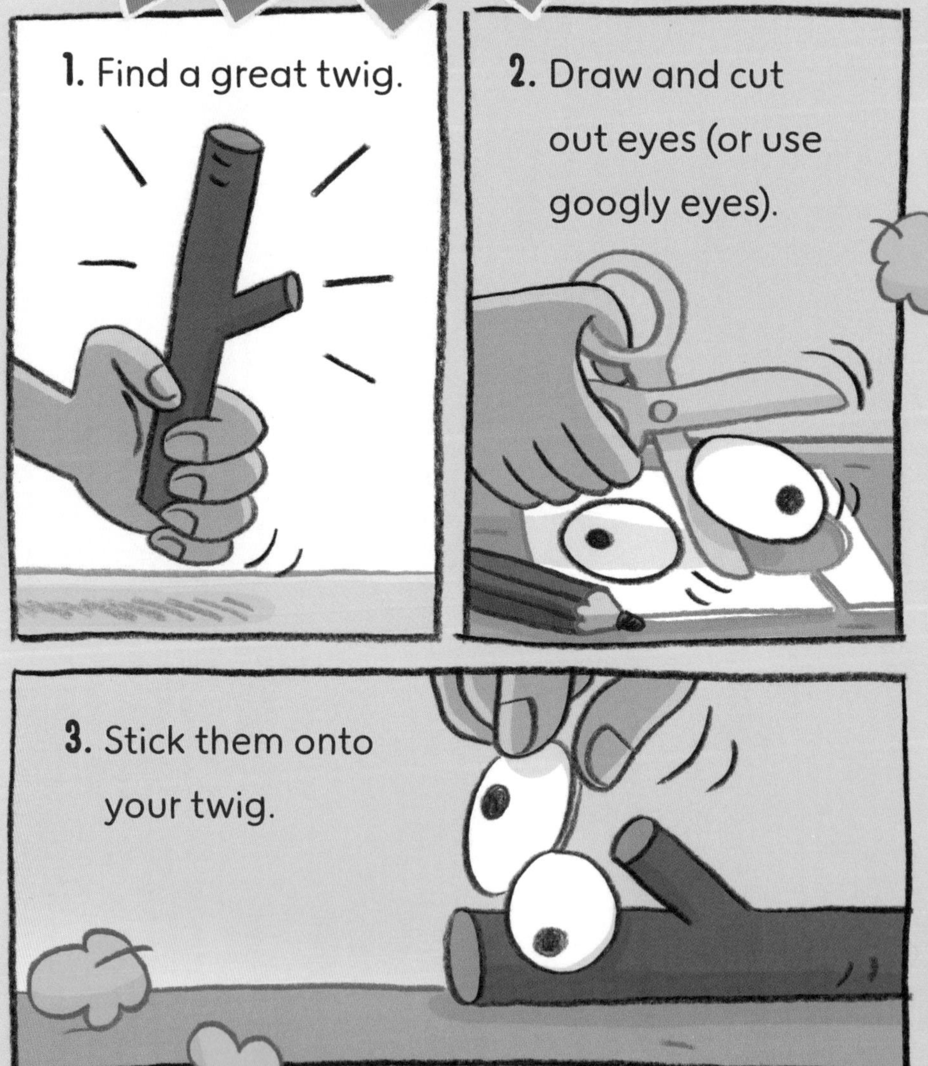
1. Find a great twig.
2. Draw and cut out eyes (or use googly eyes).
3. Stick them onto your twig.

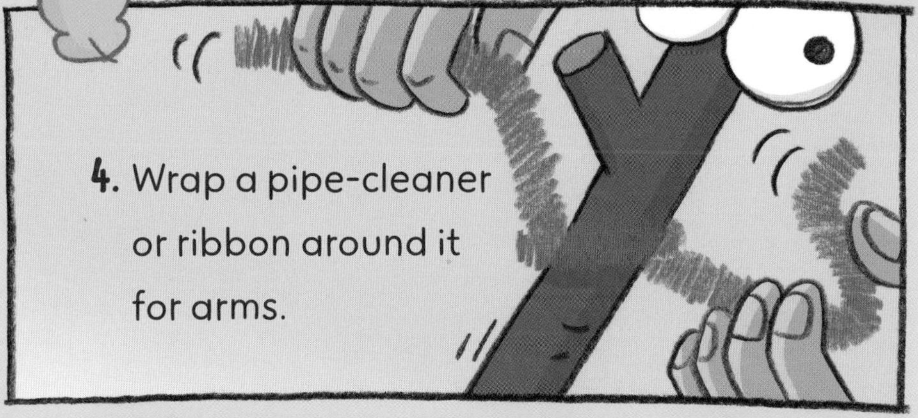
4. Wrap a pipe-cleaner or ribbon around it for arms.

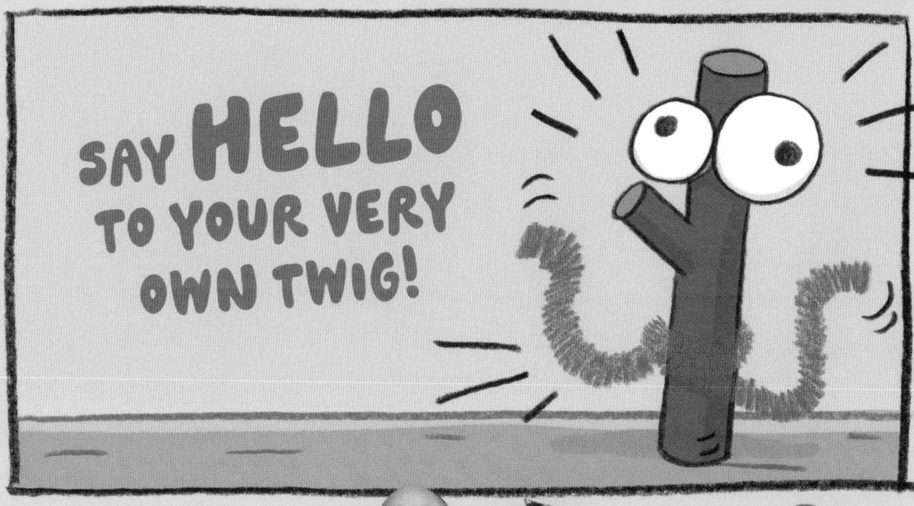
SAY HELLO TO YOUR VERY OWN TWIG!

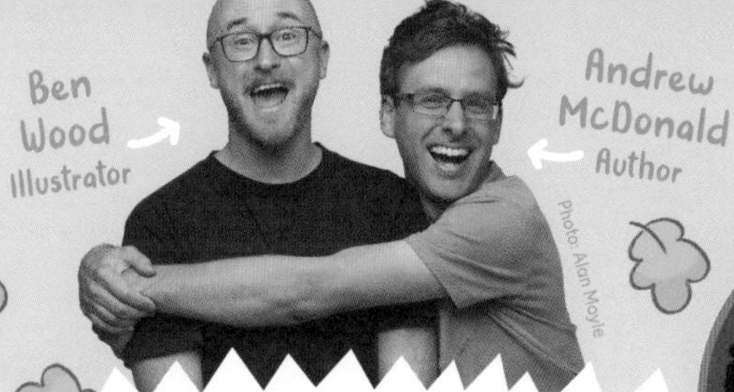
Ben Wood Illustrator
Andrew McDonald Author
Photo: Alan Moyle

Discover the world of

ANDREW and BEN!

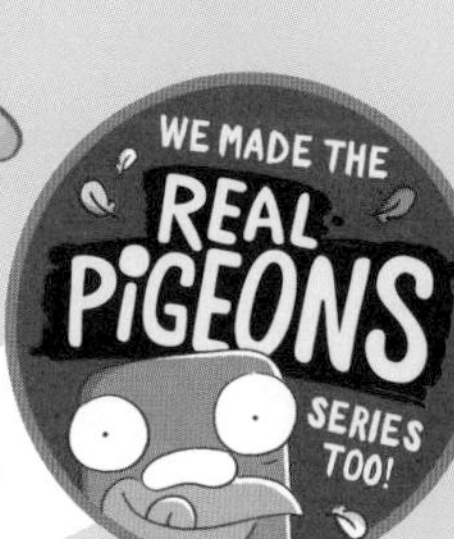
WE MADE THE
REAL PIGEONS
SERIES TOO!

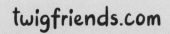

twigfriends.com

Hardie Grant, the author and illustrator acknowledge the Traditional Owners of the Country on which we work, the Wurundjeri People of the Kulin Nation and the Gadigal People of the Eora Nation, and recognize their continuing connection to the land, waters and culture. We pay our respects to their Elders past and present.

TO RAF AND EVE

Bright Light,
an imprint of Hardie Grant Children's Publishing
Wurundjeri Country
Ground Floor, Building 1, 658 Church Street
Richmond, Victoria 3121, Australia
Melbourne | Sydney | San Francisco
www.hardiegrantchildrens.com

ISBN: 9781761214356
First published in Australia in 2023
This edition published in 2024

Publisher Marisa Pintado
Design Kristy Lund-White
Editorial Johanna Gogos and Luna Soo
Production Amanda Shaw
With special thanks to Gina Gagliano

Printed in China by Leo Paper Group

MIX
Paper | Supporting responsible forestry
FSC® C020056

The paper this book is printed on is from FSC®-certified forests and other sources. FSC® promotes environmentally responsible, socially beneficial and economically viable management of the world's forests.

10 9 8 7 6 5 4 3 2 1